Dear Reader,

I'm so glad to have you with me on our journey to Seal.
I'd like to say thank you for being here with me and all my
characters. I love them all, and I hope you will too.

In *Keep Me Safe* you'll meet Anna, who has forgotten how to
care about herself, and Sorren, who prefers caring for other
people than facing a painful past. Also Ava, a little girl who
has so much life in her, but whose family life crumbles and
who has to find a way to lead herself and her mum to a place
of love and safety. All this in the surrounding of beaches and
cliffs and sea and sky.

Seal for me is a place of the soul. Death and childbirth, love
and loss all go and join the waters of our souls. The idea I love
is that we are not alone in grief and comfort, Seal is a place of
kindred souls.

Reader, I am privileged to undertake this journey with you.
My readers make my stories come alive. My writing is a
four-hands sonata, where each reader composes and creates
with me, superimposing their own story to mine.

So thank you for dancing with me all the way to the
Hebrides.

Con amore,
Daniela x

By Daniela Sacerdoti and available from Headline

Your Hand In Mine
Calling You Home
Keep Me Safe

Also by Daniela Sacerdoti

Glen Avich Quartet
Watch Over Me
Take Me Home
Set Me Free
Don't Be Afraid

Sarah Midnight Trilogy
Dreams
Tide
Spirit

Really Weird Removals.Com

Daniela
SACERDOTI
Keep Me Safe

REVIEW

First published in Great Britain in 2017
by HEADLINE REVIEW
An imprint of HEADLINE PUBLISHING GROUP

1

Cataloguing in Publication Data is available from the British Library

ISBN 978 1 4722 3500 8 (Hardback)
ISBN 978 1 4722 3501 5 (Trade paperback)

Typeset in Baskerville Std by Jouve (UK), Milton Keynes

Printed and bound in Great Britain by Clays Ltd, St Ives plc

Headline's policy is to use papers that are natural, renewable and recyclable
products and made from wood grown in well-managed forests and other
controlled sources. The logging and manufacturing processes are expected to
conform to the environmental regulations of the country of origin.

HEADLINE PUBLISHING GROUP
An Hachette UK Company
Carmelite House
50 Victoria Embankment
London EC4Y 0DZ

www.headline.co.uk
www.hachette.co.uk

This book is for Ross.

Midnight: the day-weary sun yawns last colours,
Sea-cooled gold and red fade into frosted silver.
The darkling ocean, dim green in the dying light,
Swallows final embers with rolling whispers.
Unseen, a curlew cries out without answer –
A shrill dart hurled into the black.

Early stars spark – pewter bells playing cold music.
The rising moon, thin and curved, its bone light unfurls
Across the milk-white sand, now a glistening necklace.
The wind, gentle tonight, a warm breath,
Drifts through the machair, the drowsing flowers blow
Sweet scents over the dreaming islands.
Salt and seaweed, the perfume of life and death.

This gliding night, unheard, but not silent
Is a half-dreamt song – a red-rusted drum now beats.
The eastern sky chatters with colour and fresh flight.
Corn-yellow sun, turquoise sea, orchids pink, yellow, blue.
Reddening flames lick smoking peat in morning fires.
Oystercatchers tiptoe surf for dawn-dazzled shells.

Night is, once more, a gentle lament on unplayed fiddles.
The harpsong of morning fills the air again.

Ross Walker, 'Hebridean Night, Midsummer'

Prologue

Little soul

Where I am, there is no day and no night, there is no time. There is nobody but me, and all these little flames that move and flicker, even without wind. Sometimes I feel whirlpools brushing past me, touching me with wispy, invisible hands, their breaths and sighs cold against me. I hear them whisper, talk about their lives and their deaths, and I listen.

So many stories.

So much love and pain and happiness and sadness, so many lives and so many deaths. I try to call, I try to stop them, so I can speak to them. But they never listen, they never stop. They flow and float away, invisible currents of fog inside fog. All that is left is a little flame gleaming in the distance, and a memory, a shadow of their story – and I'm alone again.

I know things now, things I used to not know before. I listened to the whispers for so long, I've known so many lives. I was a child but I'm not a child any more, for all I know and for all I have heard. I dive into the sea of souls and listen to the voices of those here with me. I listen and I know what they carry in their hearts.

I remember my time as a child. I remember when the sea came, and how it was stronger than me, stronger than those who loved me. *I'd always known the sea wanted me; I'd been nearly taken when I wasn't much older than a baby, but my father held on to me and took me home, dripping and distraught, and he and my mum said to each other what a freak accident, how could it have happened, I was watching her, I really was, I know you were, thank goodness she's here, you brought her home.*

And now the sea was back for me. I screamed in my child's heart: please let me go.

Please let me go home.

Please, sea, don't take me.

Please, sea, give me back.

I cried and cried and thought I need to breathe, I need to breathe – but I couldn't feel my tears in the water that was all around me, I couldn't fill my lungs with air. And then everything was peaceful, black and warm. I didn't hurt any more, I wasn't cold any more. I'm saved, I thought. But I wasn't saved, I was drowned.

When the darkness disappeared and my eyes could see again, there was a golden light in front of me. From the light I heard voices calling my name, calling me to go with them. The light pulled me and pulled me, just like the sea that drowned me; and the voices were tender, promising to enfold me with love, and I wanted to reach them, I wanted their embrace because I'd been so scared and in so much pain. But I needed my mum and dad. I couldn't go in there, I couldn't leave them behind. I couldn't leave my family.

And so I turned away from the golden light – and then the greyness and loneliness frightened me, because it was all so desolate, like I was the last person in the world, the only one left. I turned back, but the light and the voices were gone. I was left in the grey and the lonely.

Little lights appeared all around, over my head, under my feet; little flickering flames.

And now I am here, and I wander and listen, and sometimes I cry, sometimes I sing tunes I used to know. Everything is grey and soft, like walking in cotton wool.

I am not sure if a long time has passed or just a little while.

I don't know where I am.

I just know I want to go home.

Whispers echo in the fog, my soft sobs, the tunes I hum. They come back to me a hundred times. But then, one day – if there's such a thing as day where I am – I hear something else, something that is not an echo. Someone calling. The flames all around dance and dance, like they've heard her too, and whirlpools move the fog in slow currents. I walk among the little candles and follow the voice – joy overwhelms me, and I haven't felt joy in so long, so long, it's like I feel it for the first time. It's all new and warm, it feels like sunshine, and I want to laugh and cry at the same time, and I run, run towards whoever is calling me. It must be my family, it must be. It's me, I'm here, I cry without noise – I put my hands up in the white fog and the sound of calling and crying is everywhere, please, Mum, hold my hands and take me home – and she does, she holds my hands and pulls me through.

Everything is black for a moment, and then I open my eyes.

1

Snow in March

Anna

When Ava started inside me, sudden and surprising like snow in March, I didn't have time to ask myself the reasons for such a miracle. I was working too hard, worrying too hard. With all the practical problems and the morning sickness and trying to stay awake during my night shifts, I didn't have much time left to consider what was happening: a human being had taken up residence in my belly, and was growing, growing. Somebody with eyes and ears and hands and legs and a heart. And more; she was more than a body and its parts. A soul lived inside this body-in-the-making, a consciousness, a set of feelings and emotions and thoughts like sparks inside her tiny brain.

I fretted about how I'd look after a baby, with my shifts and little money and no family at hand to help, while the man who did this to me in the first place was lost in one crazy project or another. He was forever wheeling and dealing somewhere while I threw up and cried and surveyed the wards full of new mums, their babies beside them in plastic cots, not quite believing I would be one of them soon. I couldn't sleep, and when I did, I had strange dreams, dreams of water and the sea and grey waves swallowing me. And then Toby would caress my barely-there bump and promise me the world, promise our baby the world – I didn't believe him any more, of course, but I didn't want my child to grow up without a father, like me.

I knew she was a girl. And not just any girl – she was *Ava*. I loved her with an intensity that blew me away. Somehow, in the lottery of procreation, one I witnessed every day in my job, this baby, *this* baby and no other, among the millions of possible genetic combinations, had been given to me. An old rhyme came into my mind, one my Scottish grandmother used to sing:

> *Of all the babies who swam in the sea*
> *Ava was the one for me . . .*

While I was making beds, or fetching nappies for the midwives, or cleaning up mess, I was aware of her, like a constant song in the back of my mind. My belly grew, the fears grew, my love for her grew. In this city of eight million people, I thought as I contemplated the London skyline out of the staffroom window, there was now one more.

Months went by as my secret came into the light, my bump too big to hide. Ava talked to me in every way but words. *I know you, baby – I've known you forever*, I thought as I chose curtains for her nursery, and a Moses basket, and I dreamt of the day I'd hold her in my arms. *I love you, I've loved you forever,* I whispered to her as we lay in bed in the middle of the day, waiting for another exhausting night shift.

I lay half naked with a little thing breaking me from the inside, my body clamping onto itself over and over again. When she finally came out, after what seemed like days, I looked into her eyes, semi-blind and alien black, and I had the strangest thought: that I had fooled myself believing I knew her, this little soul that had sat inside me waiting, this creature I'd been a vessel for.

I didn't know her at all. I had no idea who she was.

I never told anyone about what came into my mind the moment she was born – about the way I didn't recognise her like I thought I would, and how that feeling of *of course, it was you all along* never happened for me. A sense of knowing the creature that has been inside you for nine months and finally getting to meet her – it wasn't like that. I didn't know her, I never had known her. She was somebody other from the little life I had imagined.

It would have been impossible to explain such a weird sensation. People don't talk about these things anyway, and your head is all over the place after you've given birth. You're bound to have strange thoughts.

I soon forgot all about it as Ava grew into herself and I grew into my new life, a life where it was Ava and Anna, our little family.

My daughter's eyes have lost their alienness and now she's fully here, fully herself. Now, I do know her. Ava

Elizabeth Hart, six years old, happy and chatty and lively and fearless like I never was, so different from me and yet so much mine, a part of Toby and me and yet herself.

But when it all began, when Ava told me about a life she had without me, with people I didn't know – that day I thought again of the moment she was born. I thought of the moment they placed her gently in my arms, wrapped in a white blanket, my blood still encrusted in her hair, and she opened those other-worldly eyes and the first thing I thought was *I love you*, and the second was *Where were you before?*

2

All that remains

Anna

I always knew it would happen one day. I always knew Toby would leave us; I was even surprised he'd waited so long. Despite all my efforts, I had failed to keep this lopsided little family together.

I dreaded the day he'd go, not because of me – all my feelings for him had ebbed away a long time ago – but for Ava. She was so close to him, even if he kept letting her down in one way or another. She adored her father; whether or not he actually deserved to be adored was of no concern to a little child.

One winter afternoon, my child-minder, Sharon, phoned me at work to say that Toby had been to the house, stuffed some of his things in a suitcase, and left. I stood there with the phone against my ear, frozen. I could only imagine how it must have felt for Ava, sitting in tears and terror while her dad rushed around packing clothes. It was like a bolt from the blue for her; as for me, I'd played the scenario so many times in my head, I nearly had a sense of déjà vu.

Sharon told me that he'd left behind a note addressed

to me, and a distressed little girl sobbing her heart out. She said that before stepping out of the door he'd spoken to Ava, that he'd told her he was very sorry, but he was going somewhere far, far away, that we'd be better off without him; that he was a loser, that he'd tried but nothing had worked out for him.

He said all that *to his six-year-old daughter.*

Anger burnt scarlet through me as I put the phone down and ran to the ward sister to tell her I had to go home at once. I was a new nurse – I had gained my qualification at last, after years of menial jobs and studying at night while Ava slept – and I was working for an agency.

I hurried out into the freezing evening air; I jumped on a train, and then another, in a daze, tears not of regret but of fury swelling in my eyes. He'd hurt Ava. He'd done the one thing I could not forgive him for. After all the years I'd forced myself to be with him, so we could give Ava a family . . .

When I barged into the flat, Ava was on the sofa watching CBeebies, clutching Camilla, her favourite doll. Her eyes were puffy and red, but she wasn't crying any more. She was sucking her thumb, which was something I had been trying to help her grow out of. She looked very small and very lost.

'Ava, sweetheart . . .' I said as I sat beside her.

She didn't look at me, she didn't move.

'Ava . . .'

'She's been like this for over an hour. She hasn't said a word,' Sharon whispered, her kindly coffee-coloured face shadowed with worry. I felt my heart quickening and my hands tingling; the familiar signs of panic.

I wrapped my arms around my daughter. She let me hold her close, and leaned her head on my chest, still sucking her thumb. I stroked her long black hair and her face – milky skin and almond-shaped black eyes, maybe the heritage of an Asian ancestor we knew nothing about.

'Everything's fine. Mummy is here . . . Where's the note?' I asked Sharon in a low voice, not wanting to disentangle myself from Ava. Sharon seized a piece of paper, roughly folded in four, and handed it to me.

Dear Anna,
    I'm so sorry. I've been nothing but bad news in your life. I'm off to Melbourne to stay with a mate for a bit, and then hopefully get a working visa. I explained everything to Ava, so she wouldn't get too upset . . .

I'm going to kill him, I thought.

. . . you deserve somebody to look after you properly. Ava deserves a proper father . . .

You're right on that one.

You and Ava are better off without me. Please remind Ava how much I love her.
    Toby

And here's where you're wrong, Toby, I said to myself. Very, very wrong. *I* am better off without you; *Ava* isn't. You stupid, irresponsible, selfish man who couldn't hold down a job, who would spend thousands of pounds on a fancy car and then have no money left to buy food, who would feed Ava ice cream for lunch and dinner and then be aghast if she threw up, who was always too busy for the nursery run but found time for a daily catch-up with his friends – your daughter needs you. Not just someone to look after us, but her father.

But you left anyway.

'It'll be okay, baby,' I said into Ava's hair, squeezing her dimpled hand. I felt her letting out a small sigh, full of the grief and loss she didn't know how to express.

It was dark outside, and Ava still hadn't spoken. Dinner-time had come and gone, and she was sitting at the table with an array of untouched plates in front of her. Fish fingers and mash, a ham sandwich, a bowl of tomato soup. Nothing tempted her.

'Let's order pizza!' I said, trying to sound cheery, or even just normal. I was getting desperate.

'What do you say? Pizza?' I repeated, exhaustion squeezing the sides of my head until I felt nauseous. No reply. 'Please, Ava. You haven't eaten anything since breakfast.'

She just sat there looking at me with a blank expression, not saying a word.

*

I phoned the hospital and then the agency, and told them that my daughter was sick and I had to take a few days off. They weren't happy, but they grudgingly accepted my unexpected leave. Then I called Sharon and said I wouldn't need her for a while, but I would keep up with her wages, of course. Finally I phoned Toby's mother. I don't know why. It wasn't like I would get any sympathy or help. Whatever her son did – rack up thousands of pounds of debt, leave yet another job, get beaten up by someone he owed money to – she just found excuses for him, and cried, and said he was such an affectionate boy and it wasn't his fault if he was *a bit immature.*

'Did you know about this?'

'About Australia? Yes. He told me not to tell you until he was ready . . .'

'Well he told Ava. *Before telling me.* He told her he was going away and she was better off without him. Ava is six years old, for God's sake!'

'He's confused. He's just a confused boy with nobody to advise him properly,' she pleaded.

'He's not a boy, Gillian.'

Oh, all the things Gillian didn't know. Toby was very much a man, a man who ranted at me whenever things didn't go his way, who slammed doors, who always knew the right thing to say to make me feel I was worth nothing. But his mother didn't know any of this. She was never to know. It would break her heart, and one heart broken was more than enough.

'You know the way it is. They are always little boys to

their mothers!' She laughed a foolish laugh. There wasn't even any point in being angry with her.

'Good to know that my daughter has a boy for a father,' I hissed.

A little silence, and then came her favourite mantra, her excuse for so much of what Toby did. 'He wasn't ready to be a father.'

As if it had been my fault. As if I'd planned it. I closed my eyes briefly, cursing the day I'd been taken in by his charm, his endless optimism. I was young, and I was alone and starved of affection after a cold, loveless childhood; I'd fallen for his promises.

'If he phones, Gillian, tell him we never want to see him again.'

'What? You can't stop him seeing his daughter!' she whined in a tremulous, how-can-you-be-so-heartless voice.

I put the phone down.

'Please, sweetheart. Maybe a cookie?' I tried again.

I'd made chocolate chip cookies, hoping that baking would channel my confusion a bit, and that they would tempt Ava into eating something.

Still no answer. She just looked at me with those dark eyes of hers, two pools of silent sadness in her white face.

I was ready for a long, long cry, but I couldn't do that in front of Ava. I gently led her into the bathroom and gave her a warm bath with bubbles, chatting to her in a low voice, though she never replied. Then I took her to her room, where I slipped her Little Miss Sunshine PJs on, dried her hair, and tucked her, Camilla and myself into her bed. We lay together, hypnotised by her magic lantern turning and turning, until we both fell asleep.

She didn't speak for three days.

Dawn rose on the fourth day of Ava's silence. I was lying on a mattress in her room, after another white night. Later I would take her to the doctor; I couldn't deny any more that something was terribly, terribly wrong. That something had broken inside her.

I propped myself up, resting my head on my hand. She slept on her back, her chest slowly rising and falling. Little Briar Rose, trapped in an evil spell. She was so beautiful, my daughter, and so small, so vulnerable. It broke my heart that I couldn't protect her from everything, anything that could harm or upset her. That I couldn't save her from this heartache, like I hadn't been protected or saved when I was a child. That I hadn't given her a better father, or, it turned out, a father at all – she would be fatherless, like I had been. Maybe I shouldn't have worked so hard all those years . . . Maybe all the nights I spent on my course books and all the times I was too exhausted to even speak had slowly corroded our family life. But I'd had no chance of an education, no chance to do anything for myself – I *had* to get my qualification. I had spent too many years watching the nurses doing their amazing job while I was stuck cleaning floors. I knew there was more in me; I knew I had more to give.

And I did it for Ava too, to give her a better future. To give her the chances I'd never had.

Tears threatened to flood out of me again, and again I stopped them. During those three ghastly days, I had only cried once, when I was sure Ava was in deep sleep; I couldn't bear the idea of her seeing me crying, and alarming her even more than she had been already.

All of a sudden, she stirred. She jerked her head towards the wall and back again. A small whimper escaped her lips, and then another, as she tossed and turned. I sat on her bed and took her little body in my arms. She began to cry, harder and harder, and her sobs rose to the sky and wrecked my heart. And the worst thing was that she was crying with her eyes closed, like all that pain was coming from the depths of her, unbounded and unchecked, exploding after four days of silence and stillness.

'Shhhhh . . . Mummy's here . . .' Tears were falling down my cheeks too. I couldn't bear it. I couldn't bear to see my daughter in so much pain.

'Mummy!' she cried, and again those dreadful, dreadful sobs – the cries of someone abandoned, all alone in the world. I could feel what she was saying with those sobs – *I've been abandoned, I'm lost* – and I held her tight.

'I'm here, baby, I'm here with you,' I whispered in her ear.

Suddenly her whole body became tense and tight; she was rigid in my arms, just like she used to get as a toddler when she was throwing a tantrum. My heart bled. Then, at last, she relaxed. Her eyelashes, damp with sleep and tears, fluttered some more.

'Ava. Ava!' I called.

Finally she opened her eyes.

'Mummy,' she said in a whisper.

My heart soared. She was speaking again.

'Ava . . .'

'Mummy,' she repeated.

'I'm here . . .'

She blinked over and over again, studying my face. Then she looked straight at me as if she didn't recognise me, and I'll never forget the words that came out of her mouth. I'll never forget the moment when, as I held her in my arms, my face so close to hers that our noses nearly touched, she asked calmly and quietly: 'Where's my mum?'

'Where's my mum?' I asked Miss Carter, my teacher.

I was six years old, a crown of tinfoil on my head and wearing a long white tunic – a shiny triangular cloth with a hole for a head, but to me it seemed like an evening gown, the dress of my dreams. I remember feeling so pretty in my costume, like a princess and a fairy and an angel all mixed together. My hair was loose on my shoulders; the other mums had woven my little friends' hair into braids and buns, but mine didn't have time. She had been out all day and couldn't come to fetch me from school, so I'd had to sneak out on my own – we weren't allowed to go home by ourselves – and go to our neighbour's. It happened often, that my mum wasn't around and Mrs Ritchie had to look after me; my sweet, loving grandmother had died three years before, and since then my life had been pretty much chaos.

When Mrs Ritchie looked after me, I tried to spend as much time as I could in the street so that she wouldn't be annoyed by my presence and then tell on us to the teachers or social workers or whoever else. My mum always said we weren't to tell anyone that she wasn't around much; that if someone asked, I was to say she'd gone to the shops.

But it was December and very cold, so I couldn't stay out for long. I waited and waited in the Ritchies' kitchen for my mum to turn up. It was the day of the school nativity play, and she'd promised she'd come. Mrs Ritchie had given me tea with her two teenage sons, and then I explained to her that I was to go to the school for the show. She didn't roll her eyes like I thought she would do. She stroked my cheek.

'I'll give you a lift in the car,' she said. 'I'm sure your mum will be there.' But as she was putting her coat on, I heard her muttering under her breath, 'As if. As if she'd give up drinking one night, just one bloody night, to go to her daughter's nativity . . .'

I knew she was talking about my mum, but I didn't want to hear. I pretended she'd said nothing. My mum would prove her wrong and turn up, maybe smelling strange and not walking so well, and saying weird, angry things; but she would turn up.

And there I was, with my tinfoil crown and my tunic over my grey uniform skirt and trainers, while the other girls wore ballet shoes and white tights, and their prettiest outfits. But I felt so shiny and special, I couldn't wait to go out on the small stage and show off my glittery angel self. My mum would love it. She'd think I was so pretty, she'd stay at home all night. She'd make us hot milk or cocoa and we'd curl up on the sofa and watch TV, and she wouldn't ask me to get her drinks, or have strange friends over and then keep me up half the night, terrified in my bed, with their yells and fights.

Tonight it'd just be the two of us.

The show came and went. I was blinded by the lights the teachers had borrowed from the local bingo hall, so I couldn't see my mum's face. But the applause was rapturous and I was sure she had loved it. At the end, we all stood together, Joseph and Mary holding a doll Jesus, and sang 'Jingle Bells'. The lights were off by then and I studied the crowd, looking for my mum's face. But she wasn't there.

Hope began to seep out of me and seemed to deflate my very bones. I felt tears gathering in my eyes and I desperately tried not to cry.

Maybe I just couldn't see her. Maybe she was at the back, hidden behind other parents. She was there, she had to be.

But something inside me kept whispering: *She's broken her promise. Again. She won't see you with the silvery crown and the long shiny white gown. She's not here, she wasn't at the show at all.*

19

I felt a warm tear slide down my cheek and wanted to die of embarrassment, but the sadness inside me was so great, I couldn't hold it in.

And then it was a blur, the teachers getting our outfits off and telling us we'd done so well, so well, and releasing us to the waiting parents.

I was left there. There was nobody waiting for me.

'Where's my mum?' I asked Miss Carter, helplessly. I remember clearly how I felt I was standing right at the edge of a cliff, looking down. That feeling stayed with me all my life, like I was forever trying not to fall.

The teachers conferred between them. What to do with me? It was the days before mobile phones, and my house phone was ringing out. Finally, Mrs Ritchie turned up. She'd seen my mum staggering home.

'Agnes is in no fit state to fetch Anna,' she told Miss Carter. 'She asked me who Anna was. Oh, she's a piece of work.'

She asked me who Anna was.

Mrs Ritchie seemed furious, her movements rapid, sharp. 'Come on, dear,' she said, almost sweetly. 'They tell me you looked so pretty in your angel costume . . .'

'Where's my mum?' I repeated, tears now flowing unchecked. A sob racked my chest. I was too upset to be ashamed.

'Don't worry about that. We'll sort it all out,' Mrs Ritchie said, leading me to her car, her lips pursed. She looked so angry. I know now that she was angry with my mum, not with me, but at the time I just couldn't tell, and I was scared. All I knew was that my mum had broken yet another promise, and that I had no idea where she was.

And then there was that other memory: how the night ended.

I never think about that. But sometimes the memory remembers itself, in spite of me.

When I came home, my mum was slumped in the living room. I brought a duvet from upstairs and covered her, and then I slept on the sofa in my angel dress, hoping I could finally show it to my mum when she woke up. We'd been allowed to take our costumes home so our mothers could wash them and return them clean.

Finally morning came. I tried to wake her up and show her the dress, but she yelled at me, and threw an empty bottle. I was afraid, but I thought if she had a shower and drank some coffee she would feel better, so I tried again to wake her – and all the drinking she'd done came out of her and onto my dress, onto my lovely angel dress, now soiled and reeking like it meant nothing, like it was a piece of garbage.

That was the beginning.

The night Ava asked about her mum, even if I was shocked, I didn't probe her – it just wasn't the right moment, not after those three terrible days without eating or speaking. She couldn't go back to sleep, so I made her some milk, and she asked for honey in it – she'd never liked honey, I thought in passing, but I had more pressing worries on my mind than her changing tastes. We watched *Frozen* for the umpteenth time, snuggled up under the duvet with Camilla.

Although Ava's strange words had chilled me, I put them down to shock. For the next few days I hardly thought about them. But there was a difference in her; something had changed after those three days of silence and refusal to eat. Yes, she was back to her lively, cheerful self, but every once in a while a weird daze descended on her, and a faraway look appeared in her eyes, like she was seeing something I couldn't see, or remembering something long past.

About a week later, on our way home from school, she was jumping in the puddles with her bright red wellies, and I was chatting about her dance class.

'. . . soon we'll have to buy you a new leotard, you've grown so much recently . . .' I was saying, when suddenly she stopped and raised her face to the sky.

'Come on, baby, we only have half an hour and we still need to get a snack and get changed . . .'

The faraway look I had noticed before was back, like she was there and yet she wasn't. She stood like that for a moment, her little nose in the air. Then she looked down at the puddle again. I could see her reflection in the still water – the red jacket, her dark hair in two braids, her face like a little pale moon.

'I remember,' she said.

I don't know why, but those perfectly innocent words sent a chill down my spine. Maybe it was the way she'd said it, her hazy, remote look; maybe because a part of me *knew* that something was happening in her mind.

'What do you remember?' I asked in a low voice. Two older boys in blazers walked past us, hands in pockets, laughing loudly, and I didn't hear her reply.

'What did you say?'

'I remember one day it was raining, and I jumped in the puddles,' she said.

Relief filled me. 'Of course, you've done it many times. Now come along, we'll be late . . .'

'My mum took me to the beach and there were puddles in the sand, and she said they were like tiny seas. One day we saw a little fish swimming in a puddle, and she took it and ran and threw it in the sea. She ran and she laughed all the way and she said the fishy was very slippery.'

Ava giggled at the memory. I could only look at her, speechless. But then she simply started walking again, skipping a little as she always did.

'Come on, Mum! We need to get to dance class!' she called, as if nothing had happened.

All through the dance lesson, as Ava and her friends jumped about in their leotards like little pink ducklings, I mulled over her words. My mind was like a stuck record, playing what she'd said over and over again.

She ran and she laughed all the way and she said the fishy was very slippery . . .

Who was this person Ava was talking about? This woman she called mother?

I was too frightened to ask.

The months that followed were the strangest of my life. On the outside, things went back to normal, just without Toby. But what was going on in Ava's mind – that was indecipherable.

She never asked for her dad. A couple of days after she'd gone back to school, I cleared out Toby's belongings and packed them into boxes to bring to his mother – there was no way I'd keep them in the house. I'd put them in a cupboard so that Ava wouldn't see them, but I'd forgotten something: a favourite jumper of his, a frayed thing he'd had since we'd got together. I walked into the room and I saw Ava holding it in her hands, just looking at it without a word. There was a thoughtfulness to her face – like she was trying to absorb something enormous, something momentous, too big to be grasped or understood.

'Ava . . .' I began, thinking that she needed to be comforted. But she let the jumper fall as if it was incandescent and turned to me.

'I'm going to watch TV now,' she blurted and ran out of the door.

She didn't want to talk about it. And so I never brought it up again, all the while worrying that she was bottling up her pain, but not knowing how to tackle the conversation.

Instead, she kept mentioning her *other mum* and what they did together. She never went into much detail; I didn't know if it was because that was all she knew, all she *remembered* – that was how she put it – or if there was so much more going on in her mind, and she chose only to show me the tip of the iceberg.

It kept happening. The weird memories kept coming.

I was giving her a bath, and she told me how she used to have a white and green striped bathrobe. 'Was this at Granny Hart's house?' I asked her.

She shook her head, foam flying from her hair. 'No. I had it in my other home.'

At breakfast, she mentioned that she used to have a bowl with a rabbit painted on it, and that she ate porridge in it. 'And no, Granny Hart didn't give me porridge!' she pre-empted me. 'My other mum did!' At her dance class, she told me she used to dance in black shoes, not pink. And that her mum had put a red ribbon in her hair for the dance show.

She didn't seem upset or sad when she mentioned these things to me, not for a while. And then, one day, as we were watching TV on the living room sofa, she hid her face in my shoulder.

'Are you sleepy, darling?'

She shook her head, her face still hidden against me.

'What's wrong?'

'I want to see my mum. My other mum,' she murmured, and her voice was heavy with tears.

As usual, the mention of this phantom woman, this

ghost hovering in our lives, took my breath away. I didn't know what to say – I just could not bring myself to ask. I could only hold Ava, cradle her soft, sweet-smelling body and stroke her hair, murmuring nonsensical words the way mothers do.

I had no idea what to do. In her short life, every time Ava had been upset or out of sorts, I'd always had a solution. If she had a temperature I'd give her medicine; if she scraped a knee I'd give her cuddles; if she was afraid of something I would hold her tight.

But if she asked me to take her to her mother, what could I do?

All this weighed like a stone in my heart and I desperately needed some advice, but I felt I couldn't confide in anyone. My own mother, well, she was a non-entity in my life, someone I saw every six months to make sure she had a roof over her head, cook her a meal and do a couple of washes, nothing more. And imagine telling Gillian.

No. I was on my own. I couldn't tell anyone what was happening. I couldn't find the words to explain that my daughter had started talking about an imaginary life she had somewhere else – another life, another *mother*.

But her pleas continued. She kept asking to see her mum, and I was at a loss.

One day, as I collected Ava from school, her teacher asked to have a word with me. I thought she wanted to tell me how Ava was doing in class – I'd told her that Ava's father had left us and was now in Australia – and I hoped with all my heart that she'd say everything was well, that Ava was coping fine. We left Ava in the office with the secretary and a couple of children whose parents were late, and went to the classroom.

'Ava is doing a lot better, it seems to me,' Miss Luther said. She was a tall young woman with dyed blonde hair and trendy black-rimmed glasses.

'She is, yes. Thanks for looking out for her . . .'

'You're very welcome. This kind of thing happens all the time, you know; children with both parents at home are a rarity nowadays, so please don't think that Ava will feel in any way different from her classmates. I'm not dismissing her distress, of course . . .'

'No, I understand.'

'She was tired for a bit after she had that horrible flu,' she continued. Ava had never had the flu, of course; those were the days she was refusing to speak, so I couldn't send her to school. 'She was picking at her food at lunch-time, a bit dreamy during lessons . . . but she soon perked up, and she's herself again now.'

'That's good,' I said.

Miss Luther pushed her glasses up her nose. She looked pensive, as if she were searching for the right words. The right words to tell me what? Just to update me on how Ava was doing, or was there something else? My hands began prickling, and a subtle wave of anxiety began to work its way up to my chest.

'You're probably wondering why I wanted a word with you,' she said, echoing my thoughts.

I nodded, nerves knotting my stomach.

'This,' she said, turning round and picking up something bright yellow from her desk, 'is Ava's Busy Book. It's an exercise book for her to use when she's finished her work, if she has a free moment. The children use them however they want: write little compositions, draw pictures, cut and paste, anything. Ava's Busy Book is so pretty. She's really very talented in art . . .'

'She is, isn't she?' I said, trying to force a smile, my throat dry. Something was coming. 'I'm sorry, Miss Luther, but what is all this about?'

She smiled. 'Have a look yourself.'

I opened the yellow book at the first page. A picture of Ava's fairy wings and wand set she'd received for her birthday, coloured with felt-tip pens. A short piece on how bees make honey, written in her neat, methodical handwriting, decorated with little yellow and brown bees dotted all around and a jar of honey in the corner. The text of a song they'd learnt in school. A series of princesses with different outfits, each with a name – Princess Diamond, Princess Emerald, Princess Moonlight . . . She really had a lovely imagination, I thought with pride.

And then there was a picture of the sea, blue and grey, taking up two whole pages. In the corner, a beach with two figures. One was definitely Ava, with her long black hair in a braid; the other was a tall blonde woman. Nice, I thought. A seascape. I turned the page. Another seascape, this time from a different angle, but the same sea, blue-grey. And the same two figures: a small one with Ava's black hair, and a tall, blonde one. And another picture – a yellow sun in the upper left corner, and again the two figures on the light brown sand. And another. And another, and another.

There were only two pages left empty in the Busy Book. Ava had filled it all with seascapes, and those little pictures of herself and the mysterious woman.

'I see,' I said, my voice shaking.

'Don't take this the wrong way, but . . . well, I've never seen anything like this. She does two or three of these pictures a day . . . as you can see, the whole book is full of them. We've been encouraging her to do something else when she finishes her work, like reading a library book, or doing word searches, but she says she really wants to draw. And look . . .'

Miss Luther stood up and walked across the room; I followed her. She pointed to a colourful display on the wall. The banner over the display said: *What makes me happy*. There were pictures from the whole class, carefully framed on blue sugar paper, each with the name of the pupil who'd drawn it printed and glued in the far left corner.

A painting of a dog, with the caption *My dog Blackie makes me happy – Adeela*. A father-and-son scene, playing football surrounded by tall grey buildings: *Football with my dad makes me happy – Connor*. A games console and two boys playing: *My best friend makes me happy – Jonathan . . .*

'And this is Ava's,' Miss Luther said, pointing at a picture somewhere in the centre.

Of course.

It was a painting of a calm bright blue sea, a yellow sun in the sky. In the foreground were the same two figures: Ava wearing her favourite dress, a bright red summer one with spaghetti straps and a ra-ra skirt, and a woman dressed in blue. The caption made my knees go weak: *Going to the beach with my mum makes me happy.*

Except that the woman was not me. It was the woman from the Busy Book pictures, tall and blonde. Definitely not me.

I looked more closely and saw that Ava had drawn a little sign on the beach: *Seal.*

'I just wanted to show you because . . . well, she seems sort of obsessed with this scene. It's a happy scene, as you can see, so I'm not concerned *as such* . . . I'm not a psychologist, of course, but it just seems a bit strange . . . I mean, a bit unusual' – of course, 'strange' wasn't exactly a politically correct word – 'that she'd draw the same thing over and over again.'

'Yes. I know.' My mouth was so dry I was struggling to speak. I had no idea what these seascapes were, but I was sure they had something to do with the things she'd been saying since her dad left – about her 'other life'. About her other mummy.

'Have you been on holiday at the seaside at some point? Somewhere she really loved? Where she saw a seal, maybe?' Miss Luther said, pointing at the tiny sign.

I nodded. 'We've been to Tenerife once. But there were no seals,' I said, my voice artificially calm. I didn't want Miss Luther to see I was upset, in case she thought there was something actually to worry about, and then Ava would be under scrutiny. I collected myself and continued.

'She had a great time there. She met a little French girl and they played together for the whole two weeks . . . she had the cutest long blonde hair,' I said, pointing to the tall, blonde figure in the display. 'I think she's remembering a happy time, now that she's had some upset in her life.' I smiled a tight smile.

'But the caption says: *Going to the beach with my mum*,' Miss Luther noted.

'She was there with me, of course. She just forgot to draw me. She only drew her friend . . . Amélie, her name was, I think. Well, if that's all, thank you for letting me know. I'll certainly tell her to use her Busy Book more . . . more usefully.' *Use it more usefully?* I felt my cheeks grow scarlet. My painted-on calm was falling to pieces. I just wanted to get away and digest what she'd shown me.

'No problem. And if you have any concerns, please come and speak to me . . .'

'I don't have any concerns at all. I mean, she's fine. We have a great support system.' We didn't. We had a child-minder – albeit wonderful – my best friend, who happened to be extremely busy and had two children of her own, and a stepbrother I never saw. More than a lot of people had, but less than a family. A lot less. 'We'll be fine. Ava is a happy child . . .'

'She certainly is.'

'And very settled . . .'

'Absolutely.'

'With a great love of the sea,' I concluded, my hands clasped together to stop them from shaking.

I sat in the car and cried. The blonde woman was her other mum. The seascape was not Tenerife. We'd never met a little French girl; *Amélie* was a film I'd seen. And what about the sign that said *Seal*? Had she invented that too?

I looked at myself in the rear-view mirror. My eyes were red-rimmed and my cheeks looked just a little bit hollow – I'd lost weight. That wasn't good. I had to keep strong; I had to keep my energy up for Ava.

I had to understand. And I couldn't carry this burden all on my own any more. I had to speak to someone.

I took out my mobile phone and called Parvati. Parvati and I had been close friends since we'd trained as nurses together, and we worked for the same agency. I wasn't one for confidences, but if I were to open up to anyone, it would be her.

'Hi, it's me . . .'

'Are you okay? Your voice sounds strange. Have you been crying?'

'No. I mean yes. Just . . . Things are bit complicated.'

I heard her sighing. 'Toby.' Let's just say Toby wasn't her favourite person.

'Not exactly. Well, in a way. Listen, I was wondering if you feel like a curry and a drink after work on Saturday? Come over and I'll tell you all.'

'Of course. Ajit can look after the twins.'

'Thank you.'

'Any time, Anna. You know that.'

Yes, of course. I knew she was there for me, just like I was there for her. There was no doubt in my mind. What I did feel doubtful about was how I could explain what was happening with Ava, and what she would make of it.

After a long shift at the hospital, Parvati came to my house for a home-made curry and a glass of wine as promised.

'So. How are things?' she asked as we settled on the sofa. Ava was in bed, her magic lantern on and Camilla in her arms.

'You mean, without Toby?' I said. I wasn't ready to throw myself into what was really bothering me. I had to find the right words, the right moment.

'I don't want to pry, but yes. You sounded really stressed on the phone.'

'I know what you're thinking,' I said, looking down into my glass of Prosecco.

She smiled. 'You always know what I'm thinking.'

'True. You're relieved that Toby is gone.'

'Absolutely. When you told me, I rejoiced,' she said, rolling her eyes. 'I mean, I'm sad for Ava, I know how much she loves him, but . . . yes, I rejoiced for you.'

'I don't miss him at all, Parvati, not for a moment. Except when I have to bring the bloody recycling down four flights of stairs.' I laughed bitterly. 'That says a lot about how things were between us.'

I pulled up the shoulder of my oversized white cardigan, falling loose on my small frame. Soft music played in the background, turned low so it wouldn't disturb Ava.

'But . . .'

'I knew there was a but. It's Ava, isn't it?' Parvati took a sip of her wine.

I lowered my head. 'She misses him so much.'

'I can imagine . . . Ava has always been a daddy's girl. She must be so upset . . .'

'She's devastated,' I said miserably, and there was a touch of anger in my voice.

'God, I hate the man even more now. I never liked the way he treated you. Putting you down for every little thing . . .'

I didn't want to be reminded of it. I didn't want to talk about it. 'Yes, well. He did that.'

'How is she doing now?' asked Parvati, turning her head briefly towards the corridor. The living room door was ajar, and we could see the blue reflection of the night light in Ava's room.

'Okay. She's sleeping and eating well, and according to her teacher, she's enjoying school.'

'So where is this devastation you talk about?'

'What do you mean?'

'You told me Ava is devastated. I don't really see any signs of it. Maybe you are overestimating the effect that her dad leaving has had on her.'

I took another sip of my Prosecco, Dutch courage for the strange things I was about to tell her. 'There's something else . . .' I said, refilling her glass.

'Right. It's something big, then. You are seeing someone? You met someone?' She smiled, her eyes shining in the light of the table lamp.

'Parvati! No. Bloody. Way. No no no no. Nothing like that . . .' I closed my cardigan over my collarbone in an unconscious gesture.

Parvati put her hands up. 'No, of course not. I had forgotten I was talking to Miss Self-Sacrifice. God forbid you should do something for yourself!'

I laughed. 'Ah, silly. Look . . .' I rested my glass on the coffee table and walked over to the kitchen. I carefully slipped a picture from under a heart-shaped magnet and handed it to Parvati. She ran a hand through her jet-black hair and studied it.

'This is lovely. Ava did it, yes? So this is Ava, and the sea . . . those are seagulls, I suppose . . . and seals! So cute. And this is you, holding her hand? But . . . she gave you blonde hair?'

'That's not me,' I said, each word coming slowly, reluctantly out of me.

'Her teacher?'

'No . . .' I might as well get to the point. 'That's her other mum.'

35

'Her . . . what?'

'Her other mum.' Just talking about it made me feel choked. I hoped there would be no tears, tired as I was after the twelve-hour shift, the wine and the weirdness of it all.

'Okay. You need to explain this to me, because I have no idea what you're talking about.' She refilled my glass. 'Now tell me.'

I studied the dark blue nail polish on my toes as I sat back on the IKEA sofa, my legs crossed, looking for the right words.

'This is the thing. When Toby left, Ava stopped . . . *functioning* for a little while. She wasn't eating, sleeping, talking . . . nothing. It lasted three days.'

'Oh . . . I remember you saying that she had a touch of the flu. You took a few days off . . .'

'Yes. That's what I said, because I didn't know how to explain the whole thing, the way she was like a living doll. It was a nightmare.'

'Oh Anna! You must have been terrified . . . You should have told me.'

I shrugged. 'Then she got better, just like that. She woke up from a vivid dream and she started talking again. Everything went back to normal . . . except the first thing she said was "Where's my mum?" And I was right there, Parvati, right in front of her.'

'Oh Anna,' she repeated. Her eyes were wide. 'Maybe it was dark, maybe she couldn't see you . . . maybe she hadn't woken up fully . . .'

I shook my head. 'No. She was awake, and she could see me fine.' I took a breath. 'And there's more.'

She pushed me gently away to look at my face. 'Tell me.'

'Ava's teacher called me in. The picture I showed you . . . she'd done *dozens* of them. All showing the same scene – the sea and this woman.'

Parvati raised her eyebrows. 'Dozens?'

I nodded. 'I don't know what's happening to my daughter.'

'It's the shock of her father leaving, that's all. A phase. She'll grow out of it.'

'Yes. Yes. Of course she'll grow out of it,' I said and took another sip of wine. There was a little silence. 'Do you think . . . do you think I should take her to a doctor?'

'Well, I was going to say. Maybe a child psychologist could help. I know my friend took her daughter to one a while ago. A Dr Craig . . . she said he was great. I can get his number for you if you want.'

I nodded wearily. 'Yes. Yes, maybe that will help. Oh God. I'm so mad at myself.'

Parvati frowned. 'What have *you* done wrong?'

'I didn't protect her,' I said sadly.

'We can't protect our children from life. And that's from someone who still hasn't removed the bed guard from her sons' beds, and they are seven . . .'

I laughed despite my tears.

'But it'll all sort itself out, with time, love and some more wine.'

'Just as well I'm off tomorrow,' I said, letting Parvati fill my glass again.

I arranged an appointment with Dr Craig, with more than a few misgivings. The following week, we were sitting in a softly lit waiting room at the private clinic. Ava was chirpy and unconcerned, playing with the toys scattered all around. I was a bundle of nerves.

'Ava Hart?' the receptionist called, and my heart started pounding. Silently I took Ava by the hand and we made our way into the doctor's office.

Dr Craig was a tall, imposing man with huge eyebrows and gentle eyes. He sat behind his dark-wood desk like a kindly king on his throne. I relaxed a little as he smiled at us, a smile that looked honest, like he really cared. I had already explained to him on the phone the crux of the matter, so he knew what to expect as he began chatting to Ava.

'Your mum tells me you make beautiful pictures. That you love drawing the sea.'

Ava nodded.

'You love drawing one place in particular, don't you?'

'Yes.'

'Right. And where is this place?'

Ava shrugged. 'I don't know. I don't live there any more.'

'But you used to?'

'Yes. I remember when I used to live there . . .' A shadow passed across her little face. I was alarmed. I didn't want her to get upset. My eyes went from her to Dr Craig and back.

'What do you remember?'

'The sea. And my mum,' she said in a small, vulnerable voice. She turned to look at me, and her eyes were so sad all of a sudden.

'So your mum lived with you in this place called Seal?'

'Yes. Not this mum. My other one.'

My stomach knotted up even more.

'Oh, I see,' the doctor said easily, like it was all perfectly normal.

Ava nodded. 'I miss my other mum,' she said, and again she turned to me, as if to silently apologise for this little betrayal. Also, I thought I read a silent plea in her eyes – to stop these questions that were upsetting her.

'Ava, your mum . . . this mum here . . .' Dr Craig said, perfectly serious, 'told me that something happened in your life recently. Something about your dad.'

Ava nodded again. I wanted to intervene, to stop this stranger from taking her back there, to the day her dad packed his bag in front of her and said goodbye. But I pressed my lips together and forced myself to be quiet.

'Your dad decided to go and live somewhere else, didn't he?'

Another nod.

'And how does that make you feel?'

My heart sank as I saw my daughter forced to face what had happened. I tried to tell myself that it was good that such strong emotions should be acknowledged and not just buried deep; that Dr Craig knew what he was doing; but inside I was crying for her.

'It makes me feel really sad.'

'And you want to be happy again?'

'Yes. But my dad isn't coming back. He said so.'

'Right. Ava, you said you had a mum there. Did you have a dad too?'

'Yes, but I can't remember him very well.'

'And you all lived together, in the same house?'

'I think so. There was the sea all around. I really, really want to go back . . .' I could see a wave of emotion running through her little body, and all of a sudden I just couldn't take it any more. I couldn't bear to see her upset.

'Doctor . . .' I murmured, and wrapped a sheltering arm around my daughter's shoulders. He raised his hand slightly, as if telling me to hold on.

'Did you like that? Did you like that you were living together in a place near the sea?'

'Yes. I want to go back there.'

'Doctor, maybe it's enough for today,' I said, more decisively now.

'Ava, I'll tell you what. Why don't you go and play with our toys while me and your mum have a little chat?' He nodded towards me and I took Ava by the hand, leading her outside to the waiting room.

'Are you okay, sweetheart?'

She didn't reply.

'Ava . . .'

She took a little breath, and looked at me. Her face was composed again. 'Yes. I'm okay. The man understands.'

'What does he understand?'

'That I used to live *there* and I want to go back.'

'Yes. Yes, he understands,' I murmured, wondering how on earth I was going to unravel all that was happening. 'Why don't you play here for a bit? I'm just going to go and have a little chat with him now.'

'Okay, Mummy,' she said, and I exchanged a glance with the secretary, who nodded imperceptibly, as if to say that she would keep an eye on her.

I went back inside and sat down, holding my breath as I waited for Dr Craig to speak.

'Our chat was brief today; I didn't want Ava to feel overwhelmed in our first session.' He didn't? All that questioning, albeit in a gentle tone, had felt pretty overwhelming to me. 'I need some time to try and unravel her . . . recollections, so to speak.'

'But what do you think?' I interrupted. 'Sorry,' I said, feeling my colour rise. 'It's just that . . . Well, it's been difficult. And I don't know what to think.'

'It's early to say, but at this stage my feeling is that Ava has been greatly affected by her father leaving, and because of this she's building an imaginary life for herself in which both mum and dad live at home. It's a sort of escape from the stress in her life, a way to imagine that everything is back to normal. A way to sort in her mind what she can't sort in her life.'

'Right.' A moment of silence, then I shook my head, my hands clutching the armrests of the chair. 'It's my fault.'

'Mrs Ford . . .'

'Miss Ford,' I said softly. It was important for me to acknowledge that Toby and I were not married. I didn't want to feel tied to him, not any more than having a child together made me.

'Miss Ford, mothers always feel guilty about something, whatever happens. Children come to me with a million different issues, some big and some small, and mothers always say *it's my fault*. Ninety-nine per cent of the time, it isn't.'

'I'm the one per cent,' I said, and to my shame, I felt my eyes well up with tears. I had cried so much since the whole *other mum* thing had begun. Dr Craig passed me a tissue from a Barbie box. He also had a Spiderman one. I thought of the children who had cried in that room and needed a tissue from the colourful boxes.

'I beg to differ,' he said gently. 'Traumatising events will happen in all our lives, whether we are grown-ups or children. All we can do is learn to get through them. Stand strong so that the waves don't sweep us away.'

Apt metaphor, I thought, considering that Ava kept talking about the sea.

'I don't know *how* to be a mother. I never had a mother of my own.'

Dr Craig looked at me seriously. Then he turned a framed photograph on his desk towards me.

'This is my son. His name is Max. When he was born, thirteen years ago now, I went into a complete panic.' I gave a little laugh, drying my tears with my fingers. 'Honestly,' he continued, 'I had no idea how to be a father, I felt completely overwhelmed by the responsibility. And I am a child psychologist.' I laughed again, and he joined me. He had managed to lighten the mood a little. 'Nobody knows how to be a parent really. We all muddle through. If you had a hard childhood, maybe that makes you even more careful, even more aware. Though it's not my place to pass judgement on you either way, let me tell you: it's plain to see that you are a wonderful mother; the bond between you is palpable. And Ava will be fine, with time and a little help.'

His words gave me some solace, but the disquiet would not go away so easily. 'Thank you. It's just . . .' A pause. I bet he was used to listening to the parents as much as the children. 'It's just that it's been so hard, by myself. Her father was hardly ever there. Even when he *was* there, if you know what I mean. Actually, when he was, it was worse. It was chaos.'

'I hear this kind of thing all the time. It's very, very hard to parent alone,' he said.

'Dr Craig, *why* is Ava making up this whole thing? About having another mother?'

'I don't think it has anything to do with *wanting* another mother. She's just fabricating an alternative scenario in her mind, an ideal life where she lives exactly where she wants, and her mum and dad are together. She's myth-building.'

Myth-building. Okay.

'This whole sea obsession. We've only been on holiday to the seaside once, in Spain. I didn't think it would have impressed her so much. And anyway, it wasn't like the place Ava describes. You know, the wind, the seals, the high waves . . .'

'Maybe she's seen a film or read a book, and reworked it in her mind? Used it as a scenario for her fantasy world?'

'It could be . . .' Yes. She always watched *Katie Morag* on CBeebies – a colourful programme set on a Scottish island. Maybe that was where it all started from. Or a book they'd read in school.

'But what should I do? When she talks about this imaginary life . . . what should I say?'

'Listen to her. Don't dismiss her fantasies, but gently remind her of the here and now. If you wish to bring her back to me, Ava and I can have a chat every couple of weeks and see how things are going.'

'Okay. Okay.' I tried to fill my lungs with air, but it didn't really work.

'Actually, I'm going to give you some homework,' Dr Craig said with a smile. I nodded. '*Ask* her about this dream of hers. Show that you want to know, that you are interested. Try not to convey any fear or distress you have about it . . . show her you want to be part of it.'

'All right. I'll do that. I . . .' My voice trailed away. It was hard to find the words.

The doctor raised his eyebrows, waiting, giving me time to think. I looked down.

'I *wanted* to give her all that. A proper family. But it just didn't work out.' I felt my eyes welling up again.

'We want nothing but perfection for our children. We want to protect them from everything, to keep them safe. But life gets in the way. Life can never be perfect. It can only be as good as we make it.'

'I suppose so.'

'Miss Ford, would you like to know what I think?'

I nodded, not trusting myself to speak.

'I think that Ava is a much-loved child, and like I said, you are a loving, committed parent. She'll be fine. And so will you.'

Maybe I should have felt patronised. But the kindness in Dr Craig's voice, his warm eyes, the way he had shown me the picture of his son, made me feel better for a moment. There was someone in my corner, someone who knew what was going on. I had to trust him.

Ava was myth-building, he'd said. It was all a fabrication, and it was all going to be fine.

I desperately wanted to believe him. But my deepest instinct told me that something had happened during that period when Ava wasn't talking – something had happened to her mind. And I had no idea what it was.

3

Heart of home

Anna

I crawled to the Friday until I finally had two days off in a row. My plan was to give Ava a proper day out, complete with shopping and play park. Some time for the two of us alone.

It was a lovely early-summer day, one of those days when London feels like the south of France – warm, sunny, the sky as blue as forget-me-nots. Ava's dark hair shone in the sunlight, and she looked so pretty in her denim pinafore, short-sleeved red T-shirt and red tights. She loved red, and most of her outfits included a bit of it, even if just a touch.

We scoured the shops in Oxford Street and collected treasures: a mini diary with a pen, a tiny box with three lip glosses in it, a hair band decorated with a small fabric flower. We laughed and giggled like girlfriends, all our cares, big and small, forgotten. It was wonderful. She didn't mention her other life at all as we explored the shops and walked the crowded streets, both excited in the buzz of this busy city.

After a few hours, though, we began to get tired. There

were so many people, and everyone seemed in a rush. I held Ava's hand, worried she might get lost in the crowd. Red buses passed by and deafened us for a few moments, bikes whizzed past; every few minutes we had to step aside so as not to bump into a fellow shopper, or a tourist, or a Londoner on the way back from work. All of a sudden, it was too much, and we both felt it.

It was time to head to our favourite play area, tucked away in the depths of a quiet park not too far from our flat, and – unbelievably for such a populated area of the world – little used. Laden with bags, we walked through the iron gates and stepped into the soft, enveloping green. In this island of trees and grass, the din of the city seemed far away – the noise of distant traffic, filtered by the trees, sounded a little like the sea ebbing and flowing.

We stopped at an ice cream van, and then sat on a bench overlooking the play park in quiet companionship. We were finishing our ice creams – decadent things with hundreds and thousands and a chocolate Flake – when a little girl about Ava's age skipped up to us. Her bunches had come undone, sitting askew on the sides of her head, and her cheeks were flushed in the heat of the day.

'Want to play tag?' she asked Ava, bouncing up and down like she was unwilling to stop even for a minute. On the bench next to us, a woman – probably the girl's mother – was surveying the scene with a smile on her face. Ava looked at me; I gave her an encouraging nod, so she finished the last of her ice cream as fast as she could and scampered off with her new friend.

I sat in the warm air, relaxing after the busyness of the shops, and watched Ava playing with the little girl. A few other children had gathered around them, laughing, climbing up the slides and frames and occasionally bursting into cartwheels.

After a while, I saw Ava stop and stand still, like the quiet in the eye of the hurricane, with the other children whirling around her.

She stood with her head bowed.

I sat up; I knew what was coming. I had developed a sense for when she was about to speak of her other life. Even if she did so calmly, matter-of-factly, something descended on her at those moments, something alien that didn't belong to her, or to me. And so I knew what was ahead as she walked slowly towards the bench, leaving behind the children she'd been playing with, and sat beside me. She was quiet for a moment.

'Are you not playing any more?' I asked, nerves churning my stomach.

She shrugged her shoulders.

'Are you tired?' I pressed.

And then it came.

'My other mum always took me to the play park near the school. I could see the sea, right there,' she said, pointing at the trees at the edge of the park. Above them I could see a pale blue sky and the outline of the highest buildings beyond.

I froze.

Her other mum took her to the play park.

Somewhere near the sea.

She could see it as she played.

She'd often said things along these lines, but for some reason, at that moment I just couldn't take it. My eyes filled up and I scrunched the dirty paper towels I still had in my hands after our ice creams. It had been such a lovely day. Why, why did she have to mention somewhere else, someone else?

'*I* am your mum, Ava!' I said, fighting to keep the tears from falling. Out of the corner of my eye, I could see the woman at the next bench lifting her head suddenly. I immediately felt guilty. I didn't want to upset Ava – things were confusing enough for her without me losing my temper – but I was overwhelmed. 'I'm your mum!' I repeated desperately, helplessly.

Ava took my hand. There was something wise, something timeless in that gesture. Her blue eyes fixed on mine, and they weren't an innocent little girl's eyes any more; now they hid a secret. A secret too big for my daughter's little heart to contain, for her young brain to wrap itself around.

'I have two mums,' she said calmly, as if it was the most natural thing in the world.

My heart sank and I sat back on the bench, every part of my body drained of strength. All around us were the happy cries of children. Birds chirping, strollers chatting, and in the distance, the sound of the London traffic. The sound that I'd just thought was very much like the sea.

My daughter was all I had. All I had in the world, my

only family, the only person who truly, truly loved me like my mother never had. I couldn't lose her. I couldn't share her.

I couldn't.

It was time to ask. I couldn't deny what was happening any more – I couldn't pretend it wasn't happening. I had simply run out of the energy to do that.

I took a breath and steeled myself. 'Where is she, Ava? Where is your other mum?'

Ava looked up towards the tops of the trees. Her little legs were kicking the air. 'Seal.'

'Seal?' I repeated. And then I remembered the sign on the picture she'd drawn in school. I knelt down in front of her, the grass damp under my knees. I took her by the shoulders and locked my eyes with hers again. 'Where is Seal?' I asked.

'I don't know.'

'Ava, listen. *Who* is your other mother?'

'I don't know. I can't remember!' She was becoming distressed. I could see she was about to cry, but what could I do?

'You *can* remember her . . . You talk about her.'

'I can't remember her name! I don't know what she looks like . . .' The deep frown on her forehead told me she was going to dissolve into tears any second.

'It's okay. It's okay, my love . . .'

'She speaks to me.'

'Who? Who speaks to you? Your other mum?'

'No . . . I don't know who it is. She tells me things. Not

all the time, just sometimes. I can hear her . . . Please, Mummy, I don't want to talk any more . . .'

I held her tight, my heart cold and heavy. 'You can go and play, darling. Everything is fine. Everything is just fine,' I whispered in her ear.

She pushed back from me and gazed at me. A change had come over her face, as though a cloud had lifted, as though she was back here, back with me. She took my face in her hands and smoothed my hair down, the way she often did. Then off she ran to her new friend, back to their games, leaving me breathless and charged, like a cat before a storm. I sat back on the bench, my hands trembling. My question hung unanswered in the chilly air, as the afternoon turned into early evening and a cold breeze began to blow.

We made our way home in silence, Ava holding her little treasures, tired and lost in thought. I kept her hand in mine all the way, never letting go, not even for a moment.

Ava was my daughter.

She only had one mother.

Ava was *mine*.

That night I sat at my computer in my pyjamas, my hair held up with a clip. Ava was sleeping already, exhausted after our long day out. I was tired too, and emotionally drained after the mini meltdown I'd had in the play park; but a million questions were surging inside me, and I couldn't quite relax.

She speaks to me, Ava had said.

There was a voice in her mind.

I didn't even know where to begin to unravel this.

I felt in my bones that things were coming to a head, that Ava's memories, or whatever they were, were more and more in the forefront of her mind. I knew that if I wanted to help her, I needed to find out more. I had to start from the little I knew to discover whether this place Ava talked about existed, or if it was just a product of her imagination, like Dr Craig had said.

Seal.

My fingers lingered on the keyboard, eager and still at the same time, unwilling to type the word into the Google box. I was afraid of what I would find. Maybe I hoped to come across some book or TV programme about a place by the sea where a little girl lived happily; something that Ava might have read at nursery or seen on TV while I was at work, like the *Katie Morag* series she loved. That way I could fully believe that she was making it all up to comfort herself.

Because what I didn't want to admit, even to myself, was that I didn't know any more. I didn't know that it was all fantasy. There was something in the confidence and surety she showed when she spoke about this other life that brought shivers down my spine. Something in the way she looked, in the sound of her voice when she told me about the sea, about her other mother, about her other *life*.

Something that made me doubt my own mind.

Letter by letter, I entered *Seal* into the search box. My heart was pounding. I took a deep breath, ready to press Enter . . . and then I hesitated. I clasped my hand over my mouth, the light of the computer shining on my face. I brought both my knees up onto the chair and curled into myself, looking out of the window at the lights of London shining in the darkness.

I couldn't help being scared.

And yet what could be worse than what we were already experiencing? Ava's recollections were not stopping; if anything, they were getting worse. I had to know, in spite of my fears; I had to find out what was going on.

My finger hovered over the keyboard for another moment, and then, finally, I pressed Enter.

I blinked as the screen changed: 694,000,000 results. A sigh came from the depths of me. What Ava was looking for was somewhere in there. Somewhere in there was the first step towards the answers I was seeking.

I needed a cup of tea. I got up to put the kettle on, and as I did, I saw out of the corner of my eye that the screen was flickering. My gaze went to the window – was there a storm brewing out there? But the night sky was clear. Maybe there was a problem with the connection.

I finished making my tea and went back to sit at the computer. Another page had opened – so that was what the flickering was. Maybe I had clicked on a link without noticing. I began to read.

It was the website of a place called Seal, a tiny island

off the west coast of Scotland, in the Hebrides archipel-ago. I gazed at the map for a while, unable to take my eyes off it. Seal was so small, and surrounded by bigger islands. Like a baby island among grown-up ones. The photographs showed a place of amazing beauty, with a sea that seemed to be a different colour in nearly every picture – green and aqua, like some Maldivian beach; then huge and grey and stormy like you would expect from a northern shore. White beaches dotted with sea-birds were side by side with flowery meadows, and deer played in the fields. The houses were whitewashed, with dark roofs and brightly coloured doors. On the main street, the buildings were painted in vivid colours, like a rainbow against the dark hills behind and the blue of the sea in front. There was a picture of a red sandstone stately home – Kilpatrick House, according to the caption – and a bridge covered in purple flowers; foxgloves, I thought. It joined two bits of land separated by a deep fjord, and it boasted that it was the only bridge 'over the Atlantic'. And then there were endless photographs of seals with gem-like black eyes, and golden eagles, and birds I didn't know the names of. It seemed like a paradise, touched only lightly, gently by human hand, not distorted and destroyed by covering every inch in concrete and leaving only man-made parks, like oases in a desert.

Was this the place Ava was talking about?

Was this the place she had portrayed in her Busy Book, over and over again?

I thought of my grandmother, Leah. I knew little about

her, as she'd died when I was three and my mum had done nothing to keep her memory alive; nor were there any photographs or paperwork, nothing that could tell me more about her – and about myself. But I did know she came from a Scottish island too. I wondered where . . . I wondered if it was anywhere near Seal. I had so few memories of her – mainly the way that she was always humming a tune, always. When I thought of her, I thought of music. My grandmother was a reminiscence of love and calm and nurturing, a short-lasting haven before the barren, chaotic years with my mother.

But Leah was long gone, and I was an adult with a daughter of my own; and here I was, sitting in a little flat on the outskirts of a city of millions of people, looking at photographs of sea and sky. They followed one another, so real, so alive that I forgot where I was. If Ava had somehow come across Seal, however it had happened, I wasn't surprised she was dreaming of it. Every image spoke of wind and freedom and sea and peace.

I loved London, my birthplace and my home, but in the last few years it had so often felt suffocating. And lonely, with thousands, millions of people, strangers to each other and to me, living crowded in the same city. Sometimes, on the Tube especially, I felt invisible. Like I wasn't really there, like none of us was – because nobody could *see* each other.

I carried on reading the website. My tea had gone cold, but I didn't want to have to interrupt my search to make myself another cup; I was riveted by what I saw, by what I read. There were details of island life, as intimate as you would expect from somewhere so tiny – Seal only had two settlements, two villages with poetic names: Roan, the main harbour, and Ollaberry, a smattering of houses right on the sea. They were at opposite ends of the island, but the whole place was so small, I imagined them to be quite close. How do people live in a village that size? I asked myself – born and bred in the city, I didn't know any different. The website said that there were 978 souls living on the island. London was a few thousand times bigger than tiny Seal. I thought that maybe in a place like that, it would be impossible to feel alone.

Reading the island website was like reading a novel. A local committee was being created to repaint the benches around the pier, and a fund-raising event would take place in the community centre; home-baking donations were welcome. The local policeman was concerned with incidents of poaching and gave his own mobile number if the public had anything to report; I tried to imagine policemen giving their mobile numbers out in London, and failed. The ladies from some association called Women's Tapestry were meeting to decide how to decorate Roan and Ollaberry for Christmas using recycled materials. A local boy had won a silver medal in a music competition called the Mod – I didn't know what that was, but the pictures were adorable, with the boys and girls in kilts or tartan skirts.

The postmistress in Ollaberry was retiring after forty-one years of service; a band called Sweet Recollections was going to play at her 'do'. A picture of the band showed four young people, three with fiddles and one with a guitar, and there was a caption: *Mhairi, Charlie and Lesley Grant, with Ollaberry guitarist Ali Reid.* I smiled, thinking of the three members of the same family and their fiddles, playing a kind of music I had never heard before. A brief list of deaths, a list of births and baptisms; Father Chris McGee had officiated, and a Father Stefano had visited the island parish from Rome. The news went on, and it felt like truly being there – like knowing what was happening in those people's lives, in their streets, in their shops, in their living rooms.

After a while, a shiver went down my spine – the cold of the night had brought me back to myself. It was past midnight; time had flown. I wrapped the cardigan I had left on the back of the chair around my shoulders and got up to make myself a fresh cup of tea. The spell I'd felt while reading the Seal website had been broken, and I was back to reality. There was no point in falling in love with this island. I didn't even know if it was the place Ava was talking about and portraying in her drawings, as much as the name and the description fitted her words and her pictures. Was this the place she had seen somewhere, or heard of, and was now creating a whole world of her own around?

But how on earth would she have come across Seal? I wondered as I waited for the kettle to boil. What had clicked in her mind to make her weave such a web of dreams and imaginings with the island at its centre?

My mind went back once more to what she'd said – that someone was speaking to her in her mind.

I had no answers to all these questions, and my eyes were closing. I switched the computer off and sat at the window for a long time, warming my hands around the cup and gazing at the orange-lit sky and the outlines of the buildings – a forest of concrete where a million strangers lived. As soon as I closed my eyes, the flickering of the computer screen came back to me; the way the Seal website seemed to have decided to show itself to me. Or maybe someone had found it for me, I thought sleepily.

The thought chilled me all of a sudden. It was ridiculous, completely ridiculous – but I got up and switched the light on, and that was how I fell asleep, the bright light in my eyes, to banish all secrets and all mysteries.

After that, the days followed one another like nothing had happened.

I didn't look at the island website again, but I thought about it all the time, in spite of my efforts to block it from my mind. Ava wasn't mentioning Seal or drawing seascapes any more, and I was crossing my fingers, hoping that maybe it was over – that this strange phase was finished and we would settle back into our old life. Or our new life, to be more precise – one without Toby.

I let myself believe that this wasn't a fragile truce – that Ava's weird island dream really was over. But part of me kept watching, and waiting. Part of me kept seeing that faraway look in her eyes, though she wasn't saying anything. During the silences, so unusual for a girl who usually chatted like a little bird, I would look at her face, observing her while trying hard to make sure she didn't notice, so she wouldn't feel scrutinised. Her round, smooth cheeks; the shadow of her eyelashes as she sat at the table reading a comic; the waves in her hair when I dried it after her bath; her tiny fingers on the remote control as she watched *Frozen* yet again; the way she jumped and skipped all the way to school, her Hello Kitty bag bouncing on her back, her red coat bright among a sea of blue uniform jackets as she ran in through the school gates – and all the time I kept wondering what was going through her mind.

And then one day I went to collect her from school before my shift at the hospital. As she stepped out of the gates, I noticed that she looked a bit dazed, and that she had that remote look in her eyes, like she truly was seeing something far in the distance, beyond the reality around her. I felt the hair on the back of my neck rise.

We went through our usual routine – snack, home-work, TV – but I could feel that something was off. I was tense, waiting for her to say something about her other life again. I wished I didn't have to go to work that night and leave her.

I was sitting on her bed in my work uniform, waiting for Sharon to arrive and reading her a bedtime story about a fairy taking a voyage across the ocean on a walnut shell – I felt like I was doing just that myself, sailing away across the ocean – when suddenly, unexpectedly, Ava burst into tears.

'Oh baby, what's wrong? Why are you crying?'

'Because I *remembered*.'

There. What I'd been waiting for all day, since I'd collected her from school, had finally come.

'What did you remember?' I asked in a small voice, bracing myself for her answer. She dried her eyes with the palm of her hand.

'The fishing boats. I liked looking at them. I miss them.'

An image came back to me, a photograph I'd seen on the Seal website: a row of fishing boats, painted in different colours, against an orange sunset sky.

My daughter missed them.

'Mum?'

'Yes, my love,' I said, trying to keep my voice steady.

'I remember things I have never seen.'

'Ava . . .'

'She keeps asking me.'

'Who? Who keeps asking you? What are they asking?'

'Please take me home.'

I was horrified to see her eyes filling with tears again, and her face crumpling in renewed upset. She threw herself into my arms, and sobs began to rack her little body.

'Where is home, darling?' I said, so choked I could barely speak.

'Seal.' Her voice was muffled in my shoulders, her hair soft against my cheek.

Seal. Of course. Of course.

'I want to go home, Mummy.'

'Yes. I'll take you home. Don't worry about a thing. Mummy will sort it all out for you.'

That was it. I was at the end of my tether with Ava's sadness and upset. I was weary of seeing her becoming more and more distressed as these strange memories gathered inside her. I had to do something, something more than clicking wistfully through a website, unwilling to take a risk and jump into the unknown.

At the end of my twelve-hour shift, I sat in the staffroom with my phone and a cup of strong coffee. The soft sound of white clogs on linoleum and my colleagues chatting over tea was my soundtrack as I went on to Travel Zone and, without giving it a second thought – there was no more time for hesitation and-soul searching – booked the flight, the train, the ferry and one of the three bed and breakfasts on Seal. I had quite a bit of holiday I hadn't taken, and anyway, this was an emergency. I was sure that my boss, Ibiwami, would sign my leave – I would find her before going home and speak to her. It was the worst time to take a holiday, in my first year as a qualified nurse, but it had to be done.

I would take Ava to Seal. I would take her home, like she'd implored me to.

We'd find out whether all she said, all she drew and dreamt about was a fantasy – whether Dr Craig was right or whether . . .

My mind could not formulate an alternative. There *was* no alternative. Not one that my head could wrap around.

But I was sure there was nothing to worry about; that we'd see the place and Ava would somehow put her fantasy in context and grow out of it bit by bit.

Yes, I was sure it was the right thing to do.

Nearly sure.

I went to collect Ava from school. I couldn't wait to tell her about our journey, but I struggled to restrain myself until we were home. We were barely in the door when I knelt in front of her and took her by the shoulders.

'Listen, my love. I've made a decision. I'm taking you to Seal.'

Ava stood with her jacket still on, her backpack on her shoulders, and looked at me in silence. Then her expression turned to something between overjoyed and disbelieving.

'You are?' Her eyes were as wide as little saucers and a pink flush had risen on her cheeks.

'Yes. We're taking a plane and a boat and I'm taking you there.' I fought against the tears that were pressing behind my eyes.

'To Seal?' she whispered.

'Yes. So you can see all the places you told me about . . .' Before I could finish, Ava threw herself into my arms and I held her tight, breathing in her fresh little-girl scent, the strawberry shampoo aroma of her hair.

'Thank you, Mummy,' she said, her words muffled in my shoulder. She pulled away from me gently and looked into my eyes. She was beaming, a big smile lighting her face up like a little sun.

'It'll be a nice holiday for us, won't it?' I said, stroking her hair. 'You know, maybe we'll be able to see dolphins . . .'

'Yes! I'm sure we will. Sometimes I could see them from the beach, and even from my window!'

I swallowed. 'Could you, darling?'

She nodded and began to take her backpack off her shoulders. 'When are we going? Now? I need to pack!' That was Ava, methodical and organised as ever.

I laughed. 'No, not now! On Thursday, the day after school finishes. Yes, we need to start getting ready, don't we?'

'I'll get my ladybird trolley!' she said, and ran to her room without even taking her coat off, her school bag abandoned on the hall floor.

I was left standing at the front door, my daughter's words playing in my mind.

Sometimes, from the beach, she could see dolphins.

My night shifts were over for the week; finally I could spend the night at home. I lay awake for a long time, watching the orange-tinged darkness through a gap in the curtains. Sleep would not come. When I couldn't take the insomnia any more, I gathered up my duvet and pillow and went to sleep on Ava's floor. Her ladybird-shaped trolley sat beside her bed, full of travelling essentials:

Camilla, her favourite red dress, and a book of bedtime stories. I lay on the rug, cocooned in my duvet, and closed my eyes, listening to her soft breathing and imagining her little beating heart close to mine.

Four days to go, and we'd be off to Seal. Off to the unknown.

When I woke up the next morning, I had a vague image in my mind, a hazy, gossamer-thin dream that had left a sensation more than a full recollection: my granny Leah, sitting in her favourite high-backed armchair, softly singing a song with words I couldn't make out. Sweet, flowing words, and a tune like a long-lost memory.

4

Star of the sea

Sorren

I stood in front of my restaurant, Star of the Sea, beside
the low stone wall that separated land from sea, salty
wind in my hair, on my skin, breathing in the sea with
the moisture-laden air. A soft drizzle was falling, and
judging from the black clouds above me, it would soon
turn into a downpour. And it'd do so suddenly, like so
often happened in this corner of the world. Today was
the day I thought about just that – about how quickly a
blue sky could turn grey and then black, and a life that
was once sunny could become a study in grey.

Today was the day I thought about her.

The wind rose and made the boats sway and dance on
the waves, straining against their ties; the sea was now
steely grey under an even steelier sky. I couldn't wait to
go out on the water, and I would, as soon as I finished
service at the restaurant. I spent more time on the sea
than on dry land, and I liked it that way. Especially
today, when it was the only place I could find peace.

It was the tenth of July. If you tried to Google it, you'd
probably find out that someone famous was born today,

and someone even more famous died. Maybe something very, very important was invented on this date; a new advance in science or technology . . . maybe someone painted a picture that went down in history, or a new land was discovered.

For me, the tenth of July meant one thing only: my sister's birthday.

'That's not how we get a Michelin star, having a break just before service,' Fraser said brightly, shaking me out of my sad thoughts. He was carrying a crate of breaded haddock, ready to be delivered to the school.

'Join me for coffee? We have time,' I said.

He shrugged. 'You're the boss.'

That wasn't strictly accurate. Fraser didn't have a boss – he really wasn't the type. His main occupation was working as an outdoors-living instructor; he travelled all over Britain to give his courses. He'd written a couple of books, and he'd even filmed a survival programme for the BBC, which had made him a bit of a local celebrity.

We went inside – from the windows in the kitchen I could still see the sea, like a living picture that changed every moment – and I stood at the coffee machine. 'Espresso, yes?'

'Yes. You having a cappuccino?'

'Mmm.'

I could see he was in the mood for baiting me, which was often. 'Real men don't drink cappuccinos.'

'This man does.'

'I rest my case.'

'Do you not have something you should be doing, Fraser?'

'Oh yes, lots. And I also need to prep for this week-end's foraging course . . .'

'A useful skill for when the Co-op is closed.'

'Very funny. Maybe you could stop reading *Deep Outer Space* or whatever and come and help me,' he said, crossing his arms. I had one of my astronomy books with me. That was my passion – stargazing. I did it almost every clear night, with my telescope.

'Sooner or later I'll fire you,' I said, pretending to be annoyed but actually enjoying our morning spat.

'You can't, you never hired me in the first place. Also, you wouldn't last five minutes without me,' he said as he disappeared into the cold room, giving me a pat on the back in passing.

Fraser was my favourite sparring partner. We kept each other sane. We'd known each other for five years now, since he'd moved to the island from Edinburgh, leaving behind a life I didn't know much about, despite my efforts to discover more about him. All I knew was that he'd had a great career as a sort of Scottish Bear Grylls, but all of a sudden had decided to make a clean break with his old life and move away, somewhere he could start again. Seal works like that for a lot of people, actually. They come here to leave something behind, to find peace by living somewhere poor in people and rich in nature, somewhere at the edge of everything. But not many remain. You might come to Seal, but it's Seal that chooses you as hers, or sends you back wherever you came from.

In the summer, when most people visit, they find themselves under the spell of sunshine and clear green-blue waters to rival a Caribbean beach; the lovely white cottages, the hospitality of our people, the music and the whisky – all the ingredients of the magic recipe that is Seal. The island wins them over. Then winter comes, and the days when we are cut off from the ferry service because the sea is too rough, when mist covers the island like a white blanket; the power cuts, the gales, the storms, the afternoons when it gets dark at four. The silence. The first winter – that is when most of the new residents of Seal decide to go back, selling up the pottery business or the organic deli they opened in a fit of enthusiasm, embracing with relief the return to the shopping centres and the cinemas and the people-ridden streets of the cities.

The few who remain are the ones who truly love Seal. The island has seeped into their blood, with its challenges and its infinite beauty, and they become islanders not by birth, like me, but by choice. And whatever you give to Seal, you get back a million-fold.

I would not live anywhere else.

But the woman I loved would not live here.

So I had to choose between her and Seal; and my island won.

The memory was painful, like the brush of nettles against my hand; better not to think about it. I finished my cappuccino quickly, and began preparing for service.

I heard the van starting – Fraser was on his way to deliver lunch to Seal primary school, like we did every day.

The kitchen door opened – to be more precise, it was wrenched open and nearly slammed against the opposite wall – and my Ukrainian waitress, Tatiana, made her entrance.

'Hi, Sorren! Lovely day, eh?' Tatiana had learnt English here on Seal, and she spoke like a local, with the tiniest foreign inflection. She looked like a model, tall and slender, with the lightest blue eyes; she also lifted the heaviest crates like a wrestler, and could drink any of us under the table.

'Hopefully it'll clear by Sunday. We want a nice day for the Blessing of the Boats,' I said.

'Hopefully. I'll get the fish, you start filleting,' she said, and disappeared into the cold room, reappearing a second later with three heavy crates of fish in her arms. She would have made a great bouncer, Tatiana, but she preferred to use her strength for the good: making food.

I had just started filleting when my mobile rang. It was Fraser. The van had broken down, with the food for the school in it. I could have asked Jim from the garage to go have a look at it, maybe tow it back if it couldn't be repaired, but whatever happened, the food would be out of the cold chain. There was no way I could serve it now. I had a sudden vision of Tatiana carrying the food herself, a crate under each arm and one on her head . . . but that would have been too much even for her.

70

'Right, Fraser, call Jim and wait there, I'm coming up with sandwiches.' And then, to Tatiana: 'I'll be gone for half an hour or so; you'll have to hold the fort.'

'Before service?'

'Just rub the specials off the board and write "kippers on toast" instead. Hopefully I'll be back in time to get something going and nobody will complain.'

'If somebody complains, I'll give them a piece of my brain,' she said with a truculent expression on her angelic features. Sometimes I was positively afraid of her.

'You mean "I'll give them a piece of my mind", Tatiana. Unless a few zombies come for lunch.'

'Yes. I meant that.'

I didn't doubt it.

We quickly made sandwiches and threw in a chocolate cake I'd made the night before – the customers would have to go without, but the children would be delighted – then I jumped into my jeep in the pouring rain. Fraser had managed to park the van by the side of the road, and was waiting for me in the driving seat. When he saw me, a rueful smile spread across his face.

'Sorren to the rescue,' he said as he climbed into my jeep. 'What do we have there?' He gestured to the boxes in the back.

'Sandwiches and cake; nothing fancy, but it'll do.'

'Ach, that *will* do. Chocolate cake is not exactly healthy eating, but the kids will be happy. By the way, Jim said he'll see to the van in half an hour.'

'Which means he *might* be there before nightfall.'

'Maybe. I say let's not count on the van for the next couple of days.'

We drove to the school, where a panicked Caty, my childhood friend, and my unflappable mother greeted us.

My mother and I exchanged a look. Today was the day. But it was buried deep in mine and Mum's hearts; nothing would show on the surface as we went about our jobs.

The teachers actually clapped as we came in, to our amazement, happy to be involved in a bit of excitement because it was the last day of school. The children, inebriated by the thought of the impending holiday, tried to follow them out of the classrooms and enjoy their share of elation, but they were quickly shepherded back inside, albeit with smiles. A wee boy in a bright blue uniform peeked from one of the doors, a cheeky smile on his face.

'We had *nothing* for lunch!' Caty was always dramatic.

'I knew you'd sort it,' my mum said calmly.

'I'll lay it all out in the kitchen,' Fraser said without looking at them, and disappeared. I gave my mum a gentle pat on the shoulder and followed him. When Caty was around, Fraser always vanished. It bothered me a little. Caty and I were pretty close, so it put me in an awkward position. I had no idea why Fraser avoided Caty, why he seemed to dislike her so much; but it would have been impossible to get a straight answer from him. Or an answer at all, come to that.

Anyway, the emergency was sorted and we were

laying out the sandwiches and cutting the cake just as the dinner lady, Ailsa, arrived. The boys and girls of Seal had been sent out to play in the drizzle; we could see them from the kitchen, hoods and hats on, cheeks red in the chilly air. There was no way they would stay inside just because it was raining; Seal children played outside all year long, in almost any weather.

When we were finished with the food, I found Caty and my mum in the staffroom, with Fraser hovering out-side the door. My mum was admiring a bracelet Caty was wearing.

Caty lifted her arm. 'Thank you, I made it myself. I really want to get into jewellery-making this summer.'

'This summer you're all mine, Caty,' I said. She had promised to help me in the restaurant. 'We're done here, girls!'

'Thank you, guys. Thank you so much,' my mum replied. 'I'll go and help Ailsa.'

'See you later, Mum.'

She rested her mug of tea on a low table and stood up. 'Wait. I'll see you to the door.'

'And I'll drop by later to the pub to say hello,' Caty told me, rinsing her mug under the tap. 'Will we see you in your *Star Trek* uniform for the blessing?' I heard Fraser snorting behind me.

'Oh, yes. I need to iron that for you,' my mum joined in.

'You too, Mother? Can a man not have a passion around here?'

Everyone laughed, and we made our way towards the

door, waving goodbye to the children queuing up for their lunch.

'So, things are well, then?' Fraser muttered just as we were on our way out. I turned around and realised he was speaking to Caty. I couldn't quite believe it. Caty, just as mystified as me, said 'yes' with that big smile of hers, but nothing more. We stepped out into the hall.

'Well, thanks for sorting this out,' my mum said. But I knew it wasn't what she wanted to say.

We held each other tight and quick, without saying a word, standing in front of the little row of coats and jackets hanging in the hall, each with a label and a child's name.

And a hole opened in my heart.

Over my mum's shoulder as we hugged, I could see it. A coat peg among all the other pegs, with a tiny image of a dolphin sellotaped above it, and a name: *Isla*.

And that was why I never liked going to the village school – that peg was a blade in my heart, every single time. I don't know how my mum dealt with it; but it was she who'd decided that the peg shouldn't be removed.

And there it stayed, a memory of my sister.

On our way back to the restaurant, I was silent. My mum's perfume lingered on me – sweet lavender – along with the look in her eyes when we'd said goodbye. I was still to face my dad – his wordless grief, the way he kept everything inside. I would see him that evening.

Yes, this was the day when my parents and I thought

about my sister constantly – not much new there – but we still didn't mention her. I always went to see them, and my mum and I hugged once, twice, three times, with whatever excuse we could think of, or no excuse at all. A way to say to each other *I know, I know, I miss her too.*

Every time I went to the house, memories of Isla enveloped me. She was everywhere, even if the room of her door remained closed – only my mum went in there. Sometimes I longed to step in and sit on my sister's bed, look around at her things and feel her close. But I always stopped myself, because I was too afraid that instead of feeling her near, I would feel her gone forever.

We had been through fifteen tenth of Julys. Three of them I had spent with Alessia. When I'd told her what this day meant to me, she'd slipped her arm around my waist and rested her head on my shoulder without saying anything.

I thought: there *is* a future.

But now Alessia was gone too, back to her own home, from my island home that she couldn't make hers. After a year in which she'd tried everything to get a bit of my time, of my attention, while I divided myself between my parents, the Sea Rescue, and anyone and everyone who needed me, and all to block Isla out of my mind. Trying to make amends, trying to never have to stop and think. Trying to look after the people around me because I'd failed the only person I should have looked after. Alessia watched me, bewildered, as I morphed back into the haunted man I was before leaving for Italy. The man who'd let his baby sister slip from his hands and be pulled away.

And while I punished myself, there was no room in my life left for love. For her.

I knew that evening I was going to find an email from her, because she always remembered my sister's birthday. Her letter would be sweet and useless; it would mean everything and nothing, because although we clung on to each other, we both knew that there was no future for us.

No future for us at all.

Fraser parked the van in the back, and I jumped down. I was about to step into the restaurant when something stopped me, something I saw out of the corner of my eye on the windswept beach. For a long, heartbreaking moment I thought I saw my sister, standing there in the rain with her long black hair blowing in the wind. Before my knees could give way and my heart beat faster, the illusion was gone. It wasn't Isla, of course, just a wee girl who looked a bit like her. She stood on the beach, and for a moment she seemed to look back at me, her little red jacket like a beacon against the white sand.

At that moment, my phone rang. It was Morag from the Swan Hotel – her husband Billy had had a stroke a while ago, and with Morag running the hotel and not being in the best of health herself, I helped them out any way I could. When I answered, though, there was nobody there. I checked my phone, once, twice. It seemed to be working fine. I tried to phone Morag back, but it rang out. It was time to bring Billy his lunch anyway. I quickly wrapped a dish and made my way to the Swan Hotel in the pouring rain.

5

A place of stones and water

Anna

We stepped off the boat, my head spinning and reeling as I tried to steady myself on dry land. Ava's cheeks were rosy with the wind, her hair tangled up with sea spray. Her eyes, wide and shining, were darting everywhere, as if she wanted to see everything at the same time. I watched her turning round and round, and held her by the arm when she swayed.

'I'm dizzy!'

She laughed her flowery laugh, and I realised I hadn't heard that lovely sound for weeks, not laughter so free, so pure.

And then three things happened: the shiny black head of a seal emerged from the waves a few yards from us; two men in yellow overalls, unloading boxes full of fish, glanced up and smiled; and an elderly woman strolling on the pier turned to look at Ava, murmuring something about her lovely eyes. With my head still spinning from the boat trip, I thought I heard whispers coming from the waves, and a sudden awareness astonished me: *Seal is happy to see her.*

'Can we go to the beach?' Ava called, pointing at the

white half-moon of sand a hundred yards away. Just above the dunes, past a flowery meadow, lay a village of brightly coloured houses so pretty it looked nearly unreal. I remembered seeing it on the Seal website, but to witness it in real life was something else entirely. Close to the pier, some men were building what looked like a raised podium, not dissimilar to those used at concerts.

Ava ran on, and I followed suit. I inhaled deeply, and it felt like my lungs were opening up, filling with oxygen and salty sea air. I stood on a seaweed-covered rock as Ava made her way down to the waterline. As she danced on the sand, aqua waves heaved and swelled not far from her, but she was unafraid. And so I wanted her to be. If there were worries to be had, I would carry them for her. Seal was behind me, the sea in front; while my daughter laughed and danced with the island, I couldn't silence the questions in my mind, the apprehension.

What awaited us on Seal?

What was to be our story here?

But the wind swept me, and somehow it seemed to cleanse me from the inside. Relief and hope and a sense of spontaneous joy coloured all my worries, my questions, and slowly, timidly, peace began to rise inside me.

Maybe it was going to be all right for Ava and me.

Ava and her cuddles, Ava and her tears, Ava and her stories.

Ava who talked of her other mother, of her old life.

There was no life before, Ava – you started in my belly, you are all mine.

London with its swarms of people and its unrelenting noise was a million miles away. Ava's red jacket was a splash of colour against the sea, her wellies leaving the happy prints of a running child. The beach was nearly deserted; a man in a checked shirt stood at the low stone wall, and a tall, red-blonde-haired woman wrapped in a blue jumper was walking our way. She smiled at me and murmured a greeting. I was taken aback – in London you don't smile at strangers, you don't greet them – so I didn't manage to rearrange my face into a smile, or reply to her quiet *hello*. She walked past, her beautiful bright hair flowing in the wind. Her Celtic loveliness belonged to the place; she seemed to have grown straight from the land, with her white skin and her incredible hair, flaming against the blue and grey.

'Mummy! Look! Shells!' Ava cried, bending down to retrieve some treasure she'd found. I was about to reply, when suddenly the air itself went dark. I'd never seen anything like that before, the way it happened in the blink of an eye. It was as if all the light had been sucked out of the day. I had read about the unpredictability of Scottish weather, but this was something else.

I looked up to the sky, where galloping black horses were coming in from the sea. The breeze turned into wind in the space of a moment, and the first few drops of rain started falling. Ava was standing with her back to the sea, grey waves swelling slowly behind her, and all of a sudden they looked threatening, like they were about to swallow her. For the first time since she was born, I remembered the dreams I'd had when I was carrying her – the grey waves and the water, water all around.

'Ava!' I called over the rising wind. Maybe she couldn't hear me, because she didn't move. I began running towards her, calling her name again and again. 'Ava! Ava!'

She shook herself and ran to me. We met halfway; I held her tight, and clung to her. 'Ava,' I whispered once more, as the rain fell on us. *She doesn't smell like Ava any more*, I realised, in one of those strange thoughts that flash through your mind like comets. *She smells like salt and wind.* I took her face in my hands. Her eyes were full of joy, her cheeks suffused with pink. I hadn't seen her so happy in a long time.

I had to ask her, even if the drizzle was intensifying and soon we'd have to find shelter. 'Is this the place you were talking about? The place you dreamt of?' My heart quickened – I was afraid of her answer. If she said no, we were on a wild goose chase; if she said yes . . .

'Yes. Thanks for bringing me back, Mummy,' she said. At her words, a wave of emotion overwhelmed me and tears began to sting my eyes, but I blinked them away. Ava raised her hand to smooth down my hair.

'Are you happy, sweetheart?' I said, holding her little fingers, her starfish hand.

'Very very very happy!' she said, and spun away, her arms wide and her face up to the sky, tiny drops falling on her cheeks, her nose, her forehead, her scrunched-up eyes. She had turned into a wave of the sea, dancing and

81

flowing, natural and perfectly beautiful. I stood and closed my eyes too, letting all my other senses take over, breathing in the salty, watery scent of the sea, feeling the rain and the sea spray on my skin . . . It all spoke of far horizons and wide spaces, and things free and new.

We spent some time playing on the wet sand, slipping sandy shells in our pockets, standing on the shoreline and then running back when a wave came in, until the drizzle began to get stronger and Ava started shivering. She looked pale and tired after the long journey. 'Mummy, I'm hungry,' she said, wrapping her arms around me and resting her head on my stomach.

'Me too,' I replied. 'Let's go and check into the hotel, and then we can get dry and changed and find something yummy to eat.'

I led her up the heathery slope, and we grabbed our trolleys and began to make our way towards the village. We didn't have to wander around for long before I recognised the place I'd booked online: the Swan Hotel, a bright green building squeezed between a pink and an orange one.

We were both dripping wet and feeling rather miserable as the stern woman behind the reception desk checked her books.

'Ford, you said?'

'Yes, Anna Ford.'

'I have nothing in that name.' She managed to turn the soft island accent into something clipped and hard.

'But I'm sure I booked. I sent an email . . .' I insisted,

slightly panicked now. I swept my wet hair away from my face. A small puddle was gathering where we stood.

'I didn't get any email. Mind you, we had a problem with email bookings, but we assumed people would phone to check.'

'But . . . I booked a twin room . . .'

'Did you get a confirmation from us?'

'No, but . . .'

'Like I said, we're full.'

As I took in what she'd just told us, the bell above the door chimed and a gust of cold air froze our backs.

'Hi, Sorren,' the woman called above our heads. I turned around to see a man in a sodden checked shirt holding a tinfoil-wrapped parcel. The guy behind the stone wall above the beach.

'Hey. Did you need me?' he asked in a deep voice.

'I always need you, you know that,' the woman said warmly, and the difference of tone between the way she spoke to us and the way she spoke to the stranger was like nails down a blackboard.

The man laughed. 'I mean, did you phone me?'

Ava took a step away from me and towards the man. I was surprised to see that she was looking at him with wide eyes, as if hypnotised.

'Hey,' he said to her. 'I think I must have seen you on the beach earlier. I recognise your jacket.'

Ava nodded. 'Yes. I saw you too.'

'I didn't phone you, no,' the woman interrupted. She turned back to me, as if she wanted to finish the conversation and see us out. 'I'm really sorry. They're blessing the boats tomorrow. You won't find anywhere.'

What was she talking about? I placed my hands on the wooden counter, desperately trying to keep my temper. 'Look. We've travelled from London. We have nowhere to stay. What are we supposed to do?' I shot her a pointed glance. Would she leave a six-year-old child, soaked to the bone, without a bed for the night?

'Sorry. There's nothing I can do.'

There was my answer. Yes, she would.

'Sorry to jump in,' the stranger said. 'We might have something. I mean, up at the Seal Inn. We're full too, but our own guest room is free, and if you want it . . .'

I couldn't even pretend to be coy. I launched into a series of heartfelt, if weary, thank yous. Maybe we were saved.

'It's no problem. Morag, here's Billy's lunch – shepherd's pie à la Sorren.' He placed the package on the counter with a smile. A million little drops were shining on its tinfoil cocoon.

'Bless you, Sorren,' said Morag.

'Tell Billy my mum and dad say hi. Mum will drop by tomorrow.'

Morag nodded with what could almost have been called a smile, and disappeared through a door behind reception, carrying the package with her. I was trembling with cold, long shivers that travelled down my body. Ava was leaning on me, even more exhausted.

The man turned back towards us. His hair was

dripping, but he didn't seem to mind. 'So yes, it's quite a small room, but if you're stuck . . .'

'We don't mind,' I sighed. 'We just want to get dry and have something to eat.'

'Sure. Come along, let me take those.' He took our trolleys by the handle, one in each hand. 'It's only up the road,' he said encouragingly, and looked straight at me. For the first time I noticed his eyes, dark blue and shadowed by long eyelashes, and his hair, wavy and thick and even darker than Ava's.

I picked Ava up and she leaned her head on my shoulder, strands of her wet hair across my chest. 'It's all right, baby. We'll get dry and have something to eat, okay?' I whispered.

We followed Sorren onto the street. As quickly as it had started, the downpour had stopped. We walked past the brightly coloured houses, the sea shimmering in the distance under a pale sun.

'So, you're up from London?' he said. He was tall, I noticed – I probably came up to his chest – and he had a reddish five o'clock stubble. His voice was gentle and deep, with a musical island lilt.

'Yes. Just here for a holiday,' I lied.

'Don't pay any mind to Morag. We're not all like that up here. She's not bad really. Just a bit dour.'

I nodded. I was too wet and cold to feel any understanding for the woman.

'Lucky I was there. I thought she'd called me . . . Anyway, I just came to bring her husband his lunch.

Billy's not well, and Morag is busy all day with the hotel. I made a ton of it, if you're hungry. Today it's moussaka.'

'Oh, I love moussaka. But did you not say it was shepherd's pie?'

He laughed, and little lines appeared around his eyes, a sign that he laughed often. 'Billy doesn't like *exotic* food, which basically means he doesn't like anything with flavour. But I was completely over making him mince and tatties and sausage stew day in and day out. Also, the man has to live with Morag. He could do with some good food . . .'

I laughed.

'So I started calling things by a different name. I fed him lamb burgers with minted yoghurt, and told him it was a beef burger with extra-light mayo – for his cholesterol. I made him pasta al forno and told him it was macaroni cheese . . . and in a way, it is. It worked,' he shrugged. 'Spicy lentil and tomato soup is a broth, Cajun fajitas are chicken rolls . . . and moussaka is shepherd's pie à la Sorren.'

'I see! You *deceive* him,' I teased. I was surprised at myself. I didn't usually joke with people I'd just met.

'It's for a good cause,' he laughed.

We stepped into a side street beside a light blue house, and into a cobbled courtyard. At the back of the blue house was a door with a sign – *Little Moon Holistic Therapies* – and on the other side of the courtyard stood a whitewashed cottage, the soft sound of a fiddle seeping from the ground-floor windows. It was the first white house I'd seen after the rainbow of the main street.

'Come on in,' said Sorren, and carried our cases inside, holding the door open for us. We stepped into a low-ceilinged room with beams above our heads and scuffed golden wooden floors beneath our feet. A pleasant smell of honeyed beer, peat and something delicious cooking somewhere filled my nostrils. I caught a glimpse of a thin blonde man and two equally blonde girls playing fiddles in a room on the left. I did a double-take – where had I seen them before? And then I remembered: the Grants, the young musicians mentioned on the website. It was strange – like I had jumped into a dream. I felt my bones warming up; a fire burnt warm and inviting on the far wall, and I longed to sit beside it. It was a place as welcoming as a hug. I let myself exhale . . .

'Hi! Oh . . . hello.'

My eyes followed the voice. A tall, fine-boned silver-haired woman stood behind the counter, dressed in a teal-coloured woollen jumper and a pleated skirt. With a touch of lipstick and pearl earrings at her ears, she looked immaculate.

'Hi, Mum. These ladies are up from London for a holiday,' Sorren explained, gesturing towards us. 'I'm afraid they got the famous Morag welcome. No sign of their reservation, and nowhere to stay.'

The woman rolled her eyes. 'I'll never understand how the Swan is still afloat. Anyway, you offered them our guest room, I hope?'

'Yes, if it's okay with you? Just as well I was there. What a coincidence,' he said. He smiled, and a dimple appeared on his left cheek.

'Of course.' The woman stepped out from behind the counter. I noticed that she had the same dark blue eyes as her son, and like his, they were shadowed by long, long eyelashes. At her feet was a white cat, who eyed us warily and then slunk away.

I let Ava slip to the floor – my arms were aching – and she stood on unsteady feet. Then, to my surprise, she ran to the kindly woman and looked up at her without saying a word. The woman knelt on the wooden floor until their faces were level.

'Oh my. All wet. And hungry, I bet?' she said, and caressed Ava's face softly. Ava stepped forward and into the woman's arms, nestling into her. The woman's eyes widened, and she met my gaze while wrapping her arms around my daughter. There was something else in her expression, something other than surprise and tenderness: there was a shadow of sadness.

Something like . . . regret.

Like she had lost something, never to be found again.

Quickly she composed her face into a smile. 'There, there,' she said. 'It was an awful long journey. Let's get you and your mummy settled.'

Ava took a step back and looked into the woman's face, then threw her arms around her again.

'Ava.' I smiled and went to pull her away, but the woman shook her head lightly, as if to say it was okay, and they hugged for a little longer. I was taken aback. Ava was a sweet, affectionate child, but, like me, not so ready to open up with strangers.

'I'll see you tomorrow, then,' Sorren said. I was confused. The way he'd said it, it sounded so personal. 'I mean, at the Blessing of the Boats,' he explained, seeing my uncertain expression.

Oh yes, Morag had mentioned that. I didn't know what it was, but I was so exhausted, so overwhelmed by it all, I just nodded slightly as he waved his goodbyes and left.

'My name is Shuna McNeil,' the woman said as she made her way upstairs with us trailing after her. The white cat had reappeared out of nowhere, the way cats do, and was following us up, twining deftly between our legs. 'And this is Andromeda, my son's cat.' The way she spoke reminded me a little of my granny, the same soft Scottish lilt.

'Andromeda?' I smiled.

'He's an amateur astronomer. My son, not the cat,' she laughed. 'We call her Andy.'

'I'm Anna. And this is . . .'

'Ava!' chirped my daughter. I gazed at her. In spite of being sodden and tired, there was a light in her eyes that surprised me.

'Ava. What a beautiful name,' Shuna said in her gentle, calm voice as she opened the door of what was to be our room for the next three weeks.

I was expecting something old-fashioned, with a

patterned carpet and dark furniture, but I couldn't have been more wrong. The room was so pretty, with light blue wallpaper and warm wooden floors. The twin beds had white iron headboards, white sheets and white duvets. There were fairy lights wrapped around the tiled fireplace and blue cushions on the window seat. And the view – oh, we could see the sea! I was speechless.

'I'm sorry I don't have a better room for you, what with the Fishermen's Mass . . .' Shuna stepped in after us and switched on the fairy lights, a golden glow illuminating her face.

'Not at all, this is absolutely perfect,' I said, and I meant it. 'What is this Fishermen's Mass? Is it the same thing as the Blessing of the Boats that Sorren was talking about?' It felt a bit awkward using the man's name like that – as if I knew him already, when I'd only met him for a few minutes.

'Yes. It's an island tradition. The priest blesses the fishing boats, then there's a Mass and a bit of a celebration of our fishermen and sea rescuers,' she explained. 'And a ceilidh later on. I hope you and Ava will be there.'

'What's a . . . ceilidh?'

'It's a party. Music and dancing and a fair amount of drinking too, I fear!' Shuna said.

'Well, I'm not sure . . . but we'll come to the Blessing of the Boats.' I didn't know if I wanted to go to a party among strangers, just me and Ava.

'The priest wears a green scarf,' Ava chipped in. 'And there are fishing nets on the ground.'

'He wears a stole, yes,' Shuna replied with a smile. 'And the podium is decorated with fishing nets.'

For a moment, I felt like the air had been sucked out of my lungs. Then I pushed the thought out of my head. Again. Maybe I was just getting paranoid. She'd probably seen a priest officiating on TV, or learnt about it in school. I thought of the podium I'd seen near the pier. Perhaps that was where she'd seen the fishing nets, though I hadn't noticed them there.

'I'll get Jane to start the fire in here,' Shuna said, and gestured at the fireplace, already piled with peat. I couldn't believe I had a real fire in my room. 'In the meantime, you can get changed and come downstairs, if you want. We're in between lunch and dinner, but Sorren brought some moussaka earlier on.'

'Can we have chips?' asked Ava.

'Ava . . .' I didn't want to inconvenience this considerate, friendly woman more than we had already.

'My husband makes the best chips you will ever have tasted, I promise you.'

'Thank you,' I said. 'Oh, and if you need a deposit . . .'

'Don't worry. We can settle all that later,' she replied, and left us with a smile. As I began to help Ava get out of her wet things and dry her hair, I thanked my lucky stars.

Half an hour later, dry and changed, we were sitting in the pub beside the fire. I'd never smelled peat before – it was a smoky, earthy, nearly sweet scent. We'd been treated to heavenly moussaka and chips – on the house,

91

Shuna had said, to make up for Morag's unpleasantness. We'd also met Hamish, Shuna's husband, who was in charge of the inn. He was tall and dark-haired, like his son; he barely said a word to us, but there was a sense of kindness about him. We had discovered that Shuna was the head teacher of the island school, but it had been the last day of term today, and she was now on holiday.

Although it was only late afternoon, having been so cold and wet and hungry, we were now sleepy with food and warmth, and lulled by the fiddlers who were still going next door. Ava was huddled up against me, her eyes at half-mast, about to fall asleep. From the window we could see the day changing colour, becoming colder, opaque – the long Scottish summer night was beginning.

'So, are you here for a holiday?' asked a young girl in a ponytail from behind the counter – she was probably Jane, the girl who had lit my fire. Shuna was standing beside her, assembling a tray of drinks.

'Yes,' I replied briefly.

And then Ava's little voice piped up, sleepy and muffled by the fact that her face was against my jumper. 'I wanted to go home.'

I felt cold, in spite of the fire.

'You want to go home? Already? But you've only just arrived! Do you miss your friends?' said Jane.

'I mean I wanted to *come* home,' Ava replied, as if it were obvious.

'Time to say goodnight, Ava,' I intervened, flustered, and picked her up.

I hurried upstairs with a thank you to Shuna and Hamish, stepped into our room and closed the door. I quickly prepared Ava for bed, even if it was early – I didn't bother giving her a bath, because she was half asleep. I simply slipped on her lilac pyjamas with the tiny moons and tucked her into bed with Camilla. She fell asleep almost at once and slept soundly.

I sat on the blue cushions, looking out to sea, until night finally closed in. The view from the window was magical. A sliver of moon hung in the sky, peeking from a cluster of clouds. It was a waning moon, and I hoped it would take all my worries and fears away with it. The fishing boats, illuminated by the lights of the pier, danced and swayed on the water. I could see that the podium for the blessing was ready, and sure enough, it was decorated with fishing nets, just like Ava had said. Maybe, if the nets weren't there when we arrived, she'd seen them from the window?

Suddenly the screen of my phone lit up – I'd put it on silent so as to not wake Ava. It was a message from Parvati.

How are things? Are you there safely?

We are here. It's a beautiful place. Things are okay.

You sure?

Yes . . . Ava seems so at home. It's a bit disquieting.

Listen, have a drink and try to sleep. Keep me posted. Thinking of you, honey. P xxxx

I would do what Parvati said – not about the drink, unless I wanted to go down to the pub in my pyjamas, but about going to sleep. I was exhausted from the journey and I had to try and get some rest, even if my brain showed no sign of slowing down.

I switched off the fairy lights and slipped into the bed beside Ava's, finding a hot-water bottle that Shuna had left – she must have put it under the covers while we were eating. Another kind touch, I thought. Funny how things had worked out, with our reservation at the Swan Hotel mysteriously disappearing and Sorren coming in just as we were standing at the counter. You could almost say it was destiny. I couldn't believe that that morning I'd been in London, and now I was in this place, so different from everything I knew, so unique – as if it had been suspended in time . . .

I was bone weary and my mind was tired of racing. Soothed by the soft sounds wafting from the pub downstairs – the Grants' lullaby – I fell asleep without realising it.

I woke with a start in the middle of the night, and looked at my watch: 3.20. Too many thoughts and worries and questions were dancing around my mind.

I got up and checked on Ava; she was sleeping peacefully, in the same position I had left her in. So many emotions, so many new things, and now she was recuperating, ready to explore Seal tomorrow – today, actually – while I would be weary-eyed and downing coffee after coffee. I sighed. There was no way I could go back to sleep. I wrapped myself in the blanket at the foot of my bed, careful to be quiet, and sat at the window again, looking out into the night. And then, by the light of a street lamp, I saw them.

The seals.

A whole pod of them had gathered there, right in front of our window.

They've come to greet Ava, I thought, and it was such a strange, unexpected consideration – so absurd – that I chased it away as quickly as it had flashed into my mind.

6

Seal people

Anna

I woke to a paradise of sea and sky after an unexpected deep sleep. Tiredness had won over excitement. From our window, still in my pyjamas, I could see that the weather was perfect: the sun was shining and the water was exactly like in the pictures I'd seen on the Seal website, aqua and green and blue. The wild flowers danced in the breeze and there was nothing amiss in that ideal picture of beauty. My heart beat a little faster in anticipation.

'Ava! Ava, wake up!' I called softly in her ear. I was excited like a small child, raring to go and explore.

Ava blinked sleepily, then sat up. 'We're on Seal!' she said as she suddenly remembered. I laughed and smoothed her hair down. She had slept like a baby, exhausted after the long journey the day before.

'Come on, let's get dressed. I have a plan,' I said with a smile.

'What plan?'

I took out a pair of jeans and a long-sleeved top from her bag and placed them on her bed. 'You'll see.'

*

It only took us ten minutes to walk from the Seal Inn to the small harbour, down a flight of stone steps and a slope of wild flowers; and then the pier was before us, happily buzzing on that sunny day.

'Here we are!' I said, and pointed to the man standing beside the hand-painted sign – *Mini Cruises of the Island.*

'We're going on a boat again!' Ava exclaimed.

'Yes! For the second time in two days.' I looked at her sideways – she was beaming. I smiled to myself; to see her happy was all I wanted.

All I ever wanted.

Ava nodded, and took the man's hand. She stepped lightly on board, and the boat didn't even sway, she was so light. Like a little seal, I thought. 'I want to take a boat every day!' she said, and I wrapped my arms around her, standing behind her as we waited for the boat to leave the pier. We'd been out for a short while only, and already her hair smelled like salt and seaweed, like yesterday.

I'd decided that today there would be no questions; there would be no attempts to learn more about Ava's connection with Seal. Today my daughter and I would simply be together, in peace, taking in the beauty of the island and shedding London and all the upheaval from our minds.

The fisherman-turned-tourist-guide kept chatting, telling our fellow tourists about the island; but I tuned out. I just wanted to breathe in the atmosphere and the beautiful landscape.

Everything was so dramatic here – the sky was huge,

full of swollen clouds even on a clear day, and the sea seemed to be everywhere, ready to swallow this little island any moment, or take it away from the mainland on an ocean voyage. The wind was so strong that it blew the cobwebs away and cleared my head. In such a place it was impossible to be worried, or full of thoughts – you could only be full of beauty and in awe of what was in front of you.

For the first time I thought that maybe the trip to Seal meant more than deciphering Ava's memories; that maybe I had lost something too, and I was there to find it again. But I didn't know what it was; I didn't know how to get it back.

Slowly we followed the island's shoreline, curious seals bobbing around the boat. The fisherman kept telling us to watch out for dolphins, but they didn't make an appearance. My eyes were on the land, and from here I could make out its very bones – this barren little rock covered in a thin layer of soil, its shores sometimes falling dramatically into the water, the jutting juncture between sea and land covered in foamy waves, and sometimes sloping gently in deserted white beaches.

Seal was a song. The song of the sea.

We reached the westernmost part of the island, some-where without gentle slopes or beaches, but only breathtaking rock faces that rose sheer from the sea, dot-ted with seabirds' nests. From a distance we could see the waves shattering at their feet in splashes of foam. We could hear the ocean breaking against the island over and over again, like it wanted to reclaim it for itself. Here, the sea was the master of the land.

And then we came to a long stretch of beach, endless and windswept, the shoreline dotted with rocks covered in slippery seaweed. A soft mist was rising from the land and rolling in slowly from the sea, and soon it was hard to see around us. The fisherman told us not to worry, that he knew these waters so well that no rock could take him by surprise, and then he fell silent, with an air of concentration.

I sat Ava down beside me and wrapped my arm around her shoulder. We were floating on the mist; sea and sky and beach seemed to melt together in a palette of creams and blacks, and I felt suspended in time and space – somewhere not quite earthly, not quite here. And then a distant call broke the silence. Someone was on the beach, running along the shore, their footsteps on the wet sand and their little squeals and calls of delight muted and faraway, though they were only a few yards from us. Even the sound of the sea around the boat felt muffled, as if the mist had enveloped us in soft cotton. I looked up to the sky – it was low and white, and it seemed like I could raise my hand and touch it. The air was so full of salty moisture, we nearly couldn't tell where the water ended and the air began.

As I gazed into the mist, I thought how easy it would be, in such a moment, to see anything you wanted to see – to mistake that piece of driftwood among the waves for a seal, or to think that the two seals swimming near the weed-covered rocks were mermaids. It felt as though any time now, a Viking ship would materialise from the mist, a sea monster carved on its prow and a line of shields along its side; a seal woman would rise up from the water, her long black hair rippling down her back, shedding her skin as she walked . . .

The air was full of magic, and I didn't want to break the spell with words. We sat in silence in the rolling boat, droplets of moisture in our hair, slowly advancing in this dream world.

And then, as suddenly as it had come, the mist rolled away, swept by strong winds. The white sky was blue once more, full of stray clouds galloping towards the west, and we could see the shore again. The man made a joke about the weather on Seal changing every five minutes, and the boat was full of laughter after the eerie silence that had enveloped it when the fog was upon us.

I laughed too, and then I turned my head towards Ava and saw that she was standing beside me, steady in spite of the swaying boat, pointing with her arm perfectly straight somewhere towards the shore. I followed her arm, but there was nothing there except heathery hills and slopes, and the ruins of a stone cottage lying abandoned and eroded by the sea winds.

'Ava, what are you pointing at? What do you see?'

There was no reply. She just stood there, her arm out, in silence.

'Ava?'

For a few seconds, it was like she hadn't heard me. And then, gradually, her arm came down.

'Ava? Ava, what did you see?'

She blinked once, twice, as though waking up from deep sleep. She turned to me slowly, as if she was seeing me for the first time.

And then she knelt on the little white bench, kicking her legs behind her and resting her chin on her arms as the wind blew in her air. 'You know what would be nice, Mummy? An ice cream! A chocolate cone!'

At that point, I realised that I had been holding my breath the whole time.

7

The blessing of the boats

Anna

Early next morning, the sound of pipes filled the air, and the island seemed to come alive. It was the day of the Blessing of the Boats, and the pier and the main street were packed with people. There were a few market stalls selling local produce and souvenirs, and the queue for the ice cream van seemed to never get any shorter. We stood beside Shuna, who in turn was standing with the island's schoolchildren, all lined up in their bright blue uniforms.

'Look, there's Sorren.' Shuna pointed. He was with a small group of the Sea Rescue, beside a boat that bore the name *Oystercatcher*, painted in red on the side. He was squinting in the sun, wearing a light blue shirt with the sleeves rolled up, jeans and a bright orange lifejacket. Next to him was an older guy in a wheelchair. Sorren leaned towards the wheelchair and listened attentively as the man spoke to him, then crouched to take out a blanket from the bag hanging on the chair, and wrapped it around the man's legs. *He's kind*, I thought all of a sudden. I gazed at him a little longer than I should have, and when his eyes met mine, I looked away, embarrassed.

Two priests celebrated the Mass – Shuna whispered to me that one, Father Michael, was from Seal, and the other, Father Chris, was from nearby Eilean. Given that my mum is an atheist – I'll rephrase that: my mum is an I-don't-know-and-I-don't-care type – I had never been to Mass before, and the solemnity of the rite, together with the beauty of the Gaelic singing, moved me deeply. The choir sang with the background of seagulls and waves, so that it really seemed like a song of the sea.

As the priests sprinkled holy water on the boats, every-one stood still and silent. Those boats carried their sons and husbands and fathers, so I could understand why it was such an important matter. Ava stood beside me, clutching my hand. A couple of times, she seemed to anticipate what everyone else was going to do, like the standing and sitting, as if she'd been to Mass before; but it could have been my imagination. Probably she was just imitating the people around her.

The end of the Mass arrived, and with it the last song from the Gaelic choir. We were standing just beside the choristers, and I felt their voices resonate through my body. They sang beautifully, so beautifully that to begin with I didn't notice, not for a while.

I didn't notice that Ava was singing along with the rest of the children.

We were in the community hall, at the evening ceilidh. Sorren and Shuna had convinced us to go, though I felt a little shy among all these people I didn't know.

That night I definitely needed a drink after the emotions of the day, and I was grateful when Sorren slipped a whisky into my hand and a juice into Ava's. The whisky was so strong, it burnt my throat – but in a good way. I kept thinking of Ava singing with the Gaelic choir.

I'd refrained from asking her how she knew the song – I could foresee the answer, anyway. Something along the lines of 'I've heard it before', or 'I used to sing it', or something equally baffling. I knew that I had to start investigating Ava's memories, that it was the reason we'd come in the first place; but the idea of asking anyone frightened me. Would they think I was crazy? Would they think my daughter was crazy?

I was also scared of the answers I might find. It all seemed so absurd, so unfathomable – but there had to be a simple explanation.

Our little party consisted of Shuna and Hamish, Sorren and two employees of Star of the Sea, his restaurant – an Eastern European girl, Tatiana, and a quiet man called Fraser, who looked like the archetypal Scot, with auburn hair, light blue eyes and a kilt he wore extremely well. Sorren's friend Caty was also there. As soon as I saw her, I realised that she was the stunning girl who'd said hello on the beach. She was expansive and cheerful, with an infectious smile. Her beauty was simply breathtaking; with her strawberry-blonde hair down her back, she could have been an actress, or a model. Her warmth was a perfect antidote to my shyness; she sat beside me and began to chat like she'd known me forever. I couldn't believe that I was among strangers, and yet I was beginning to feel so much at home, in spite of my usual reserve. The whisky helped, warm and honey-coloured, and the music was flowing and crazy and wonderful, with the fiddles – the Grant family, of course – and the accordion talking to each other, and a singer whose voice made hearts melt.

Ava was playing and dancing with a group of local children and looked perfectly at ease. I was glad we had brought her favourite dress, the red one with a ra-ra skirt, to be worn with black leggings. Her hair was down and held back by a thin red hair band with a tulle flower. She was the prettiest little girl there. I was biased, of course, but I was so proud of her, her eyes shining, dancing in time to the music without any of my awkwardness. I followed her with my eyes like you would follow a cherry blossom in the breeze. Suddenly Shuna's expression as she saw Ava all dressed up to go to the ceilidh came back to me – tenderness, and a touch of sadness, the same as I had noticed when Ava had thrown herself into Shuna's arms.

The music, together with the heat of so many bodies in a small place, went to my head, and I began to relax and smile like all was well with the world. It was a rare feeling for me, and I revelled in it.

Suddenly Catriona was gone, dancing with a tall blonde man, and in her place beside me was Sorren. His eyes were grey in the semi-darkness, and he wore a blue, green and white kilt, with a simple white T-shirt. Most of the men were wearing kilts, I'd noticed. I made a mental note to tell Parvati, who was a fan of romantic novels, and who especially loved books with kilted men on the cover. The thought made me smile.

'Having fun?' Sorren asked. His accent made everything he said sound like music.

'The time of my life, honestly! It's just great,' I said, and I meant it.

'So, what are your plans for the holiday?'

Well, my daughter has been saying strange things about having another mother and another life here on Seal, so we came to see if we can sort that whole thing out, you know.

'I . . . Well, no plans really.' I shrugged. 'Sightseeing. Exploring the island. Going on the beach . . .'

'The beaches here are beautiful. Maybe not as warm as Spain or Italy, but still beautiful.'

'I'd like to collect some shells. I had a shell collection when I was a child; I kept them all in a jar. They were my gran's. She was Scottish, by the way, so who knows, maybe some of those shells were—'

'The Gay Gordons!' Shuna interrupted us. 'Come on, Sorren, show Anna how we dance here!' She got up, followed by Hamish, and took our hands to make us stand up too. We faced each other for an awkward moment; Sorren looked a bit like a deer caught in headlights – as did I, I imagined. 'Come on,' Shuna encouraged us, before disappearing into the dance.

With a shy smile, Sorren took both my hands in his – his skin was very warm.

'I can't . . .'

He shrugged. 'Don't worry, anyone can dance the Gay Gordons!'

And before I knew it, he had swept me off my feet and into the dance. The steps were very easy even for someone with two left feet like me, and I learnt quickly. I felt my cheeks redden, and laughter was coming spontanously, joyfully, from my lips – how long had it been since I'd laughed so heartily? All the while, I was looking into Sorren's face as he guided me, gently but firmly, so that I knew exactly what to do. It was easy to guess from his style of dancing that under his mellow exterior was someone who knew how to take charge. His hands held mine or rested on the small of my back, his arm was around my waist or my shoulder – a thousand points of contact and a thousand little sparks.

When the dance finished, I was out of breath and happy and feeling like a little girl who'd spun round and round until she'd made herself dizzy. I threw myself back into my chair, still smiling. A blonde woman in her twenties approached Sorren as soon as he'd let me go, and wrapped her arms around his waist – quite proprietorially, I thought. A sudden bout of jealousy squeezed my heart. How ridiculous – Sorren could dance with whoever he wanted; I couldn't monopolise him all night. He certainly seemed quite popular with the ladies.

The celebrations went on long into the night, and then we went back to the Seal Inn for a nightcap. I carried Ava to bed and left her in our room with a kiss, the nightlight we'd brought from London plugged in. When I went back downstairs, a few stragglers were there still, and we sat beside the fire listening to the Grants playing low, sweet tunes. Finally, even the last customers went home – or were carried home, depending on the state of them – and the McNeils were left to clean up. I offered to help, but Shuna convinced me to have a last dram and sit with her beside the fire, while Sorren, Catriona and Tatiana restored the place to order.

'So you're here for a bit of a break,' she said. She wasn't prying; I could feel she was genuinely interested.

'I . . . Yes.' But the need to open up, to tell my story, was irresistible. I don't let my guard down easily, but there was something about Shuna – the smile lines around her blue eyes, the kindness of her face – that made me want to offload. 'We just went through a . . . stressful time.'

'I'm sorry to hear that.' Her gaze was full of warmth, and I could see that she was someone who was used to listening, someone people confided in.

'My partner left us . . . Ava's dad.'

'Oh, what a shame . . .'

Was I really telling a total stranger such details about my life? Must have been the whisky, or maybe the way Shuna felt so much like a *mother*. 'It was a huge blow for Ava.'

'I'm so sorry . . . You know, I find that life has a way of sorting itself out,' she said, and somehow those clichéd words seemed to take on a new, deeper meaning. Like an omen of peace.

I shrugged. 'Well, we have each other, Ava and I . . .' I began, and then I saw Sorren watching us. Had he heard what I'd said about Toby leaving us? Swiftly, as he noticed me looking, he began to wipe the table in front of him, concentrating resolutely on his task.

When I couldn't keep my eyes open any longer, I tiptoed upstairs, so as not to wake the guests who were sleeping already. I got washed and changed quickly, and slipped into Ava's bed instead of mine. Her back was turned to me, and I rested one arm around her little waist and my face in her hair, holding her tight.

If I should lose you . . .

But I would not think about that. I'd think of the swaying boats in the sunshine, and the dance, and how I felt alive moving in time to the music. I was about to fall asleep when suddenly I remembered how Ava had sung along with the Gaelic choir.

No. She was just miming, following the words at random, making up a language of her own. I was too tired to mull that over, to think about anything; the evening of music and dance and whisky, and the craziness of the last few days, made me fall into a deep, deep sleep, entwined with my daughter.

8

A life for others

Sorren

Dawn was breaking. The long Scottish summer day was beginning, and we were still up. Fraser, Caty, Tatiana and I were sitting on the pub's deep red sofas, nursing cups of strong coffee. There had been something about that night, something magical – the perfect combination of music and companionship – and we didn't want it to end. Nobody wanted to return to their everyday lives.

My parents had gone to bed; in the past they'd always been the first ones at a party and the last to leave, but they weren't so young any more, and their resilience was fading. Anna had gone too, after a chat with my mum. I'd heard them talking beside the fire about Ava's dad. It seemed so weird to me that someone could receive such a gift from life – a woman like Anna, and a daughter like Ava, so funny and lively and vulnerable – and reject it. Take off and leave, stop taking care of them, stop making sure they were safe and happy and protected.

This unknown man had everything, and he'd just let it all go.

When Anna and I had danced, being close to her had felt so natural. It was difficult to put it in words. I hadn't felt like that in a long time. She smelled sweet and fresh, like sugar and rain. She smelled like Seal in spring. And her big dark eyes, her strawberry lips – her face was perfect, framed by her brown hair down to her shoulders. Her voice was soft and low, like a caress.

I'd only known her a couple of days, but it felt like much longer somehow.

But enough of that.

She'd be here for a short while and then she'd be gone, back to her life in London. No point in having ideas when she'd be leaving so soon. What had happened with Alessia had made things clear for me; it had forced me to choose between her and the island. And I wouldn't leave Seal. My parents needed me.

I never wanted to make such a painful choice again.

No. Nothing could happen with Anna. I was fascinated by her, and maybe we'd spend a bit of time together while she was here, and then she'd leave for London and that would be it.

'Well, I'd better get going. I'll see you at the restaurant in . . . three hours?' Caty looked at her watch and got up slowly, reluctantly.

'And me,' Tatiana said, and they waved goodbye. I watched them go with regret. Real life was on again. Fraser and I were left to finish our coffee.

'If I wasn't working tomorrow . . . *today*, I mean . . . I'd consider hair of the dog,' Fraser said.

'No way. I need you sober for service,' I laughed. 'But I'll do you a fry-up.'

I made my way to the kitchen, thinking I would get things organised for the guests' breakfast, so that my parents would have an easier start to the day. I began to assemble the perfect Scottish breakfast, slicing black pudding and getting bacon and sausages going. Fraser joined me, and quietly began to crack eggs. As we worked in silence, I tried to find some order in my thoughts.

Since Alessia had left, I'd simply never thought I would find anyone else. It wasn't like I was against it – like I wanted to remain alone for some reason; it was more that Alessia had carved such a hole in my heart and in my life, I couldn't see how anyone would be able to fill it. She had blown me over with her liveliness; when she was around, it was like the sun had come out. While we were in Verona, life was perfect. She teased me when I tried to speak Italian, we cooked together, we travelled around Italy in her parents' old Fiat. I know it sounds old-fashioned, but I thought I had found the woman who would be my wife. I never wanted to be parted from her.

When the year's training at the cookery school was over, it was decision time. Alessia was happy in Verona; she wanted us to settle down in Italy, but I felt the pull of Seal, the pull of my parents and how much they needed me. No, that's not the whole truth – how much *I* needed *them* too. The loss of Isla had changed things. It had created an invisible cord that bound us, though none of us would ever have put this into words.

And so I returned to Seal with Alessia.

The rest is history. She tried to be happy here. But her forced smiles, her sleepless nights gave her away. After a few months she told me, tears streaming down her cheeks, that she loved me – she would never stop loving me – but she was going back to Italy.

She said that I put everyone's else needs before mine, before ours. That there was always something more important, something crucial, something I had to sort out – the Sea Rescue, or my parents, or anyone and everyone who needed me.

She said that I couldn't allow myself to be happy. *I don't understand. You are punishing yourself every day of your life. And me with you.* I remember so clearly, as if it had happened a moment ago, the way she leaned her forehead against the window. How the rain outside mirrored her tears. The way her *I don't understand* sounded in her Italian accent, like all the consternation in the world was encased in those words.

I couldn't say, not even in my thoughts, that if she was leaving, it meant that her love for me wasn't strong enough. I couldn't put the blame on her, though many times after she left I was tempted to do so.

I couldn't, because she asked me to go back to Italy with her, to free myself from the past and finally live my own life.

And I said no.

After Alessia left, my mother pulled me aside.

'You don't think you should go to Verona, do you?' she

said in her gentle way. I was stunned. This was the most she'd *ever* commented on my love life. Not even when Alessia and I had started to argue, not even when she'd seen Alessia becoming more and more miserable as time passed. She'd always been there for me, but without ever passing judgement, without ever interfering. In my family, these things were not discussed, but there was always a silent togetherness, like each one of us knew what the others were going through, at all times.

'No,' I said drily. 'I can't. I have too many . . . responsibilities.'

'You know that we would be fine, your father and I, don't you? We would miss you very much, but we would be fine.'

'I know.'

'When you left to attend your course in Italy, we knew you might not come back to the island,' she went on, but I shook my head. I didn't want her to continue. I couldn't say what was on my mind. I couldn't put into words the jumble of thoughts and desires and regrets that fought in me: my love for Seal, the impossibility of leaving my parents after what had happened to Isla . . . and on the other side, my love for Alessia and the desire – the need – for a life with her.

I couldn't say how in my heart of hearts, I was sure that what had happened to Isla was my fault.

I couldn't let myself be happy and leave my parents behind.

I couldn't leave my sister's memory behind.

'I'm not going,' I said, in a tone that ended the conversation. My mum never mentioned Alessia, or me leaving, again.

I did what I always do when I am low, or confused: I went out to sea and sat in the swaying boat, alone but for the seagulls and a pod of seals lying on their rocks in the sun. I threw Alessia's letter in the blue-green waters of my island.

Since then, there had been nobody. Not even a fling. I might have seen girls I was attracted to, and a couple of times someone tried to catch my attention, but I never let anything happen.

Because Alessia was still in my life. She wasn't letting me go, and I wasn't letting her go either.

She wrote to me. Every month or so I got an email from her, a long, long letter in which she told me about her life, how she missed me, how she wished things had been different. She told me about meeting Pietro and how they'd moved in together; and still, even though she said she was happy with this Pietro guy, she kept writing to me.

I waited for those letters like a lifeline, like mouthfuls of oxygen, and when they finally came, it was a relief so great I felt like I could breathe again; and yet I cursed them too, because it meant I was still bound to her, bound to the past. No wonder there couldn't be anyone if my heart was shut and bolted, if I lived for those letters and the deceit of them – the deceit that we were still close, that there was hope. Every time, I wondered whether this was the letter in which she'd tell me she was coming back, that we would try again . . .

'She's nice,' Fraser said suddenly, shaking me out of my reflections.

'Who?'

'Anna.'

'Suppose so.' What? Had he *noticed*? Or, God forbid, was he interested in her too?

'I was just saying. She's here on her own . . .' He shrugged.

'Yeah. She broke up with her daughter's dad.'

'Oh.'

'Go for it, Fraser,' I said with a brittle laugh. *Oh please don't*, I thought.

'Nah. Not me. But I have seen the way you look at her.'

I stirred a pot of scrambled eggs like my life depended on it, and said nothing.

'Whatever.' He shrugged again. Conversations with Fraser could be extremely frustrating. He said three words and he meant three hundred. 'Maybe she'd like to go out on your boat,' he said. 'You know, see the island from another angle. I can cover here, if you want to take her.'

'One or two slices of bacon?'

'Three.'

'Coming.'

'Sorren?'

'Mmmm?'

'Ask her.'

I didn't reply.

9

Trace your footsteps in the sand

Anna

The day after the ceilidh, I woke up feeling strange.

Strange as in *cheerful*.

I hadn't felt properly cheerful in a long, long time – as long as I could remember, probably.

I was full of hope as from the window I watched the green-blue sea and the sunny sky unfolding in place of the city landscape I was used to seeing. I opened the window and breathed in the chilly sea air. My arms were covered in goose bumps; the cold wind woke me. I closed my eyes in silent joy. I knew my problems hadn't gone anywhere; I knew that all the issues remained, but this was respite, and I wanted to feel it. It was like being at an oasis in the desert – even with your feet in a fresh pool, even drinking from your hands in greedy gulps, even lying in the shade of a palm tree, you know that you are still in the desert. You know you still have miles to go, but for now, the water and the shade and the rest are all you need, all you can think of.

I still had miles to go, but for now I could lay down my burden.

Ava was still sleeping, clutching Camilla. I woke her with a kiss, and she opened those big brown eyes of hers. 'Morning, baby. Did you have fun yesterday?'

She nodded, still between sleep and waking. 'What are we doing today?' Her long eyelashes sticky with sleep; that baby smell she still had when she was just awake.

'We are going to have breakfast and then go and explore. Sound good?'

She smiled her wonderful, slow smile that started with her lips and ended with her eyes, bathing her whole face in joy. I loved her smile. I loved seeing her happy. 'Sounds good.'

Yes. Coming to Seal had been the right decision. Here her distress would abate, she would find an outlet for her strange memories, and everything would go back to normal. Well, the new normal – without her dad.

While Ava was getting dressed, I took a little yellow notebook out of my backpack and sat on the bed. I opened it to a blank page, and my stomach clenched.

This was where I was recording the pieces of Ava's jigsaw to try and put them together.

She knew what the priest would wear.

She seemed to know what to do at Mass.

She sang along with the Gaelic choir.

I wasn't sure whether to record the way she had stood and pointed in that strange, trance-like way when we were on the boat. Yes, she had been pointing at a ruined cottage, but she hadn't said anything about it. I decided to omit it, and turned to the first page of the notebook. I went through what I'd written previously, a slow chill travelling down my spine.

Her other mum made her porridge.

She had a bowl with a rabbit on it.

From the play park she could see the sea, she could see dolphins.

The time had come to start asking questions, I thought.

But I would not let my apprehension ruin the day. Ava and I would unravel everything together; we would figure our way out of this strange labyrinth we'd found ourselves in.

'Are you ready, Mummy?'

'I sure am!' I said, and slipped the notebook in my handbag.

We went downstairs, Ava skipping down the steps. Since Toby had left, she'd been so low in energy; it was lovely to see her bouncy again. Hamish was serving breakfast, delicious-smelling bacon rolls and eggs, and hot, inviting coffee, while Shuna was nowhere to be seen. We ate quickly and stepped onto the sunny road, and for a moment I crouched in front of Ava.

'So, darling. I'd like you to tell me what you remember. I'd like you to take me to the places you know . . .'

Ava nodded. 'I'll try. I'm not sure . . . Sometimes I remember, sometimes I don't . . .'

I offered my hand, and she took it. 'Well, we'll do what feels right. You'll be my guide.'

She smiled and walked ahead, with me following. Her hair, up in a ponytail, blew in the wind and she had taken off her hoody – she didn't seem to suffer from the cold like I did, her soft white arms bare in the chill breeze that came off the sea.

We walked down towards the main street, and the view was breathtaking – the harbour nestled in a little fjord crowned by brightly coloured houses, the boats, from the smallest to the biggest ones, swaying on the waves. The sea mirrored the bright blue of the sky, and puffy clouds blew across, carried by the wind. On both sides of the harbour was the pure white beach, and between the beach and the village lay a strip of meadow filled with brightly coloured flowers, yellow and purple and orange. The beauty of it all took my breath away.

Did you used to play there, Ava? Among the sweet bright flowers?

On the hills above the harbour, several white cottages were scattered among the pines, and right on the sea stood a stately home built of red sandstone, at its feet a small bridge that from afar had a bright fuchsia tint – the foxgloves I'd seen on the island website. For some reason, that brave little bridge, daring to provide passage above an ocean, made me smile.

'That's Kilpatrick House,' I pointed out to Ava, leaning towards her. 'Shall we go and see it after we explore the village?'

Ava nodded so hard her ponytail bounced up and down. A fresh bout of wind threw her hair in my face, and again I noticed its fragrance – salt and wind, the scent of the sea.

We found ourselves in the main street, among the

multicoloured houses – a rainbow village under the golden sun. I imagined that in the dark of winter, those houses would shine brightly between the grey of the sky and the grey of the sea, always cheerful even on the grimmest of days. A place built to make the heart sing, that was what Roan seemed to me.

'Where are you taking me?' I asked Ava jokingly, but there was an edge of apprehension to my question. What would she say? What would she show me?

She shrugged. 'I don't know yet.'

We passed a small Co-op, a hairdresser, an ice-cream parlour with children's pictures taped all over the window, a souvenir shop with stands on the road overflowing with beach equipment and postcards, all hosted in brightly coloured buildings. Once again it struck me how small the place was, this little village lost in the middle of heathery hills, barren moors and sparse pinewoods. It was a blink-and-you'll-miss-it hamlet, and the sea was everywhere you turned. I kept looking at Ava to see if she recognised something – but then I decided to just relax and see what would happen. She skipped happily along the road, her backpack on her shoulders, chatting about everything and nothing.

Finally we came to a small fenced play park, and she stopped. Was this the place she had mentioned to me when I'd taken her to the park in London? I held my breath.

'Can I go on the slide?' she said, and without waiting for an answer, she ran towards it.

There was a red-haired boy on the swings, probably a little younger than Ava, wearing a stripy Breton top and blue shorts. He looked like a mini sailor who had just come off a transatlantic journey, his plump little legs kicking the air as he tried to go higher and higher. In the wordless, no-nonsense way in which children make friends, he scuffed the ground with his feet and jumped off the swing, then climbed up the slide after Ava.

I sat on a bench, enjoying the fresh air on my face and in my hair, and closed my eyes for a moment. I just couldn't get enough of the sea air, as if I'd known it before, as if I'd known it forever and now I'd come back to it. Funny, I thought – whose homecoming was this? Ava's or mine?

'Is that your daughter?' said a voice not far from me. It had a lilt just like Shuna's. I opened my eyes and saw a tall, matronly woman beside me, her light red hair in waves past her shoulders and her skin a perfect porcelain. She had a full, feminine beauty, and a warm alto voice.

'Yes. That's Ava. And that's your boy?'

'Yes. Alexander, but we call him Sandy. And this is Angela.'

Only then did I see that her hand on the other side from me was resting on a wheelchair. She pushed it towards me so that Angela could say hello in a small, birdlike voice, and wave her thin hand. She was a tiny thing with the same red hair as her mother and her brother, dressed in pastel colours and with a pair of glasses perched on her small freckled nose. The wheelchair seemed too big for her. She was lost in it, like a little doll sitting among the cushions of a double bed. At that moment, Ava squealed as she ran with Sandy, and my eyes went to her – to my daughter running free and happy – and then back to Angela, sitting in her wheelchair like a bird with broken wings. My heart ached.

'And how old are you, Angela?' I asked.

'Seven.'

'Oh, my daughter is nearly seven.'

'Does she like *Frozen*?'

I laughed and exchanged a look with Angela's mum. 'Oh, goodness, does she like *Frozen*! Let's just say I've watched it about fifty times . . .'

'I have an Elsa doll,' Angela said, and her mum, without needing to be asked, freed a backpack from the back of the wheelchair and fished a doll out of it. Within ten minutes, poor Sandy was left to run around on his own while Angela and Ava played *Frozen* with the Elsa doll and the Barbie Ava always carried in her own backpack.

'By the way, I'm Carla.'

'Anna. Lovely to meet you. We're on holiday here for a little while.'

'Yes, I guessed from your accent. Where are you staying?'

'At the Seal Inn.'

'Oh, with Shuna? She's great. You know she's the head teacher of the island school?' I nodded. 'She's done miracles for Angela. She fought tooth and nail to get her full-time support during school hours; she made sure she would never feel . . . excluded, you know. Shuna is the best.'

As she said that word – *excluded* – I could sense her own heartache.

'She's great with Ava.'

'I can imagine. With what happened to her family, you know—'

'Mum, can we show Ava our salad?' Angela piped up.

Carla laughed and looked at me. 'Would you like to see our allotment?'

'We'd love to,' I said.

We gathered children and jackets and Sandy's ball and a lost hair band – the debris of play-park expeditions – and followed Carla along the main street. 'Everyone is so friendly here,' I said.

'It's because it's such a tiny place, you know. We love tourists, I suppose!'

I smiled, thinking how a couple of nights before, I'd been dancing at a ceilidh, and now I was chatting with a fellow mum, our children playing together. This island had welcomed us more warmly than I could ever have imagined.

'So what brought you here, Anna? Do you have family in Scotland?'

'No, I . . . Well, we just . . . We'd heard of the place and wanted to see it, that's all,' I hurried to explain.

'This is our allotment!' Angela said proudly. We had

come to a small piece of land right at the edge of the village, with a hothouse at the centre of it. A sign said 'Community Garden', with the symbol of the Highlands and Islands Council.

'Volunteers from the village take turns looking after it. And then we all share the produce.'

'It's a wonderful idea!' What a great feeling it must be, I thought, to be part of such a close-knit community, to look after everybody's interest, to build something together. While I gazed at a row of cabbages, all lined up like green flowers, Ava and Angela were conferring in low voices.

'Mum! I'm going to go to Angela's house and we'll play *Frozen* in her room and have custard creams because they're her favourite!'

'Well, not now. But it would be good—'

'Absolutely!' Carla said with a smile, taking her mobile out of her handbag. She had read my mind. We exchanged phone numbers, and Ava gave Angela a hug. They kept looking at each other with starry eyes, the way you do when you're seven and you've just found a new best friend.

'Ava, was that the play park . . . you know, the one you told me about?' I said as soon as we were out of earshot.

She shook her head. 'No. From the one I remember, I could see the sea. From the top of the slide, I mean,' she said. She was skipping along, not at all upset by my question.

'Did you see anywhere . . . anything you remember?'

'I remember Carla.'

My heart skipped a beat, and then began to pound hard against my chest. I stopped and knelt in front of her.

'Not her face. Just her voice. She's Catriona's sister.'

'And . . . you knew her?'

She nodded.

'Did you know . . . did you know *Sorren*?'

All of a sudden, her eyes widened and her breathing became faster, shorter. 'I think so,' she said, and I could hear a hint of tears in her voice. Why? Why was she upset?

And then I remembered how she had stared into his eyes, how open she'd been with both him and Shuna. That was not typical behaviour for Ava. But then being open and chatty wasn't exactly typical me either – maybe it was just the island working its strange magic. And yet, if she said she knew Sorren . . .

I opened my mouth to ask more, but Ava threw her arms around me and hid her face in my neck.

'Don't ask, Mummy. It makes me sad.'

But I had to take that chance. I had to. 'What, sweetheart? What makes you sad?'

'That I didn't see anyone again for a long time. A very long time. Please, Mummy. I don't want to speak any more . . .'

'Of course, sweetheart. Sorry. Let's go.' I was torn, always undecided between probing Ava and not wanting to upset her.

*

Kilpatrick House sat on a small hill surrounded by pine trees and green fields. The view from there was incredible: the village of Roan, and past it, the lovely machair – Shuna had taught me the word – with its wild flowers swaying gently, the white beach and the vast expanse of the sea. The house was sheltered from harsh winds by its surrounding trees, and a lovely smell of pine resin filled the air. There was a little play park under the pines, and Ava and I played there for a bit before buying a ticket to see the house. We toured the inside, room after room of antiques and family portraits of long-gone people, and Ava completed a treasure hunt where she had to find several objects and score them off on a sheet. What impressed her most was the photograph of Lady Stella, a little girl a bit younger than her who had lived in the house.

'Was she a princess?'

'In a way, I suppose.'

'Where is she now?'

'I don't know. And you're a princess too, Ava, aren't you?' I smiled and held her hand.

A pair of peacocks came out of the pine copse, their feathers blowing in the island wind. I heard Ava exclaim, and I turned around to see her standing in front of a peacock showing off its beautiful tail. Then she looked somewhere over my shoulder. 'Hello!' she called, and ran past me to a small cluster of people. One of them was wearing a suit and a Visit Scotland badge; the second was a woman in her fifties with long, wavy grey hair pinned up and dangling earrings; and the third, the tallest of the three, had raven-black hair and was wearing a checked shirt with the sleeves rolled up. It was Sorren.

'Hello,' he said as I reached Ava, and for a moment he was the colour of beetroot. I was happy that I wasn't the only one who blushed. 'Sorry, I'm not stalking you or anything. Just bringing Lady Kilpatrick her lunch. Usually it's Fraser who does the rounds, but he's busy today. So here I am.' He lifted a tinfoil-covered plate. 'Casserole!'

'Oh.'

He took a breath. He seemed positively flustered, and I couldn't help smiling a little – just a little. 'Come, I'll introduce you to the owner of the house.' He gestured towards the woman. 'Anna, this is Linda Kilpatrick. This is Anna and Ava, up from London for a holiday.'

I extended my hand, and Linda Kilpatrick shook it.

'So what do you think of our island?' she said with a smile that lit up her eyes.

'We're loving it, aren't we, Ava?'

'Yes . . . Oooh!' She jumped back a little as a peacock came so close to her it nearly pecked her shoe.

'They like a conversation,' Linda said. 'The peacocks. Seriously,' she continued as I laughed. 'They come up to whoever is around and they look up like they want a chat. They're not interested in food; they're very spoiled birds and only eat their own special stuff. But they like a bit of action.'

'Excuse me,' Ava said. 'Can you tell me where Lady Stella is?'

'Stella . . . She went. Long ago. She doesn't live here any more.'

'Was she a princess? The princess of the castle?'

'Well, you could say that, I suppose. Anyway, I'm sorry, I have to leave you. Neal and I must talk shop, and my mother has been alone all morning. You know how it's been with her,' she said to Sorren, who nodded sympathetically. 'Enjoy your stay! And you, young lady,' she added, ruffling Ava's hair before walking inside with the man in the suit.

Sorren, Ava and I were left alone. Sorren crouched and began to rummage in the cool bag he had with him. He took out a little parcel wrapped in a white linen napkin.

'I didn't want to give it to you in front of Linda, but . . . Well, I got this for you. You mentioned the shell jar you had as a girl . . .' He opened his palm, and on it there was an exquisite shell. 'It's a cowrie.'

I was astounded. He'd remembered what I'd said about the shell collection. His thoughtfulness made me speechless for a moment. 'This . . . this is beautiful. Thank you.'

He shrugged. 'It's nothing. Listen . . .'

'Yes?'

His mouth opened, then closed. 'Never mind. It's okay.'

'I'll see you around, then . . .'

'Yes. Yes, of course.'

'Oh, Sorren. You know Carla . . . Is she Catriona's sister?'

'Yes. Her older sister.'

Right. Well, maybe Ava had heard it from Angela . . .

or maybe it had been mentioned, and I hadn't heard. I murmured a goodbye to Sorren, trying not to look back as we walked away. Trying to pretend my stomach hadn't filled with unexpected, unwelcome butterflies.

I stood on the bridge across the Atlantic and watched him step into his jeep. My eyes swept the beautiful Kilpatrick House, and something caught my eye – a figure standing at an upper floor window. I was pretty sure whoever it was was looking straight at me. I squinted a little to see better. It was an old lady, her head crowned in silver hair. I'm not sure why – probably it was a tourist and I was just making a fool of myself – but I raised my hand and gave her a wave. She waved back, a gesture so slight you could easily have missed it.

Ava and I walked on hand in hand, and as we turned away from Kilpatrick House, I wondered what it was that Sorren had wanted to say, and then didn't.

That night, when Ava was asleep, I took the yellow notebook out of my handbag and wrote one sentence only:

She remembers Carla.

I put the pen down, and read that sentence over and over again until the words were dancing before my eyes. I looked over at Ava in her bed, the light of my bedside lamp casting a warm glow on her cheek, her hand uncurled on the pillow. I bent over her and gave her a kiss, light as a feather, so as not to wake her up. Once again, I noticed her scent – salt water. And the same scent was in our room, salt water and seaweed and wind, the smell of the sea.

She remembers Carla.

Still, the day hadn't been only about Ava's memories. Something else was happening. Something unexpected. The island was working on us both. It made Ava's eyes sparkle, it made my worries ease. My daughter's skin had changed scent; my heart was softening. Ava's face had lost that anxious, lost look she'd had since Toby had left; the crease between my eyes was smoothing.

Seal was changing us from the inside, I could feel it. Both of us.

And that frightened me. Because when you relax, and open up, and soften – that's when you start *feeling*.

I reached for the shell Sorren had given me, and felt its smooth surface under my fingers. He had remembered this little thing about my childhood. He had taken my memory, and held it, and celebrated it.

And with that, he had come closer than I could bear him to be.

Stepping across the room in the darkness, I slipped the shell into my jacket pocket.

That little piece of emotion, that little bloom of possibility, had to go. It could not be allowed to grow.

Because when you soften up and start feeling . . . that's when you start suffering.

That night, I had a dream. It was a simple dream, so simple, and yet it took my breath away and made me wake with tears in my eyes.

I dreamt someone was holding both my hands – I

could feel his fingers threaded with mine, I could feel his hands so much bigger than mine. When he pulled me to his chest, he felt strong, and safe, and as his arms closed around me, I let myself go with a big sigh, like I was exhaling all my worries, all my cares.

I woke up in the middle of the night swept by waves of emotion. Loneliness weighed like a stone in my heart, and at the same time I felt full of tenderness, as though my heart had turned liquid.

10

A planet and its moon

Anna

Early the next day, Shuna offered to teach Ava how to crochet, and I decided to go for a walk, alone. They seemed so at ease together when I left them, the dark head and the grey one bent together over the little lop-sided scarf Ava was making. With my mum lost to her demons and Gillian pretty much indifferent to her grand-daughter, it was simply magical to see Ava with someone so much like a granny. I had sweet, sweet memories of my own grandmother – how I wished that Ava would have some too . . .

I went for a slow, gentle walk along the beach. The machair shone with wild flowers and brimmed with life, seabirds swooping over it, bees and butterflies dancing among the flowers. I was lost in thoughts and memories and emotions, trying to process all that had happened since we'd arrived on the island. My eyes caressed the expanse of the sea, and I took a deep breath. It was like the open horizon, uncluttered with buildings and towers, was finally allowing me to breathe. As if the same build-ings and towers had been weighing on my chest with their tons of iron and steel and cement. Now, in a space empty of everything but oxygen and water, my lungs could expand, my heart could beat calmly, slowly.

Strange how that blue-grey sea under a vast sky had begun to feel familiar so quickly. Like it was natural to walk out of the door and step onto the beach instead of a busy street. Who knows, maybe it was my grandmother's genetic memory being passed down to me, because these were the landscapes she must have looked at when she was a child.

I wondered what she would say if she knew I was here.

I still missed her. She was the only family I had ever known, and yet I knew so little about her. My mum had had a happy childhood in a loving family, but she didn't seem to fit with them; she didn't fit in school, she didn't fit anywhere. It seemed she could only bear the weight of life if she had a bottle in her hand. She and my grandparents became estranged, but she came briefly together again with her mother when I was born. My grandmother, by then a widow, looked after me until she died. I had vague, sweet memories of her as the only loving, steady presence in my childhood – the scent of talc and lavender, home-made biscuits and cups of warm milk, hugs and woollen blankets, the soft sound of her black-and-white TV as I fell asleep. When she died, I was heartbroken – I still remember it, though I was so young. I remember the feeling of loss, of abandonment, as I went from loving arms and a safe, calm home to my mum's chaos.

As I was growing up, my mum never told me anything about her – she had nothing but indifference for both her parents, even hatred at times. All I knew was that they came from somewhere in Scotland. My mum told me nothing about my father either, except that he was English and very, very young. In a way, it was like I'd been adopted – I knew nothing about my roots. I *had* no roots. My mother had got rid of all my family history, even photographs.

I didn't know who I was, I suppose. I didn't know what was behind me.

But I knew what was ahead of me – I knew what the next link of the chain was: Ava.

I'd sworn that Ava's life would be different, no matter what. She would have security, a safe, steady home. She would study, she would do whatever she wanted, be whatever she wanted to be – a doctor, a teacher, an actress, a lawyer; any dream she had, I would help her fulfil it. I barely finished school, moving as I was from foster family to foster family, then back to my mum for a short while, until she'd fall off the wagon again and someone would notice that I'd been left home alone for days, without food or money to buy it, and I was shipped off once more. I wanted an education, but it was near impossible to get one. I worked hard in school – I loved its routines, the timetables, the rules, so different from the chaos of my home life. I stayed on as long as I could, but then I simply had no money to continue. I had to support myself, so I settled for the first job I could find. I had always loved looking after people – it made me feel useful, wanted – so I became a hospital assistant.

There, at the hospital, I fell in love with nursing. The job seemed amazing to me, the skill to make people better, to heal and to help. To *care*. Being a nurse became my dream and my goal, as my mum drifted from man to man and lived on alcohol in whatever way she could find it. I lost count of how many times I tried to convince her to stop drinking, offered to pay for a clinic, for help; how many times I cleaned her up, cooked for her, washed her sheets and her clothes; how many times I threw some useless, semi-conscious loser out of her flat and put her under the shower, making her the strongest coffee I could while she recovered herself under the cold water . . .

Time wasted, energy wasted. My mother didn't want to be looked after. She didn't even want to be loved. She just wanted to be left alone, to be left to destroy herself.

But I was different. I wanted to be useful, I wanted to be *someone*. I wanted to be needed, to be loved. And when Toby arrived in my life with a ready smile and wave after wave of affection, of cheerfulness, I couldn't resist. A part of me knew already he couldn't be trusted, but he won me over with his easy warmth and eternal optimism. If we didn't have money to make ends meet, never mind, we'd get by somehow; if I was bored out of my head by my glorified cleaning job, never mind, he'd take me to Hyde Park and we'd kiss under the trees and have ice cream and go home to eat fish and chips in our half-furnished flat, and suddenly living for today seemed the only way to be.

Toby didn't believe in rainy days and could not even conceive that things might go wrong – he had a complete, blind trust in life and in himself. So different from my mum, who in spite of a happy childhood and a loving family always felt betrayed, short-changed, angry. I'd lived in the rain for years, and Toby was sunshine – yes, he couldn't hold down a job, and sometimes people came looking for him because he owed them money, and once or twice girls called the house looking for him. But I was blind to all that. Blind for a year, until this life of no-tomorrow tired me for good. I still wanted an education more than anything; I would be a nurse. And I could do it, I was sure of that. There was no future for Toby and me, and even if a part of me still loved him, I was getting ready to tell him we had to go our separate ways.

And then Ava happened, and I had to put my plans on hold.

I didn't resent her for a second. I didn't resent that little spark of a life who had come to show me what true love was; because I adored her, I adored her from the moment I knew she was there.

Toby was beside himself with joy. He caressed my tummy and spoke to the baby; he bought me grapes and anything I craved; he came to antenatal classes with me. When Ava was born, they fell in love with each other.

And that was it. I couldn't leave him now, even if my love for him was long gone and I had grown tired of his inability to work a normal job, to stop seeing other women, to act like a grown-up. I was determined that Ava should have the family I'd never had.

For my mother, I'd been an accident along the way, not a much-cherished gift like Ava was. And in my adult life, I'd never been able to shake that feeling off – that I was not wanted. I had sworn that for Ava it would be different; that she would feel precious, and beloved. I would do anything for her.

But I couldn't let my dream of training as a nurse go. And so I did it all: looking after Ava, working, studying part-time. Toby wasn't happy – he told me over and over again that I wanted too much, I was overstretching myself; surely if I had barely passed my school exams, a nursing course was going to be too hard for me? But after three years of spreading myself so thin I was transparent, I had reached my goal. I had qualified.

By then, things between Toby and me were strained. I had come to know a side of him I'd never imagined. He was dismissive. He would find every excuse, every occasion to put me down with words and actions. Little, cruel things to make me feel I didn't matter, I didn't exist.

I would come home after work and find that he had cooked just enough for him and Ava; there was nothing for me. I would be speaking on the phone and he would say horrible things about me in a loud voice, for whoever I was speaking to to hear. I would be putting make-up on at the bathroom mirror and he would make some comment about how not even a ton of make-up could make me look half decent. It was an entirely new Toby, one I didn't know, and he was slowly, slowly grinding me down, mangling my heart, destroying me. Yet he was Ava's father, and so I would not leave, I would not throw him out.

I'd just started working as a nurse when Toby left. And now here I was, far away from all I knew, chasing after Ava's strange memories and mysterious remarks.

Life is strange and unexpected, that I'd always known. But to end up on an island in the west of Scotland and watch my daughter sing in Gaelic wasn't exactly in my plans.

A cold wind was rising, and I dug my hands into my pockets. Inside, there were a few grains of sand – and a shell.

The shell Sorren had given me.

I wanted to keep it close to me – I wanted to let it go. I wanted Sorren to stay away from me, away from us. I was Ava's mum, and that was all, that was my reason for living.

All of a sudden, the shell felt heavy in my hand, too heavy.

I gently, carefully placed it on the sand.

A few drops of rain began to fall on my hands, my arms, my head. I walked away from the shell, from the sea, and towards the fire of the inn. I'd sit with my daughter and Shuna, have a hot cup of tea and snuggle up safe in the warm. All that mattered now was making sure that Ava could navigate through this moment of upset and find peace again, and then we could go back to our lives;

I could go back to my work. I was determined not to do what my mum had done, to go from man to man and never be settled, never be satisfied, always needing someone to cling to. No. It was me and Ava now, and I would not let myself be drawn to someone only to be left alone and disappointed again.

Sorren

'Wake up, Sorren!' Catriona said gently as I stared at a fish I'd been filleting for the last half an hour. I realised suddenly that she'd been looking at me all morning, that whenever I glanced up, her eyes were on me. She seemed worried about me. She always seemed to worry about me or think about me; I was lucky to have such a good friend. But I was fine, really. Just a bit distracted.

A lot distracted. I didn't seem to be able to concentrate on anything.

Up at Kilpatrick House, I'd tried to invite Anna somewhere, but the words hadn't come out. I'd made a fool of myself, I suppose, all flustered like a teenager with his first crush. God, the embarrassment.

A part of me wanted to check my emails right then, hoping that Alessia had written to keep me safely where I knew I belonged – the nowhere land where she had a life, a life with Pietro, and I had no life at all; and we danced a strange dance of broken hope and regret and refusal to let go.

What was it with her, that I couldn't stop thinking about her?

What was it about Anna that was doing this to me?

Her neck was so white, so slender, like the stem of a flower, her hair blowing around it as she danced.

Her smile was slow and secret, as though only a few people were allowed to see it.

Her dark eyes were just a bit slanted, slightly almond-shaped; and on her milk-white skin there was a hint of freckles, just like on Ava's nose.

And Ava – the way she *shone*. The way she was always jumping and moving and chatting and smiling, like there was too much life inside her to be contained.

I knew a girl just like her, who shone into my life, into all our lives . . .

What was there in Ava that reminded me of Isla this way?

Something made me want to protect her, to make sure she was safe.

And then, on the way home, I was walking down the main street, past the rainbow houses, when something rolled in front of my feet, something bright yellow. It was a bucket and spade set, tied together with a loose net, fallen from one of the stands on the street. I picked it up and Fiona, the owner of the shop, appeared at the door.

'Ah, Sorren, I am so sorry! It just fell of its own accord,' she laughed as she took the toy from me.

'Not at all. Actually, let me buy this. I know someone who might have a use for it,' I said.

With the bucket and spade under my arm, I made my way towards the Seal Inn.

Anna

I saw him coming from my window, and it was strange – my heart soared as I realised he was coming this way, and then sank as I thought that he was probably coming to see his parents . . . and then it occurred to me that whatever the reason he was here, I was not supposed to feel all in a flurry. Watching him from the window like Rapunzel, honestly. Worse than a teenage girl.

I sighed.

'Ava! Anna! Sorren is here for you,' I heard Shuna calling from downstairs. We ran down and he was there with his warm smile, his trademark check shirt and those blue eyes so clear and open. He was holding a bright yellow bucket and spade in his hands.

'Get some treasures for me, will you?' he said, handing them to Ava.

She beamed. 'Thank you, let's go to the beach!'

'Good idea,' Sorren said. 'Actually, I was thinking . . . If you want, I'll take you out on my boat and show you around a bit.'

'I . . . Well . . .' I looked at Ava, but she was busy opening her bucket and spade, with Shuna's help. 'It's a bit late now.'

He laughed. 'Not now! I meant tomorrow, maybe.

Listen, I'm about to start service at the restaurant . . .
Why don't you and Ava come up for a bite?'

All of a sudden, I was afraid.

I wanted to say yes, but I was afraid.

'Maybe we should have a quiet evening. Ava didn't
sleep much last night, and . . .'

'Of course. I understand,' he said, but he seemed crest-
fallen. 'Let me know if you want to go out on the boat . . .'

'Yes please! Mum, please?'

'Of course. I'll let you know.'

Back in our room, both of us ready for bed, I blinked
once, twice as I saw it on my bedside table.

I was so sure I had left it on the beach, but there it was,
a few grains of sand scattered around it, lying there as if
the tide had left it behind.

The cowrie shell that Sorren had given me.

11

Surviving

Sorren

The life jackets were in place, properly folded and ready to be used, tucked away in the depths of the *Oystercatcher*. I ticked another item off our list, meticulously kept with the monthly logs. Every week, Fraser and I went to the lifeboat base to do the routine maintenance checks. The rescue crew took turns so that it got done every day. Everything had to be kept in perfect order, because emergency calls could come at any moment, and we had to be ready. My work with the lifeboat rescue was all-important to me. After we lost Isla, I was desperate to make sure no other family would have to go through what we'd gone through. And that was one of the bones of contention with Alessia: that I did my own shifts, and I covered the absentees' shifts, and then I did some more, and then I just went and sat there, in case they needed an extra pair of hands . . . The Sea Rescue was a call I couldn't ignore, though I knew very well I was overdoing it.

'So, Anna. I heard you saw her up at Kilpatrick House,' Fraser said casually, like it was just another topic of conversation. He was checking the ropes, crouching beside the *Oystercatcher* in her dock. Seagulls screamed above us in a cloudy sky, and the sea gently lapped the shore, but there was a hint of disquiet in the water. Soon the wind would rise and the weather would change; I knew it with the surety of an island man.

'Oh, you heard, did you?' I said, raising my eyebrows. Of course. Everyone knew everything about everyone else on Seal. He'd probably heard it from Caty or Tatiana.

'I did, yes. This is done,' he said, patting the ropes all coiled up like snakes.

'And?'

'And what?' He laughed, showing off the kind of smile that demonstrated why he'd become so popular in his brief stint on television. He had that rugged handsomeness that many women sought, though he was very much unaware of it. Whenever he worked for me at the restaurant, there were always a few pairs of eyes that followed him across the room, and a few attempts at starting a conversation. Attempts that Fraser, being Fraser, always seemed to thwart.

'I'll do the gear, then,' I said grumpily. We had to check that the crew's life jackets and helmets were all where they should be, so they could be found and worn without delay. Fraser walked behind me.

'You haven't asked her out,' he said in a perfectly reasonable voice, as if *of course* that would be expected of me.

I rolled my eyes as I began checking the helmets. 'Why

don't we talk about what's happening with you instead? The golden bachelor of Seal?'

'The golden bachelor of Seal? Nah, that's you, not me . . .'

'It's not me getting fan mail, Fraser!' I laughed. He had mentioned the fan mail thing once, and I would never let him live it down. 'Come on, there must be someone.'

'I have nothing to say about that.'

Wait a minute. Did he look a bit flustered? Just for a moment? I stopped what I was doing. 'Fraser? I don't think you're giving me the whole picture here . . .'

'There is *nobody*,' he said, and put his hands up. 'I'm too busy. By the way, can you come up to the house and give me a hand with something for the foraging course?'

'You're just changing the subject.'

'Yes, I am. Honestly, I have nothing to say.'

'Neither have I, so stop asking about Anna.'

'Mmmm.'

'If you really want to know, I did ask her to the restaurant. She said no. She said Ava was tired.'

'Ask again. If it's another no, then you'll know for sure. Otherwise, it might be that Ava really was tired.'

'You should have a column in a magazine,' I laughed.

'Shame I can't follow my own wise advice,' he said, and once again I looked at him.

'Fraser, what's going on?'

'Nothing's going on.' He shrugged.

I gave up. I knew him. If he didn't want to talk, he

wouldn't talk. 'Right. Let's get this wrapped up and go. I'll see what I can do with your foraging thing.'

We walked to his house, a cottage just beyond the sand dunes. It was a mirror of his life, in a way: remote and encased deep in nature. When he first arrived on Seal, the cottage had consisted of three crumbling stone walls; with my help, he'd rebuilt it himself. Back then, we barely knew each other, but our friendship had grown easily, naturally. I found him restful, with his long silences and the way he saw so much and said so little. At the same time, he challenged me, he pushed me out of my comfort zone – he was like a truthful mirror to me.

'So, what do you need me for?' I asked as we stepped into his kitchen. He'd built the kitchen himself too, with reclaimed wood, most of it driftwood, and the result was unique and stunning – I'm not a decor buff in any way, but I know my kitchens – with copper pots and drying herbs hanging from the rafters, and an ancient stove he had salvaged and polished. In the middle there was a huge wooden table, now covered in items of food and herbs. I could recognise blueberries and rosehips and nettles . . . and what was that? A basket of empty shells . . . mussels, razor clams, scallops . . .

'That's just to show them what they look like,' he said as he saw me looking. 'I'm taking them on to the beach to collect real ones. And then we'll cook some stuff on the beach, and some up here.'

'The people from your course?'

'Yes. I have a couple from Japan, too.'

'Cool. So what do you need me for?'

'I need a nice tried and tested recipe for dulse soup. I made it yesterday and I wouldn't inflict it on my worst enemy.'

'Yeah, it's a funny thing, dulse soup. Even if you get it right, it's not the most appetising dish on the planet. Do you have any dulse handy? I'll show you and you can take notes.'

'Cheers, mate,' he said, and grabbed a plastic bowl full of seaweed from the fridge.

'Potatoes?'

'Straight from my garden.' He took a canvas bag from one of the cupboards.

'Cool. No need to peel them, just chop them.'

We set to work. 'Look, about Anna . . .' Fraser began, and there was an uncharacteristically serious expression on his face. 'I don't want to keep going on about it; I know when a joke gets old. It's just that I *see you*, mate. And it's time you moved on from the past.'

I took a copper pot from the rack, threw the potatoes and the dulse in and covered them with water. I was glad to be busy, so that Fraser and I wouldn't have to look at each other while we were talking about such emotional things. All of a sudden, I felt the need to open up a little. After all, Fraser always seemed to have a wise word. He seemed to see things, to observe people and understand the subtext of situations like I could never do.

'The way you look at Anna . . . Well, there have been girls, but you never looked at any of them like that.'

'Look, Fraser . . . After Alessia . . . honestly, I can't go through that again,' I said, wiping the table.

'You don't want someone who might leave here. I understand. Coffee?'

I nodded. 'It wasn't just that. She wanted me to choose between her and my parents . . .'

'She didn't. She wanted you to start living again, that's all.'

'How come you know so much about what she wanted?'

'We spoke. Many times. She didn't know where else to turn. And we were worried about you.'

'There was no reason to worry. Anyway, she went, she's not here, problem solved.'

'Yeah,' he said unconvincingly, and placed a cup of coffee in front of me. I took a sip, and immediately grimaced.

'Good God, I'll be awake for three weeks after this!'

'None of that Italian fancy stuff you make. This is survival coffee.'

'As in, you drink this, you might survive it or you might not . . .'

Fraser grinned. 'Anyway, your mum spoke to me about you quite a few times too.'

'She did?'

He perched himself back on his stool and shrugged. 'Your mum and I talk quite a lot, you know. She got me through a couple of rough times.'

'Right.' I was surprised, to say the least. But then that was Fraser; there was always something you didn't quite know or you couldn't quite guess.

'You want to know what she said? About you, I mean.'

'Go ahead.'

'That you'd rather be alone than take a risk.'

I was speechless for a second. I'd thought I was keeping all my secrets to myself, my innermost feelings and fears and resolutions. Instead, they had been out there for everyone to see. My parents. Fraser. Caty, obviously. They'd known all along. They'd been reading my heart. All of a sudden I felt like a fool.

I took a breath.

'Shuna wanted you to go to Italy with Alessia,' Fraser continued.

'Yes. I think I'd guessed that.'

There was a moment of silence. I was done with that conversation. I felt too vulnerable, too open.

'On the other hand, when it comes to taking risks . . . look who's talking. I don't see *you* taking many.'

Fraser didn't reply. He stayed silent, sipping his coffee like I had said nothing. If he didn't want to speak, if he didn't want to talk about his least favourite subject of conversation – himself – he would just stay quiet and pretend you didn't exist.

But that wouldn't work today. I refused to be the only one under the spotlight. 'As far as I can see,' I said, 'there hasn't been anyone for years. Unless you have a secret life I know nothing about.'

'No. There is nobody.'

'Well, being alone is as bad for you as it is for me.'

Fraser looked at me. His eyes said absolutely nothing. But he began to tap-tap-tap on the table.

I waited.

He shook his head and tapped some more.

'I . . . How long will this take? The dulse soup?' he finally said.

My eyes widened and I sat back.

'It's Tatiana!'

'What?'

'Tatiana! Of course!'

'Sorren . . .'

'It has to be. You two get on so well, and now she's broken up with Yuri . . .'

'Sorren, you are delusional. It's not Tatiana.'

'A-ha! So there is someone!'

Fraser rubbed his forehead with his hand. 'You are unbelievable. Leave me alone and ask Anna out again, okay?'

'I don't know. I'll see.' An image of Anna's sweetheart face, her high forehead, her soft brown hair danced in front of my eyes. 'Anyway, I *will* find out who it is you're interested in.'

'You'll never find out,' Fraser said simply, and there was something in his voice that made me realise the conversation was over.

'This will take another twenty minutes or so,' I said, stirring the pot. The kitchen smelled like the Black Lagoon. Any second now, some fish-like creature would rise from the pot, complete with gills and stringy seaweed hanging off its arms. 'Have a taste,' I added, handing him the wooden spoon.

'Mmmm. Tastes of . . . er . . . the sea.'

'Well, that's one way of putting it,' I laughed.

'It's the food of our ancestors,' Fraser said very seriously.

'No wonder the average life span was thirty-five years. See you later, Fraser,' I said, making my way towards the door. On the door frame hung amulets from his travels – a tablet in Arabic, a silk talisman with Chinese writing, a blue Turkish charm made of glass.

'Oh, and Sorren?'

'Mmm?'

'Ask her again.'

12

The bridge on the Atlantic

Anna

Days went by, and there were no more entries in the yellow notebook. All we knew was sea and sky and our inner worlds unknotting; our faces turning a light golden colour and freckles sprouting on both our noses. And Ava's hair always smelling of salt and seaweed, even just after a shower. A scent of sea that pervaded her and our room.

'You're smiling again,' she said to me one morning, as we were cuddling in bed, her soft little limbs tangled with mine.

'Am I?'

She took my face in her hands the way she often did, half playful, half solemn, and smoothed down my hair. 'Yes. You're smiling a lot, Mummy.'

She was right. The Hebridean wind was slowly blowing away the worst of my fears and cares and troubles; life seemed so much easier, and so much more beautiful, in a place surrounded by ocean and with not even a thousand people in it. The sun rose and fell on an Anna I never had the chance to be in London; an Anna who was not constantly afraid, constantly striving. And along with my slow change came Ava's change – her memories seemed to take a back seat for a while, overcome by the joys of the present day.

Whatever I had expected to find on Seal, it certainly wasn't as good as what we'd actually found.

Sometimes it felt like I, too, had known this place before. That it wasn't only Ava, with the memories of her other life, who had come home.

'Mummy, look!' Ava lifted up her new apron for me to see, under Shuna's smiling eyes. It was red, and had her name embroidered in white on the pocket, beneath the words 'The Seal Inn'. A mini version of the aprons Shuna, Hamish and the staff wore.

'Oh, it's gorgeous! Shuna, you shouldn't have!' I said. I was so touched.

'It was a pleasure! I know ours are blue, but I thought red would suit her better,' Shuna said. She was right. Red was Ava's favourite colour.

'Can you tie it for me, Mum?' I moved her hair aside and tied the strings around her tiny waist. She looked so happy.

Shuna had truly taken Ava and me under her wing. She had recruited Ava to be her helper in the kitchen and around the bed and breakfast, and Ava, who loved being given little jobs and responsibilities, was in her element. She followed Shuna around holding fresh sheets for the beds; she cracked eggs for the breakfasts; she dried dishes, acting all solemn and responsible. And now that she had her own apron, she looked 'just the ticket', as Shuna said.

'What can I do, Shuna? What can I do?' She jumped up and down, and Shuna and I laughed. It was wonderful to see Ava so happy – there was nothing I wanted more.

Shuna handed her a cloth. 'Well, you could wipe the table for me, if you like.' And then, in a laughing aside to me: 'See, this is what I do. I get my guests to do my job for me.'

'I can't thank you enough, Shuna. You're really making her time here so special,' I said, and something tugged at my heart. How I would have loved to tell her the whole truth, all that had been happening. To show her the notebook. To have someone to share this burden with.

But of course, I couldn't. It was all too strange to be put into words.

'I wish we could stay longer than three weeks,' I said, imprudently, and immediately regretted it. Ava was alarmed.

'I don't want to go, Mummy!'

'No, of course not, not yet, darling . . .'

When I'd decided to come to Seal the plan was to stay three weeks, but Ava was so happy there I was desperate to stay longer. Given how meagre our savings were, I wondered how long our money would last.

'Sorry to ask, but do you need to go back to work, Anna?' Shuna said.

I nodded, and took a deep breath. 'Well, it's not so

much that . . . I work for an agency, so I can take off as much time as I like. The problem is our savings . . .'

'Oh, Anna, look. It's just great to have Ava here, to have you both here. Please don't think you have to go because . . . We can agree something, and . . .' She was too delicate to come out and say it directly, but I knew what she was trying to offer. I couldn't accept, of course.

'No, Shuna, we'll pay our way. No question of that.'

'I don't want to go, Mummy! I don't want to go!' All of a sudden Ava seemed nearly panicked.

My head began to pound and my ears started buzzing, full of an indistinct, muffled white noise. Shuna said something else, but I couldn't hear her words.

'Are you okay, Anna?'

'Yes . . . yes, I'm fine. Just a bit . . . I don't know. A bit dizzy.' Floor and ceiling were dancing, and they threatened to swap places. Shuna's voice came from far away, and a tune filled my ears, though the Grants weren't playing.

'Come. Come and sit down.'

'No, I'm fine, I'm fine,' I smiled. The tune was fading into the distance, and the everyday noises of the pub were coming back. 'It was just a moment. Sorry.' I reached out to Ava and stroked her little face. 'Don't worry, sweetheart. We'll sort something out,' I said.

But I had no idea how.

All day I fought a lethargy that I couldn't quite shake off. I was in the middle of a bedtime chat with Ava when my

eyes threatened to close. I barely made it to my own bed
before I fell into a dense, heavy sleep, taking me quickly
and completely. My last thought, sketched and confused,
was: why is Shuna enjoying Ava's presence so much she
has even offered to put us up for free? Why have they
taken to each other so quickly? And then I couldn't think
any more.

I must have slept for a few hours, because when I
opened my eyes, the eerie grey light of dawn was coming
through the window. I thought my eyes were closed –
they *felt* closed – but I could see. I wasn't sure whether I
was awake or asleep, and my limbs and my head felt too
heavy to move. And then I thought I saw someone come
in – a little girl with black hair. Ava? Was she awake
already? She sat down beside me, and I felt the bed yield
softly under her weight. She rested a small, cold hand on
my cheek and leaned down to whisper in my ear.

'Foxgloves,' she said in a sweet, childish voice.

It wasn't Ava's voice.

'Who are you? What . . .' I murmured, but I didn't
know if it was in my dream, or if I really was saying those
words.

'Go where the foxgloves are.' And then a soft, faraway
tune resounded in my ears. The voice of a woman humming a melody, a melody I'd heard before. The music
was so sweet, I didn't want to wake up . . .

I came to with a jerk, all my muscles tense. My head
felt heavy, and so did my limbs, like I had a high fever. I
laid my hand on my forehead – it was cool. I wasn't ill.

The ceiling seemed to move above me for a moment, and little multicoloured particles danced before my eyes. Slowly my body returned to normal. I rolled over and, with a long, long shiver, shook off the last of the dream, then sat up shakily, blinking in the muted light. I opened the curtains to see choppy sea and foamy waves, and for a moment, I was transfixed by them.

And then I remembered the words I'd heard: *Go where the foxgloves are.*

The girl. The girl who wasn't Ava. And the sweet, low tune . . .

Ava was fast asleep, lying on her back, unguarded and trusting like only children can be. I sat back on the bed, in a daze. *Go where the foxgloves are.* I *knew.* I knew where the dream wanted to take me.

I pulled on a pair of leggings and a sweatshirt, and walked downstairs slowly, putting one foot carefully in front of the other, suspended between sleep and waking. I stepped out in the grey light, the sky fused with the sea, soft mist rising from both land and water. The strange hour between night and day, the hour that was both and neither.

I walked in silence, the ever-present wind cold on my face, freezing my hands.

The red silhouette of Kilpatrick House appeared in the distance, with its crown of pine trees on the barren, heathery hill. A soft mist was rising from the ground and the air seemed almost silvery. The foxglove-covered bridge was shining in the dim light. Everything felt like a dream; and it had been a dream that had commanded me to go there. It was absurd, and strange, and inexplicable – but then pretty much everything had been absurd, and strange, and inexplicable since this island had come into our lives.

The place was deserted, of course, and in the eerie light of dawn it felt like walking on earth before life had started. The sea reflected the sky in primeval colours, and the silence was complete.

I walked slowly towards the bridge, each step punctuated by the noise of the waves breaking against its stony structure. Suddenly I realised that there was a black silhouette against the flowers, and that I'd been looking at it all along without seeing it. But now a hint of pink was opening in the sky, making the foxgloves shine, and the silhouette was suddenly in relief against them, stark and immobile. I stopped for a moment to make out the details, and saw an elderly lady dressed in a long nightgown and, incongruously, long dangling earrings. Her silver hair was down past her shoulders. She stood on the bridge, her face white in the unearthly light, her gnarled hands resting on the flower-covered stone. Immediately I had the feeling that I had seen her somewhere before.

'Hello?' I said gently. I was expecting to see the confused, frightened face of a dementia sufferer who had wandered off and didn't know where she was, but there was none of that. This woman looked sharp and alert.

'You found me,' she said, smiling. The high cheekbones,

the slightly sloping eyes, a very light blue – she had a truly Scottish face, features I'd seen over and over again on the island. Suddenly I realised where I'd seen her: it was the silver-headed woman I'd spotted at the window the first time I'd visited Kilpatrick House.

'I did. Your hands feel cold. Come with me and we'll get you a nice cup of tea,' I said in my most soothing tone. I took her arm and gently began to steer her towards the house.

'You have a funny accent. Where are you from?'

I laughed. 'London. I have a funny London accent, I suppose.'

'What are you doing here at this time of morning?' She spoke as if we were making small talk. The wind was dancing in her hair and mine.

'I could ask you the same thing!' I laughed again. 'Come on . . .'

As we walked slowly in the direction of the house, I wrapped an arm around the old lady's waist, trying to keep her warm. I was making for the heavy main door, but she led me towards the back. A small wooden door was ajar, and we slipped in.

'Hello?' I called. 'Linda?' My voice resounded in the dark, silent house, and the hair went up on the back of my neck. A clock on the wall said it was a quarter to five. 'Linda?' I called again, not daring to go any further – it already felt like I was trespassing.

'Who's there?' A voice came from somewhere in the depths of the enormous house, and Linda appeared down a set of stone steps, blinking, a hand keeping her tangled hair back from her forehead.

'What are you doing here?' she said, and blinked again. She probably thought she was dreaming. I was about to say something when she looked over my shoulder. *'Mother!'*

'Morning, darling,' the silver-haired lady said with a smile.

'What's going *on*?' Linda rushed towards her and took her hands. 'My goodness, you are frozen!'

The old lady shrugged, her dangling earrings quivering. 'I forgot my cardigan. This lady with a funny accent promised me tea.'

'You wandered out again! Mother, I told you . . .' Linda began in a voice that was somewhere between weary and alarmed. 'I was asleep, I didn't even hear you . . . Do you have any idea of what could have happened?'

'Well, I did what I had to do.'

'What . . . Oh, never mind.' Linda turned to me. 'I can't thank you enough,' she said.

'It's no problem. I just saw her on the bridge . . .'

Suddenly the elderly lady looked straight at me with her light blue eyes. 'You are Anna,' she declared.

'I am, yes.'

'I'm Lady Kilpatrick.' Yes, of course. Linda's mother was the lady of the house. When Ava and I had visited, we'd seen framed pictures of her in her twenties, dressed in a polo neck and tweed knickerbockers against the backdrop of a stony mountain; another of her in a white silk dress and pearls, her hair curled in two wings in the fashion of the forties. She'd been beautiful then, and in a way she still was; even in her white nightgown and with her grey hair down, there was something regal about her. No, not regal – vaguely sacred. Like a prophetess of some kind.

'Now, let's put you back to bed, Mother . . .'

'No, no, I'd like to go to the beach.'

'Oh for God's sake, it's five in the morning!'

'Then I'll sit and look out of the window.'

'That's a good idea. Come along . . .' Linda said, softly this time. There were deep shadows under her eyes and my heart went out to her.

Unsure of what to do, I followed them through to a small sitting room. It was a pretty ordinary room for such a grand house, but when I saw the view, I understood why Lady Kilpatrick wanted to look out of the window. From such a privileged position she could see half of the island – brightly coloured Roan at the foot of the hill, and the rounded shape of the land as it rose from the sea, ending with dramatic cliffs at the north-west end. I made a mental note to take Ava there – it looked like an aerial shot from *The Lord of the Rings*.

'There you are,' Linda said. She took a cardigan from the back of an armchair and wrapped it around her mother's frail frame. Then she sighed, and I could sense the weight on her shoulders. 'Anna, can I make you some tea? It's the least I can do . . .' She opened her hands.

I was cold, and pretty confused myself. After all, a dream had told me to come here in the small hours of the morning. I could certainly do with some tea.

I began to follow Linda into the kitchen, but in the doorway I turned around to say goodbye to Lady Kilpatrick, and our gazes met. She looked very small and fragile, but her big blue eyes were still lively and alert, and her face was serious – again the prophetess.

'She told me to go and see the foxgloves, Anna,' she said simply, and a long, cold shiver travelled down my spine.

'Yes, Mother. It's fine. Now stay there and get warm. I'll be back in a minute,' Linda called from ahead of me. She sounded exhausted.

In the kitchen, I wrapped my hands around the warm mug that Linda handed me. It was heavenly.

'Thank you so, so much, Anna,' she said again. 'Oh, I just can't do this alone any more. I have this enormous house to manage, and ... it's just too much. She's gone down so fast. I need to start looking for someone to help. A carer, or a nurse. Only getting a nurse to come to the island is harder than you might imagine.'

It was my time to blink, over and over again.

Could it be ... ?

'By the way, what were you doing out so early, Anna?'

Good question. 'I couldn't sleep,' I lied smoothly. There was no way I could have explained about the dream, about how I too had been told to go to the foxgloves. 'If it's okay with you, I think I'll head home. I'd like to check on my daughter. Please give Lady Kilpatrick my regards.'

'Oh, of course. And thank you again. It doesn't bear thinking about . . . If she'd fallen off the bridge, or gone to the beach on her own . . .'

'But she didn't.' I got up and took her hands, mirroring what she'd done to her mother.

'No. Not this time anyway . . .'

I squeezed her hands, and the words nearly came out: *I can help.* But everything had happened so fast, I just couldn't process it all. I said nothing.

I walked back to the inn deep in thought, a soft drizzle on my head and arms, the chill, salty Seal wind blowing from the sea. Who had told Lady Kilpatrick to go to the bridge? Did she have the same dream as me? I closed my eyes to the moist wind and hurried home. I couldn't wait to see Ava.

13

The black sky before dawn

Sorren

I sat beside my telescope in the dark garden. The sea ebbed and flowed in the distance. It was such a clear night that four planets were visible. Venus was low in the sky; Jupiter shone bright with its moons around it, like a shepherd and its sheep; Mars was blinking red, Saturn blue and cold and distant. And the moon, the crescent moon hanging low and white, perfect from afar and scarred by meteorites when seen through the telescope – if only I could hold her in my hands, and protect her from anything that crossed her path, save her from all harm. My eyes swept lovingly over stars and constellations, their harmony and perfection taking my breath away as if it was the first time I saw them. The sky was covered in stars, stars like dust.

Maybe each and every star was a soul.

The soul of someone long gone, or someone who had just left; a new light in the sky.

I looked over through the French windows, into the dimly lit house. It was so rare for me to be at home and awake; usually when I had finished at the restaurant I went straight to bed. The place looked surreal, somewhere nobody really lived. I felt like a stranger looking into somebody else's life, like when you're walking down the street in the evening and wherever curtains haven't been drawn, you can see inside. Each house like a small theatre, its inhabitants acting out their lives.

In the small theatre of my life, beyond the French windows, there was a table with a bottle of Talisker on the left and a laptop on the right.

My laptop meant email – I refused to have it on my phone; it would have been too distracting.

Email meant Alessia, my weekly stab in the side, my only moment of joy. My endless regret and my reason to be.

A mixture of desire and unease filled me – oh, I wanted her; oh, I wanted her out of my life.

Maybe, in that closed laptop, black and silent, waiting to come to life again, a letter from Alessia was waiting for me; maybe it was the letter that would change everything.

And what if it did?

You can't hold an email in your arms, you can't kiss words; words won't lie beside you and be there when you wake up. The Alessia I knew wasn't there any more. She was now an email address, and words that reached me in my solitude, while she lived as a married woman, haunted by the memory of me.

In our letters, we talked about *us*. But there was no *us*.

Did I still love her? Did she love me? How could we

know, when in the last three years of separation we'd become two different people, two people who didn't really know each other any more.

How long would it be until she wrote that something was happening, something important – the next step in her married life? How would I feel then, when she became a mother and was tied into her life even more, and we exchanged letters that were pale reflections, memories, ghosts of memories – while our lives went on without each other?

Since she'd left, I'd been here on my own, waiting and hoping and making sure my parents were all right, making sure that all I'd taken on got done. I'd been glad to forget about myself. Time passed. And I sat here in an empty house that not even a cat wanted to live in.

I gazed up at the stars once more – their infinite numbers, the light that travelled from millions and millions of miles away, millions of years ago – and I made a decision.

I went inside and picked up the laptop. I carried it back into the garden – I needed the cold, cold night and my island all around me before I could make the jump.

I had to do it.

The words came easily, as if I'd been thinking them for a long time, as if they'd just been waiting for the right time to come into the light.

Dear Alessia,

For three years now you've been writing to me. You've built yourself a new life, and still you write to me. It's like you live in a dream world where you and I are together, a parallel reality where things didn't go the way they went. I like living in this place where we never broke up and we know every detail of each other's life and we still keep this bond between us like a lifeline. Whatever happens, you and I can reach out to each other.

And that is beautiful.

Except I am not getting on with my life. I am not living my life.

And you're married, but you're still writing to me – so maybe you're not truly living your life either.

I look into my heart and I wonder how we can still love each other if you belong to another man, if I live in hope of something that will never happen.

If neither of us makes a step, a real step, towards the other.

It's like a suspended reality where our feelings were sort of preserved in formalin and have become a shadow of what they used to be.

I need to set you free and I need to set myself free. I want us to move on and live our lives. I need something real, something I can touch, someone who's at my side.

I'll always be there for you, I'll always care about you.

But I have to say goodbye. For me, for you, for your husband, for the woman I hope I'll find one day.

Arrivederci amore mio,

Sorren

I pressed Send before I could change my mind, and away my words flew, into cyberspace, all the way to Italy, where Alessia would read them. She'd sit at her computer and tuck her long dark hair behind her ears the way she always did – and maybe she would cry like I was crying.

If it was a good thing that now we'd finally live in our own worlds instead of a dream world, why did it hurt so much?

Even the most precious things must be left behind sometimes; the tide comes and pulls them away, and if you hold on to them, you'll drown.

Amore mio, I let you go.

Anna

'Linda? It's Anna. Sorry to bother you . . . It's about what happened this morning.'

I'd thought about it all day, torn between wanting to put myself forward and worried about sounding crazy. But then Linda had said she needed someone to help. I took heart, and asked Shuna for Linda's number.

'Yes. I can never thank you enough . . . She's okay now.'

'Please don't thank me. It was just a fortunate . . . coincidence. I just wanted to let you know that I'm actually a nurse—'

'You *are*?'

'Yes, so I was think—'

'Oh Anna! I phoned an agency this morning and they say they can't find anyone to come to the island at such short notice, that it's really difficult to get people to come to Seal. I asked my cleaning lady, you know, Moira

Duggan, the hairdresser's sister?' Weirdly enough, I did know her. She had been up to the Seal Inn to take part in Shuna's women's association meetings. I was beginning to be familiar with the fabric of the island, its family ties, its friendships, its rivalries. 'Just to maybe stay a little longer while I work, but she said she couldn't. And now you turn up! A nurse! What a coincidence . . .' She echoed my words.

Yes. Serendipity, you might say.

I felt dazed again, as though I was watching what was happening instead of living it – like I was still lying on my bed just before dawn, having that strange dream-vision. It had all been so fast.

Linda was still talking. 'I run this place, look after my mother and try not to drop any plates . . . It would be amazing if you could give me a hand.'

'Does she have dementia?' I asked. I could feel my professional gears beginning to turn, and it was such a good feeling.

'Not as such. Nothing was diagnosed really. She just seems to live in a world of her own. Sometimes she's perfectly lucid, sometimes . . .' Linda paused. 'Would you be available two or three days a week? I could be flexible, of course. I'm pretty desperate at this stage.'

'I . . . I think so. I need to get organised, sort things out for my daughter.'

'Yes, of course.' Linda sounded deflated.

'But leave it with me,' I said. 'I'll call you later.'

*

'I think I might have found a job,' I said to Shuna, stepping back into the kitchen. Ava, wearing her little apron, was standing on a chair, solemnly wiping some shelves.

'You . . . you found a job? When?'

I shrugged. It was still sinking in. 'Sort of . . . This morning. Linda Kilpatrick lost her mum. I found her.'

'She *lost* her mum?'

'Well, she's asked me to look after Lady Kilpatrick a couple of times a week.'

'But that's wonderful! What a coincidence!' That word again. 'Only yesterday you were saying you needed to work . . . Oh, this calls for a celebration. We'll bake a cake, won't we, Ava?'

'So we don't have to leave?' Ava's face was still tense, her gaze going from me to Shuna and back.

'Not for now, no,' I said. My lips were beginning to stretch into a smile, as what had just happened sank in. 'Shuna . . .' I began.

She read my mind. 'Don't worry about that. I'll look after Ava for you when you have to work. It's not a problem.'

Finally my smile was free to bloom. Never mind the mysteries, the dreams, the secrets. Shuna was right: that moment called for a celebration.

14

You are my love

Anna

'Just as well I have help today!' Shuna said in an exaggerated tone. Her eyes met mine over Ava's excited face. 'It's going to be busy; Hamish and I couldn't possibly cope on our own!'

'You have me!' Ava said delightedly. She was wearing her apron over a fresh summer dress, and she'd insisted on having her hair in a ponytail, just like Jane.

Shuna stroked her dark head. 'Thanks to your mum, who's generously lending you to me. Good luck for your first day of work, sweetheart!'

'Thanks,' I replied, and 'Thanks!' Ava piped up. Shuna and I laughed. Sure, it was Ava's first day of work too. She was well aware of her responsibility as Shuna's helper at the Seal Inn, a role that she would cover whenever I looked after Lady Kilpatrick.

I left Ava folding napkins with great care and set off for Kilpatrick House. I was ridiculously early, but nerves wouldn't allow me to sit still any longer. As I walked down towards the main street and across the village, I heard a voice calling me.

'Anna! Anna!'

It was Catriona. I waved back and she ran towards me, her long strawberry-blonde hair down her back. Hers was a beauty that could not go unnoticed, with that hair somewhere between gold and red and those eyes so light they were nearly transparent. I was happy to see her – she'd been so friendly to me at the ceilidh, and Anna had been to her niece Angela's house once already.

Yet still there was a tiny, near-imperceptible part of me that tensed up when she was around.

She and Sorren seemed so *close*.

But why should that concern me? I was being silly. So what if there was something between them, or there had been in the past? It wasn't like anything could happen between Sorren and me. Between anyone and me, for that matter. It was too soon, I had too much on my plate; it just wasn't possible.

Why, oh why, did my mind keep going back to Sorren? I felt positively angry at myself. It seemed that this new person I had morphed into was pretty much unable to rein her thoughts in.

'Hi, Catriona . . .'

'Hi! Are you going somewhere?' she smiled. She looked more like an artist than a primary school teacher, I thought, with a purple top and green skirt, and beads around her neck and wrists. 'Because if you fancy, we could go for coffee and cake?'

'I was just on my way to Kilpatrick House for my first day of work . . .' I began.

'Oh yes! My sister told me you got a job there. Lady Kilpatrick's lovely, you know?'

'Yes, I had that impression.'

'Also, the house is gorgeous. Full of freezing peacocks.'

I laughed. 'They did seem pretty windswept!'

'Yes, those poor peacocks are out in all weathers – except the coldest winter days, of course – but they've adapted. They're Hebridean peacocks! Anyway, do you have time for that coffee before you start? I'm on my way to the restaurant, but I'm early.'

Oh. She was going to see Sorren. But then she saw him every day – they worked together.

I could see him too, if I wanted. But I'd refused his invitation . . .

Now, Anna, stop. My recriminations were nonsense. It was too late anyway; he wouldn't ask again.

I smiled and took Catriona's arm, and five minutes later we were sitting in the Design Gallery, the local café and souvenir shop, coffee and carrot cake in front of us.

'You know, I think I saw you the day I arrived. On the beach,' I said.

'That's not possible, Anna. I haven't been on the beach for a few days now.'

'Oh . . . but I'm pretty sure it was you, or someone who really, really looked like you, with a blue jumper and that incredible hair . . .' I gestured.

She smiled. 'It must have been someone else. Or you had a vision of me, maybe.'

I laughed. 'Me, visions? Unlikely!'

And then I thought of my dream, the foxgloves dream, and I was silent for a moment. Catriona said something about it being quite busy at Sorren's restaurant, and it brought me back to the present.

'Do you work there every summer?' I asked. My mind kept going back to how much time she and Sorren spent together, and I silently berated myself for it.

'No, I've only worked for him occasionally before, the odd weekend . . . when the book festival is on, during the Easter holidays, you know, when it gets busier. Usually in the summer I teach English to foreign students in Glasgow or Edinburgh. But this year Sorren was short-staffed . . . Also I fancied a summer at home.' She stirred her steaming cup. 'So, you're enjoying Seal, are you?'

'Oh yes. Ava doesn't want to go home!' I laughed, though there was an edge to my laughter. I had no idea how I would drag Ava back to London, and that wasn't a joke.

'I could never live anywhere else. It's beautiful all year round, but my favourite season is the autumn. The light is golden, and the sky! It changes every moment . . .'

'It's a shame we won't be here then,' I said, and something squeezed my heart.

'Have you been on one of the mini cruises? That's worth doing as well.'

'Oh yes, we've done that. Sorren offered to take us on his boat as well.'

All of a sudden, Catriona's expression changed. Her

face fell, but then, just as quickly, she composed herself, though she kept looking down.

'Sorren is going to take you out on his boat?'

'Well, he offered, but we couldn't . . .' I felt flustered, and I didn't like it. Why was it such a big deal? And why did I feel the need to justify myself to Catriona? I took a sip of my coffee and looked at her again. She was so fair, so unique – a vision of beauty. But there was a deep crease between her eyes. There was an ache in her, I could feel it, vague but persistent. I sighed silently and leaned back on the chair.

'Catriona . . .' I began, without even knowing what I was going to say.

But she interrupted me. 'Sorren and I . . . we've known each other a long time,' she said softly. 'You know, he had a girlfriend for a while. A few years. An Italian girl.'

Oh. 'What happened?'

Catriona shrugged. 'She left. She didn't like the island. And Sorren won't leave here. He . . . he belongs here. And he won't leave his parents. He looks after them, you know. He looks after a lot of people.'

'Shuna and Hamish seem quite able to look after themselves,' I said. 'I mean, of course they wouldn't want him far away, but . . .'

'It's more complicated than that. Maybe Sorren will tell you, if you . . . you know, if you go out on his boat, or somewhere else with him,' she said, and every word was like a hard stone falling between us.

Yes. Now I knew what her ache was.

And then her tone changed. She tried to sound casual. 'Anyway, you know, his Italian girlfriend went, but his friends remained. *I* remained.' Right. 'I've known him since I was born, Anna.' She smiled. It was too big a smile. 'Well, must dash. It was lovely seeing you . . . Bye then,' she said, and rushed off more quickly than was natural.

Catriona and Sorren.

I didn't know if her feelings were reciprocated, but I knew for sure that Catriona was in love with Sorren, and had been for a long time.

It made sense, after all, I thought dejectedly as I sat alone in front of my cold coffee. Catriona and Sorren made sense. They fitted together. She lived here, on his beloved island. She belonged here, like him.

Yes. There was no room for me in his life; there could be no room in it. I'd just upset him, and make things difficult when they could be so simple.

Catriona

I knew him so well. I knew what his eyes said, I knew what he said without words. I saw the way he was looking at Anna, I sensed between them what was unspoken but not any less *there*. Since Alessia had left, there had been women interested in him, but he never seemed to notice, while I held my breath. And then there was me, orbiting around him like a little moon, unable to tell him what was in my heart.

Yes. A planet and its moon.

Sorren had been part of my life forever. I'd known him since I could remember. I could recall exactly when I first saw him not with the eyes of a child, but as a future woman. I was twelve, he was fourteen, and I had tagged along to his house with my older brother. It had snowed all night, and we walked on, calf-deep in snow, scattered snowflakes still falling here and there. My brother always seemed somehow annoyed by my presence – I was the wee sister who got in the way – so different from the way Sorren was with Isla. Isla, sweet Isla, jumping in the snow, fingers red after taking off her mittens, diamonds sparkling on her hat and her hair, making snow angels with her eyes closed. She was at our house so often that Carla and I joked she was like another sister, even if when we were all together we looked so different, Carla and I with our red-blonde hair, Isla so dark, with amber skin that spoke of Spanish ancestors.

Sorren was as kind to me as he was to Isla, always keeping an eye out for me. Today he was helping me up every time I fell, carrying big armfuls of snow to build our snow dinosaur – more interesting than a simple snowman. His mop of black hair was damp, and his cheeks were red, and he had a smile that was so wide and cheerful, it made his eyes look like half-moons.

When Sorren was around, I was at my happiest. He made me feel safe, looked after.

He made me laugh.

He made me feel older than my years.

As my brother threw snowballs against a tree, Sorren and Isla stood beside me. 'Try closing your eyes and putting your face up like this,' he said to wee Isla, looking up to the white sky. 'Snowflakes feel like little kisses. See?'

Even if I was a child, I think I fell in love with him that day.

My life isn't always straightforward.

Sometimes I see things. People who aren't really there, or places the way they used to be many years ago. I also have subtle premonitions of something that is about to happen; my strange ability takes many forms. It runs in my family, the McCrimmons, and it's usually passed down to females only, though my cousin Torcuil, in Glen Avich, is an exception. It's difficult to explain what this gift means, unless you are one of us and you've grown up with it.

I remember when Isla drowned. I *knew* it was going to happen, but by then it was too late to do anything. I was at teacher training college in Glasgow and I'd come home for the holidays. My mum and I were sitting together chatting in the garden when the sky began to cloud over and the wind started blowing. I was stepping into the kitchen through the French doors when I saw something – someone – who should not have been there. A wee girl with a French bob and a sleeveless dress, big black eyes and arms at her sides – Stella Kilpatrick.

It wasn't the first time I'd seen her – she was there every time I went to Kilpatrick House, often sitting on a branch of one of the oak trees around the house. To me, the dead don't look any different from the living – no white skin or strange gait like in horror films, nothing like that – though there's something subtle there, more a feeling than something visual, that makes them look not quite right. Like sepia people in a full-colour photograph.

'Stella?'

Out of the corner of my eye I saw that my mum had stopped in her tracks and was watching me. She hadn't inherited the Sight, but she knew how it worked because she'd often seen it in her family. She knew I was seeing something. Stella stood and said nothing. Then, slowly, she raised her arm and pointed somewhere over my shoulder. I turned around, but there was nothing there; nothing but the sea. All of a sudden I was so intensely afraid I felt sick, and my knees gave way – Stella was trying to tell me something, and I knew, I knew it was something terrible. Her lips moved, and her voice came out in a sweet, low, distant whisper.

'*Isla.*'

I had to hold on to the door frame to stay standing. And then I saw her from above, as if I were a seabird flying over the beach – Isla, alone on the sand, the waves swallowing her.

I shouted to my mum to phone Shuna, and I ran to the beach myself, in time to see the tragedy unfolding – in time to see Sorren's little boat fighting on the waves, and then capsizing, as tears ran down my face and I prayed and prayed for Isla's life.

But my prayers went unanswered.

Sorren was in pieces. I held his hand at the funeral, and he clung to me. It's horrible to say, but part of me was happy that he needed me, even if it was because of such a tragedy. Carla and my mum were sobbing like their hearts would break, but I kept it all inside, a sea of grief I had no way to express, holding Sorren's hand so tight I must have hurt him, as he did the same.

That night he begged me not to go home, to stay with him. We slipped out to the beach and we spent the night awake, sometimes talking, sometimes in silence, until we saw the sun rise on the sea that had taken his sister away.

Everything had changed.

Every time I was back from college, we went out with the same crowd of friends, but nothing ever seemed to happen between us. He often said I was like a sister to him, just as we'd thought of wee Isla as our sister.

I used to cry for love of him.

When I got my job at Seal Primary and moved back to the island, a boy from Eilean, Luke, began to come to see me on the ferry. I really tried, but I couldn't be with him. After a few months, I had to tell him that things weren't working out.

'I know why,' he said. He seemed a gentle man, but as soon as I told him it was over, he became aggressive all of a sudden.

'I told you, it's just not working out for me. I'm sorry.'

'You played a game with me. To make Sorren jealous.'

'I didn't!' I certainly hadn't. But I'd tried to use Luke to get Sorren out of my head, and maybe that was just as bad.

'Well let me tell you. You and Sorren will never be together. And you'll pine for him like an idiot . . .'

At that point I simply walked away.

But Luke had been prophetic. He was now married to a Frenchwoman and had twin girls. As for me, ten years on, I'm still pining, and I can't stop. Nobody else is like Sorren. Nobody can live up to his kindness, and the way he laughs, and the soft sound of his voice when he speaks to me . . .

Just after I finished with Luke, Sorren left for Italy. He was in two minds about going, and there was a lot of soul-searching and pondering during the few months before he went. Shuna and Hamish were keen for him to go, and he'd grown so passionate about food and cooking, it seemed a waste for him just to cook for the inn instead of training properly. Studying in Italy was the chance of a lifetime, and I knew he had to take it; but it was hard to see him go. It was hard to advise him for his own good, and ignore my desire to keep him here with me.

A short while after he left, I had a dream. I dreamt of a girl wrapped in white sheets, her amber skin making a beautiful contrast; I saw her brown hair on the pillow, and I heard her calling Sorren's name.

I woke up with a stone in my heart and a knot of tears in my throat.

When Sorren called me to catch up and told me he had met someone, it was no surprise to me. A few months later, he came home with Alessia.

Alessia was quiet, a bit melancholic – a sort of romantic figure, constantly homesick and speaking to Sorren in a soft, gentle voice. She was the opposite of me. No wonder Sorren hadn't fallen for me, if that was his type.

I was nearly relieved, as strange as it may seem. What I feared most had happened. I thought I would get him out of my head at last.

My mum and Inary – my cousin and best friend – kept telling me it was the right time to move on, to at least try and see someone else. I was beautiful, they said. Beautiful in a way that made people do a double take when they looked at me. And I was wasted longing for Sorren still.

But I didn't see much use in being tall and slim and fair when it didn't turn Sorren's head; when he'd fallen for someone small and soft and dark.

Seeing them together, though, seeing how much they loved each other, was too much for me, even if I was still his little moon, orbiting around him like I'd always done. After a lot of tears and sleepless nights, I resolved to move on. *Move on* – how many times I had heard that word from my mum and Inary over the years.

Move on from Sorren, he's no good for you.

But then Alessia left, and Sorren didn't follow her. She'd asked him to, she'd asked him to go with her to Italy, and while he was pondering the choice, talking to me about it,

I was full of hollow panic. How would I manage without him? I would be lost in an uncharted land, where I had no compass, no stars above to guide me.

But Sorren knew his own mind, and knew what he wanted. And what he didn't want.

He made his choice. He stayed.

And something happened between us, because it was always like that: that when something hurt him deeply, like Isla's death or Alessia's abandonment, he'd turn to me.

One night on the beach, he said that maybe we should put an end to all our woes and get together. He said it jokingly, drunkenly – we had a bottle of whisky with us – but then he looked for my lips, and I melted inside as we kissed.

I thought I'd die from bliss.

It was like I had so often imagined it would be, and more.

Sorren, the amateur astronomer, told me once that in 2002, a dull star in an obscure constellation became six hundred thousand times brighter than the sun. Nobody knew why. And then it went back to being what it had been before, a star like any other.

That was what happened to me that day on the beach, when his lips were on mine and his arms were around me – I was six hundred thousand times brighter than the sun.

And then our eyes met in the gloom, white moonlight gathering in pools on the rocks and the sound of the sea enveloping us, caressing us. For a moment, I could see the desire in his eyes, then suddenly he laughed and said, 'You'll always be like a wee sister to me.'

That word again. *Sister.*

His arms came around me once more, but this time it was different – it was a brotherly hug and it left me cold, so cold I got up and said I was tired and that I wanted to go home, and walked away without a backward glance.

The next day he searched my face to see if what had happened the night before had left any trace. I was careful to show him that nothing was wrong, nothing was amiss. I was still Caty, his friend, his wee sister, the girl in the background. The girl whose lips felt to him like warm, sugary, comforting tea, the essence of home – the opposite of passion – while the truth was that this cup-of-tea girl trembled to her very core at his touch, and cried and cried to a silent, indifferent moon.

I'm still trying. Still trying to move on from him and stop loving him like I do.

I was a woman who could be six hundred thousand times brighter than the sun, and my life shone like never before. And now I am back to being a dull star, in an obscure constellation.

Sometimes, very rarely, he hugs me, and I wish I could be in his arms forever. I think there is nothing I know as well as his eyes – those blue eyes with the little brown speckles and the long, long eyelashes – and the scent of him, the scent of the sea, the scent of home. Sometimes, when we speak on the phone, I close my eyes and listen to his voice like you would listen to a song. I dream of his strong arms and his strong hands, and the way he stands so straight, so proud; the dimple in his left cheek when he smiles; the way he listens when people speak to him, like he really cares; the kindness he shows to all around him. His way of being himself, his way of being Sorren.

My Sorren, never quite mine.

Anna

Linda had run me through all Lady Kilpatrick's medications. I had a printed sheet in a poly pocket with everything I needed to know – including that sometimes she talked to flowers and other assorted objects. And according to her, they talked back.

When Linda was finished, she took me to the dining room, where Lady Kilpatrick was waiting for me. She was standing at the window, wearing a dark woollen dress. At her throat there was a coral cameo, and she wore lovely matching dangling earrings.

'I don't like to sit,' she said as soon as I came in, without even saying hello; but her tone was soft. 'I don't like to rest. I know I don't have long left in this world.' Linda snorted and rolled her eyes. 'I want to enjoy it as long as I can,' she finished in a resolute tone.

'Good morning, Lady Kilpatrick,' I said, smiling.

'Call me Mary,' she said, and came to hold my hands.

Her skin was cold and dry. Her long silvery hair was done up in an old-fashioned knot at the back of her head, and she had two tiny combs woven in at either side. 'I wasn't born a lady. Not at all. I was born Mary McInnes. I *am* Mary McInnes. Lady Kilpatrick is just a . . . a nom de plume.' She returned my smile.

'Well, I'll leave you to it. Behave, Mother,' Linda said, and though her words were stern, she came to leave a light kiss on her mother's cheek and looked at her with tenderness. 'I'll be around the house or the grounds if you need anything. You have my number.'

I smiled inwardly, wondering how it would feel to live in a place so big you needed to phone someone instead of just calling their name.

'Right then, Mary. We need to take our morning medication before breakfast.'

'*Our* morning medication? It's not yours. It's mine. Nurses always speak like that. And they call you sweetheart and darling,' she said.

'You don't like that?'

'Oh no. I love it. Stella always calls me that. She's my sister, Stella. Her name means star.'

'That's lovely. Does she live here?'

Mary nodded. 'Yes, she's here in the house. She fell out of the tree house when we were children and broke her neck. She's the one who saved Linda when she caught meningitis, years ago. I saw Stella at her bedside; she never left. Yes, she saved her.'

'What a thoughtful sister,' I said. I'd worked with the

elderly long enough not to be surprised by anything they said. I just went with it.

'When I finish swallowing all that rubbish, you and I can go for a walk.'

'I'd love that. But we . . . you need to wear your cardigan. There's a stiff breeze outside and we don't want to catch a cold!'

'We don't, no,' she said, and there was a mischievous light in her eyes.

Mary and I walked slowly around the grounds. Peacocks and tourists were dotted everywhere, and sometimes you didn't know who was watching who. The peacocks very much owned the place and sat on the stairs of the gift shop, underneath the picnic tables, in the middle of the flower beds like lazy, colourful pets. Lady Kilpatrick took me to the gardens, where we strolled among tidy lawns and splashes of bright flowers – such beauty in the middle of the heathery, barren hill. From there I could see the sea – on Seal, you could see the sea from pretty much everywhere; after all, there was more sea than land all around you.

'So, you and Sorren McNeil are together,' she said suddenly.

I gasped. 'Mary! Not really, no.'

'Why not?'

'Why not? Well, I . . . There are quite a few things . . .'

'Life is short, Anna. Look at me, so old and sick. I was like you only yesterday,' she said matter-of-factly, without bitterness. 'Beautiful and full of hopes and dreams . . .'

'Oh, I don't know about hopes and dreams,' I shrugged.

Yes. What were my hopes and dreams?

That Ava would be healthy and happy and loved like she deserved.

But what about me? What were *my* hopes and dreams?

'Let me tell you. After I had my children, you know what I did? I started climbing mountains.'

'You did?' It was hard to imagine this frail, fragile lady conquering peaks. Or maybe not, actually – something in her eyes told me that she would have the grit. And the hunger. And then I remembered the photograph Ava and I had seen in the house – Mary in tweed, against the backdrop of a mountain.

'I did it for Eric. That was what Eric used to do. He used to travel around Scotland on foot and climb the Munros. All the Munros he climbed, but three.'

'Who's Eric, Mary?' I asked softly.

'Eric is the man I *adored*,' she said, and I was surprised to see her eyes shining with tears.

I waited for an explanation, for more stories, but she said no more.

She spent the rest of the afternoon looking out of the window at the ever-changing sky.

15

What mothers know

Anna

It was raining so hard, there was no way Ava and I could go anywhere. Raindrops bounced off the glass of our window and blurred the landscape; I couldn't tell where the sea ended and the sky began. We had a long lie-in, snuggling up under the duvet and chatting, and then went downstairs for breakfast. Shuna was serving cups of tea and coffee and slices of cake to the morning mums, sitting with prams, babies and toddlers, sippy cups on the tables in front of them. Carla was there with Angela and Sandy. As soon as she saw Ava, Angela started waving and smiling, and Ava ran to her at once. But Carla murmured a hurried greeting and looked away.

You can tell your sister it's okay, I'm not seeing Sorren, I wanted to say, but I couldn't. Carla's coldness hurt. I decided to ignore it.

'Good morning, Anna. It's miserable today, isn't it?' Shuna said with a smile. She always wore a smile; it reached her eyes and made them soft, like she was looking at the world with love and compassion.

'Yes. We aren't sure what we'll do today . . .'

'Why don't you stay in and have a quiet one? Ava and I can crochet, if you want, or do some cooking. Would you like to spend the morning here, Angela? If that's okay with you, Carla . . .'

'That would be good, but we have a swimming lesson, don't we?' Carla said, still not looking at me.

'That's a shame. We can make cupcakes, Ava.'

'Yes!' Ava was instantly consoled. 'I can wear my apron!'

So Hamish and Jane took over pub duties, and we spent a peaceful morning, with Ava and Shuna making cupcakes, and me doing all the little chores that needed to be done and getting things ready for lunch. There was a sense of contentment being in the kitchen together.

It was a moment out of time, in a way.

I hardly ever thought about my childhood; it was too full of black memories for me to want to remember. But since we'd arrived on Seal, those memories had slowly come to the forefront of my mind. As though things I had kept buried deep, deep down, where they couldn't hurt, were coming up and shaking me.

As I worked in Shuna's kitchen, once again I realised how much I had missed out on. I had never sat in the kitchen with my mother, busy colouring or doing my homework while she cooked or read or ironed. She'd never touched my hair the way Shuna did with Ava. And in turn, she had never been a proper granny to Ava, not like Granny Leah had been in the three short years she was with me. My mum just wasn't interested; she had her own chaotic life and didn't want to be bothered with mine. And now, history was repeating itself – Ava was not to have a family life either . . .

But no – she had *me*. And although we weren't a traditional family, we would be enough to each other.

Still, as I watched Shuna stroking Ava's hair softly, praising her as she squeezed wonky icing on the cupcakes, a mixture of sadness and longing clutched at my chest. I held my breath; I never wanted this moment to pass. The sense of serenity I was experiencing, with three generations together in the same room, was an entirely new one for me. And it felt so soothing, more than I could ever say.

'Carla seemed a bit off with you today, didn't she?' Shuna said as we washed dishes together, far out of Ava's earshot.

'Mmmm.'

'Come. Let's sit and have a cup of tea and a blether.'

We sat together while Ava decorated her cupcakes, focused and quiet in her Ava way, and chatted about something and nothing. All the while, the question *Is Sorren seeing Catriona?* on my tongue, unable to come out and unable to disappear. In the end, I felt like I was burning. I had to know. But then Shuna would realise I was thinking about Sorren. And I wasn't supposed to.

'Carla is a good woman. Really. She has a lot on her plate, with Angela, you know . . .' she said finally.

'Yes, I can imagine.'

'Also, she's very protective of Catriona.'

Right. 'Well, she doesn't need to protect Catriona from me,' I said, more curtly than I would have liked.

'No, of course not. So . . . have you seen Sorren recently?' Shuna tilted her head to one side.

I looked at her.

Of course.

My worry that she'd realise I was thinking about Sorren made no sense. She was his mother, she was a woman of a certain age who had seen a lot and experienced a lot. Of course she'd guessed what was happening – or not happening – between Sorren and me.

'I . . . Well, no. I hope . . . I don't know.' Great. I was making a lot of sense. 'I . . . I went for coffee with Catriona,' I said, as if that was an answer to her question, and quickly took a sip of my tea.

'Ah, my dear, lovely Catriona. She's like another daughter to me. You know, she and Sorren grew up together.'

I nodded, and felt my heart sink. They were so tightly linked. Even their families were close. They shared so much history. I'd been right to say no to spending the evening with Sorren. I felt stupid for having thought of him at all. And yet, the way he'd looked at me . . . I couldn't have dreamt it, could I? And Sorren didn't seem the type to string someone along. I was confused.

'She's very . . . she's very fond of Sorren. But Sorren doesn't see her that way. For him, she's like a sister . . .'

Shuna was still talking, but I had no idea what she said next. I felt my mouth stretch in a smile.

'You okay?'

'Me? Yes! Yes, sorry. I'm really, really good.'

'Of course.' Shuna smiled. And she looked at me like she *knew*.

'Let me see those cupcakes, sweetheart!' I turned around, expecting to see Ava's little dark head bent over her work, but she wasn't there. 'Oh. She must have slipped out while we were chatting,' I said, and got up to look for her.

'Jane, did you see Ava? She was in the kitchen . . .'

Jane stopped with her arm in the air as she dusted the liquor shelves behind the bar. 'I didn't see her, no, sorry.'

My heart skipped a beat. How could I have missed her walking out of the kitchen? I had a radar for Ava, the way mothers do.

I ran upstairs to our room. 'Ava?'

She wasn't on her bed. She wasn't at the window seat, nor on my bed. She wasn't in the bathroom. I turned around and around, checking the whole room. The sea watched me from the window, still and calm.

'Ava? Ava?'

I tried to walk downstairs at a normal pace – there was nothing to worry about; Ava was somewhere close, no point in panicking – but I found myself running.

'Shuna, Ava isn't in our room.' I could hear a slight tremble to my voice.

'She isn't? I'll check the back,' Shuna said, and went out of the back door. In the meantime, I scoured the two rooms of the pub, but there was no trace.

Jane and Hamish joined in, searching the courtyard and the ground floor. A few punters looked up, alarmed by our calls and our expressions. I disappeared upstairs – I wasn't sure which rooms belonged to the inn and which to the house, and I couldn't hurtle in on people, but I was so scared that I knocked and opened a few doors. Shuna and I found each other on the landing of the second floor.

Shuna was deathly white. 'Has she gone outside, do you think?'

I shook my head. 'I don't think so. It's not like Ava.' But I looked towards a window, and panic rose. 'Oh, what if . . .' My voice trailed away. The beach. The sea. Strangers. A million possibilities, some of them terrible. I didn't want to finish the sentence. I turned away from Shuna and ran downstairs once again. I was about to dash outside, looking for my daughter, when a little voice, a voice as familiar as my own, sounded somewhere above me.

'Ava!' I swung round and flew back up the stairs to our own landing, panting so hard I could see stars at the corners of my vision. There was Ava, looking somewhere between dazed and scared, clutching something black to her chest.

'Mummy, I'm here . . . I'm sorry.'

I knelt in front of her and held her to me. 'Oh Ava! Where were you? Did you not hear us calling?'

I was about to shout to Shuna that I'd found her when I saw what she was holding in her hands, and for some reason I froze. Our eyes met.

'I found my dancing shoes,' she said. Little black shoes, like ballet shoes but with long laces.

I remembered what she'd said to me weeks before – that her other mum used to take her dancing, but she wore black shoes, not pink.

'Ava, where were you?' I whispered.

At that moment, Shuna arrived beside us. I hadn't even heard her coming down the stairs. 'Hamish, Jane! We've found her! She's here, she's okay! Oh, thank goodness, Ava, we . . .' she began, then suddenly stopped frozen, just like I'd been. Her mouth was in a small 'o'.

She came to kneel on the carpet beside us.

'Where did you find those?' she asked softly.

'I'm sorry, Shuna, I don't know where . . .'

She didn't look at me as I spoke; she just kept staring at Ava. This was between them, I realised. A silent dialogue was happening between them, a conversation I had no part in.

Wordlessly Ava pointed to the room across from ours. The door was ever so slightly ajar, and it struck me that I'd never seen it open before.

'They're my dancing shoes,' Ava explained once more, this time to Shuna.

'Ava . . .' I said hurriedly. I wanted to stop that conversation in its tracks; it felt . . . *dangerous* to me. Like Ava would end up saying something we couldn't have explained. But Shuna spoke.

'Highland dancing,' she said, turning towards me with a strange smile, a smile like she was very happy and very

sad all at the same time, the two feelings conflicted inside
her so that she could wear a smile and still have tears in
her eyes.

Suddenly I remembered the Highland dancing display
at the Blessing of the Boats – the girls had worn just those
kind of shoes.

'Ava, these aren't yours . . .' I said tentatively.

'No. They're my daughter's,' Shuna whispered, and
got up as swiftly as a young woman would have done.
She stood for a moment in front of the room Ava had
pointed to, and then, with an imperceptible sigh, she
pushed the door open. It was a silent invitation: I took my
daughter's hand, Ava still clutching the shoes, and we
stepped in together.

The room was in semi-darkness, the curtains drawn.
Shuna switched the light on – a yellow fabric lampshade
that illuminated Ava's hair, giving red reflections to her
dark locks – and now I could see what was inside. It was a
little girl's room, the bed made up with pale yellow covers,
a Care Bears picture on the wall, a little white desk with
books and stationery on it, a row of heart-shaped stickers
on its drawers. There was a cardigan on the bed, a book
on the bedside table, as if whoever slept here had just
stepped out, but was returning at any moment. The room
was kept waiting.

Waiting for someone who was never coming back, I
guessed at once.

Shuna's daughter, the girl who owned those shoes, wasn't
at university, or living somewhere else, or away for work.

No.

This was the room of a lost girl.

Suddenly I remembered Carla's words: *With what happened to her family* . . . They had stayed with me, but for some reason I'd never asked for an explanation.

A murmur came from me. 'Oh Shuna . . .'

She gently took the dancing shoes from Ava and placed them beside the wardrobe.

'I'm so sorry. I can't apologise enough . . .' I began. Part of me wanted to scold Ava for having wandered in where she didn't belong, but I was so relieved at having found her, and so bewildered by it all, that I just couldn't – not then. 'I'm sorry,' I said again, and it wasn't just an apology, it was overwhelming compassion, for whatever had happened.

'But *I had to*!' Ava was on the verge of tears too.

I took her hand. 'It's okay, sweetheart. It's okay . . . Come on, let's go . . .' I said.

'No, no. Don't go. Please stay a moment.' Shuna was almost pleading, and I stopped dead. Of course we would stay, if that was what she wanted, but I was afraid, though I didn't know why.

And then I noticed something I hadn't seen before. There was chaos on the floor, colourful scraps of fabric scattered around a tin box – as if the contents of the box had exploded. Ava's Barbie doll lay on the mound, dressed in flowery material held together with a ribbon.

'Ava, what were you doing?'

'I was making clothes for my doll . . . Am I in trouble?'

'Oh darling, no, you're not in trouble,' Shuna said. She went to sit on the bed and patted the space beside her. Ava sat next to her, and Shuna wrapped an arm around her shoulders. 'I don't mind you coming to play here. I really don't.'

'We'll tidy everything up . . .' I offered, and knelt to put the scraps of fabric back in their box.

'No. No, please don't. Don't tidy anything,' she said, still smiling. Her smile was different now, brighter, but her expression still had that strange combination – radiant and sorrowful at the same time. Her eyes were red-rimmed, her cheeks wet; and still she smiled. 'Let her play.'

'I *always* played like this. My mum and me made clothes for my dolls,' Ava explained.

I felt the blood leave my face. Shuna looked at her, eyes wide, then glanced towards me.

'Really? My daughter and I did that too. We got scraps of fabric from Mrs Miller, the dressmaker . . .'

She had misunderstood. Ava and I had never played with fabric, never made clothes for dolls; I'm useless with a needle and thread. What Ava meant . . . well, who knows?

I always *played like this. My mum and me made clothes for my dolls.*

Shuna's eyes met mine, and I had to say something. Something that Ava couldn't deny, something that wouldn't prompt her to say, 'No, Mummy and me never made clothes for my dolls; it was my other mother' or anything equally unsettling.

'Ava loves dolls,' was all I could muster in a small voice. The walls of that room were closing on me and I wanted out, I needed out.

'Yes, I noticed that when Angela came to play. If Ava wants to play with Isla's things, I'm happy for her to do so. If it's okay with you.' She looked around. 'This is the first time anyone other than Hamish or me has stepped into this room in many years.'

Isla. So that was the lost daughter's name.

Isla, Sorren's sister.

For a moment, just a moment, I saw myself dragging Ava away, downstairs to the pub and out onto the pier and the ferry, away from the strangeness, the mysteries.

I was afraid.

But all of a sudden, a sweet lilac light filled the room. Shuna had opened the curtains. The sea was grey and purple, and calm, and beautiful. She switched the electric light off, and this sanctuary, this place frozen in time, became a soft haven.

'So, Ava, will you come here to play?' she asked. Ava smiled and nodded, and it happened again – a wordless conversation between them.

'Shuna . . .' I began, and a jumble of words tried, and failed, to make its way out. 'Thank you,' I ended up saying – I couldn't find any other words. She knew, she knew that I wasn't just thanking her for letting Ava play in Isla's room.

'Thank *you*,' she replied, with another of her motherly smiles. Once again, what was she thanking us for?

Because we were there.

Because I let Ava be a little bit hers sometimes.

And maybe because we'd opened the door that nobody opened.

'Can I wear my shoes sometimes?' Ava said.

Shuna turned slightly towards where the shoes lay. 'The dancing shoes? We need to look at the size . . . I think they're a bit big for you. Maybe if we have time I can take you to have a Highland dancing lesson, and if you like it, I'll buy you a pair.'

'That would be lovely, wouldn't it, Ava?' I said, stretching my face in a smile to mirror Shuna's. Shuna didn't seem to have noticed that Ava had called them *her* dancing shoes; or if she had, she hadn't read anything into it. Of course she hadn't – who would? Only someone who'd gone through what we'd gone through, the memories, the strange guesses about another girl's life.

Isla, the little girl lost. The little girl who made clothes for dolls and did Highland dancing.

Isla; her life, her memories.

Ava leaned her head on Shuna's shoulder. 'Can I go back to play now?'

'Of course, my love . . .'

Isla and Ava. Ava, my daughter.

And then I realised that Ava, normally a curious child, hadn't asked Shuna anything about this room: *Who sleeps in this yellow bed? Who is Isla? Where is she?*

No, she hadn't asked anything.

'Hello?' A voice came from downstairs. It was Sorren.

My heart quickened all by itself, without any conscious thoughts triggering it – the sound of his voice was enough. Shuna's hands went to her eyes, drying tears that weren't there any more, trying to erase all traces of them. Foot-steps up the stairs – Sorren framed in the door of Isla's room.

'Mum? Anna? What are you doing here? What's wrong?'

'It's okay, Ava was having a wee play . . .'

Shuna kept it low-key, but Sorren's expression didn't relax. He knew that there had been a moment of high emotion – I was sure he could feel it in the air; he could read it on our faces.

'Come with me, Ava.' Shuna held out her hand. 'We can have a wee snack and then go back to make dolls' clothes, okay?'

Sorren and I were left alone. His eyes were dark, his lips in a tight line. He stood in front of me, white with anger.

'Sorren . . .'

'Do you have any idea what you've done, Anna?' he whispered, and his soft voice was more intimidating than if he'd been shouting.

'What . . . I know Ava shouldn't have gone into your sister's room, but—'

'Don't even mention my sister. Don't mention her,' he said, again in that quiet voice.

'Shuna asked Ava to stay here, to keep playing! She said nobody had touched Isla's things in years . . .'

'Stop it. Stop it, Anna. You know nothing about my family. *Nothing.*' The force of his words, the unfairness of them, left me breathless.

'We won't trouble you again,' I said. My eyes were full of tears, and I was horrified to hear my voice breaking instead of showing the fury I felt. 'You know, Sorren, I might know nothing about your family, but you know nothing about me, you know nothing about what brought me here! So just go ahead and preserve your sister's sanctuary forever, and don't bother listening to what your mum actually *needs*!'

I slipped inside my own room and slammed the door. Then slowly I let myself slide down to the floor, my back against the door. Warm tears fell on my cheeks, and I had to stop myself from sobbing. Sorren's steps resounded down the stairs; he was gone.

I sat at the window, rain tapping on the glass, my arms around my knees, my breathing still ragged.

If only I could explain to Sorren why Ava had gone into that room in the first place. If only I could tell him all that we'd been through: about Toby, about Ava's silence, about her memories. But it was too late. He had refused to listen. Even if Shuna had said she wanted to talk about Isla, that she wanted Isla to still be there among them, and not just a lost memory . . . Sorren would not listen.

It was too much. Too much for me to take in. Between the incident in Isla's room and Sorren's anger, I was overwhelmed. I looked for the yellow notebook in my handbag and went through the pages. Every note was a chill down my spine. Then, with shaking hands, I made another entry.

She used to do Highland dancing.

She used to make clothes for her dolls.

Who was that 'she'?

Who used to make clothes for her dolls; *who* used to do Highland dancing?

Was it Ava?

Or was it Isla; had it been Isla all along? Isla who lived on the sea, who could see dolphins from her window, who had a bowl with a rabbit on it, and ate porridge, and danced to the sound of fiddles and pipes.

The girl who had died and was not coming back. Except through memories . . .

All of a sudden I realised I was cold, so cold that I was shaking. I didn't want my daughter to have the memories of a dead girl. I didn't want to solve the mystery any more; I wanted to forget it. I wanted to leave the island and never come back.

And then Shuna's soft eyes, her kind smile – the way her hand felt on my shoulder and on my arm, like a mother's – came back to me and squeezed my heart again.

And Sorren's face. Sorren, who was so angry with us I was sure there would not be a way back. I thought of everything that could have been, and hadn't even begun to be.

It was too much. Desolate tears began to fall again, and I dried them with the palms of my hands. The rain was falling even harder now, and all the light seemed to have been sucked away by angry clouds. I grabbed my bag and ran downstairs, mumbling something to Shuna about ferry tickets. And then I was out, not caring about the wind and rain, headed to the ferry office.

Sorren

I walked home in the pouring rain, darkness inside me, shaking hands in my pockets.

Unshed tears filled my throat and made it hard to breathe.

Sooner or later, I would have to cry for her, for my sister.

Sooner or later, the tears that had strangled me all these years would have to come out.

It was like that for my mum and me: she didn't talk, I didn't cry.

My house was empty, silent. Weird, I thought: I wasn't alone, I wasn't a lonely person, and still my house was a place that had never come to life. Like I never really lived there. Like I lived with my parents still – except I was the parent, and they the children I looked after.

The image of Anna and Ava standing in my sister's room, touching her things, burnt me. I was full of anger towards her still. A sanctuary, she'd called Isla's room. A sanctuary, in a home for living people.

I poured myself a large whisky and revived the embers

of my peat fire. I knew I had gone too far. I knew that I had taken out on her my rage at what had happened, and none of that had been her fault. My hands were still shaking a little – I wasn't used to anger; I felt like I'd been poisoned by it.

My mum had opened up to Anna. She'd told her things that she never even told me. A stranger had had to come from nowhere and unearth my mum's deepest secret – that she actually wanted to speak about her daughter, that she wanted to nourish her memory and keep it alive, when all those years we had nurtured and protected the silence around her in any way we could.

A stranger had come to listen to what my mum couldn't say to her closest family. To make me feel things I'd been sure I'd never feel again.

Anna had come.

And I had sent her away.

I had done it again. I had turned my back on love, or the possibility of it.

My phone started ringing. It was Caty. Then my mum called, and Fraser. All looking for me, asking why I wasn't at Star. I sent Fraser a message with an excuse – a cold, a headache – knowing he wouldn't buy it. I sat there in my living room and drank my whisky; every sip a thought of Anna, of her stricken face when I had spoken to her so harshly, so cruelly. And Ava – had she heard me? Did she think I was angry with her?

Oh Anna, I thought as the warm liquid slipped down my throat. The incandescent embers were full of images of her – her dark eyes blinking fast as my words hit her, her cheeks shining wet under the light of the landing, the way she'd thrown her hair back in anger and upset, the tears in her voice.

What have I done?

What I kept hidden in my heart, eating away at me, was that Isla's death was my fault.

I was there and I couldn't save her.

I was only sixteen, and still I couldn't help blaming myself.

I was out fishing on my boat and I was about to turn back – black clouds were gathering and I knew the weather was about to change, but I couldn't have predicted a storm of that intensity. I was nearly at the beach, just past the jagged rocks to the west, and already struggling to keep hold of my paddles, when I saw that Isla was there, playing on the beach by herself. She was unaware that the tide was coming in, and would not be able to gauge that the wind would make the waves higher and stronger and faster. I began to shout, calling her name over and over and over again. And then something happened, something I still had no explanation for – she fell, she slipped into the sea. Maybe she slipped on seaweed, maybe she tripped on something, on her own feet, like sometimes happens, but the way it looked from where I was, it was a freak accident, something that couldn't have happened, that should never have happened.

I couldn't get there in time.

I dived in, trying to get to her. I was half frozen myself, swimming on and on, waves hurling me against the rocks and breaking up my boat like a bunch of twigs. She was nowhere to be found, already underwater, swept away by the currents. I ended up having to cling to the rocks, hit by the waves over and over again, unable to get back to shore. The flash storm had been so sudden, so savage, that she didn't stand a chance. It was a miracle I hadn't drowned too; it was a miracle someone saw me and called the Sea Rescue. Like I was meant to survive, and she wasn't.

A few days later, they found one of her shoes washed up onto the beach.

It was black and shiny, with a daisy on the side.

The other was never found.

I lay in my hospital bed with a broken hip and a few broken ribs, my injuries too painful to allow me to move, but not painful enough to distract me from the ache in my heart. My mum came to see me, but she couldn't speak. Tears came out of her eyes even when she wasn't crying – like she had become pain itself. That didn't last long, though: after the initial shock wore off, she locked her sorrow inside and buried it deep – though not deep enough that my father and I couldn't see it.

When my dad told me that they'd found one of Isla's shoes on the beach, I asked if I could have it. I kept it close to me, under the sheets. Nobody could convince me to part from that shoe.

*

We'd always called her a child of the sea. She was forever on the beach, forever trying to come out fishing with me. She was unafraid of the water, unafraid of the big grey expanse that had been her friend, her companion since she was born. Something tells me that she'd been unafraid until the very end, until the waves swept her off her feet and dragged her away – as if she could never conceive that the sea could hurt her. That one day it would be her death.

Yet it had tried to claim her once before, when she was a toddler. My dad was with her; she was just paddling, the water not even up to her knees. I was playing on the beach, and my mum – I'll never forget – was trying to sweep the sand off our towel with her hands. Isla fell, somehow, and ended up underwater. My dad dived in without a sound, too shocked to say anything or even shout at us, and brought her back, soaked and cold and scared, but alive.

'I don't know how it happened. She was just standing there, and she fell. I don't know how it happened . . .' he repeated over and over again, as if my mum would blame him for the accident. My mum held her and dried her and calmed her down, and not long afterwards Isla had forgotten all about what happened and was laughing and toddling about like she always did.

But we hadn't forgotten. We were disquieted in a way I can't even explain.

Lying in my hospital bed, I dreamt of Isla's death again and again, my brain desperately trying to change the ending. I'd find her and lift her aboard unharmed. I'd take her home to our parents and we'd sit in front of the fire. Our mother would dry her hair. I'd have a whisky, she'd sip a hot chocolate. We would thank our lucky stars for having courted danger this way, and survived; my mum would say a grateful prayer. When I left the hospital, I took the dream with me, the same nightmare over and over. I thought I'd never sleep again.

Every morning for a long, long time I woke up in despair, because I knew that wasn't how it ended. There had been no fire, no hot chocolate, no drying of hair and being sent to bed after a talking-to, somewhere between relief and anger at the risk she'd taken.

No. Isla had not come home. Isla was gone forever.

That was fifteen years ago. Or yesterday, depending on how I felt that day. My parents seemed to have made their peace with what had happened, even if the pain was etched all over their faces, never to be erased. I wanted it to stay that way, so I tried not to talk about her.

But their pain was clean, it was pure – it wasn't tinged with guilt.

They weren't the ones who didn't save her.

That was me.

16

Don't take me away

Anna

'The last ferry is at half four,' the woman at the office told me. Yes, we had enough time to pack and leave and never see Sorren again. I strode back to the inn with the ferry tickets under my jumper, to protect them from the rain. My hands were shaking and I was cold, because I hadn't even taken a jacket and the wind was rising fast, turning into a gale. Cold, thick drops of rain fell on earth and sea.

I stepped into the kitchen from the back door, a little puddle forming where I stood.

'Oh Anna. You really went to buy tickets!' Shuna said in dismay.

I nodded and took the sodden tickets out, then made my way upstairs with Shuna following me.

'How can I convince you to change your mind?' She stood at my door as I was folding clothes and stuffing things into our bags. Sorren's shell would remain where it was, of course. I had a good mind to open the window and just throw it out, actually.

'I'm so sorry, you can't change my mind. We can't stay

if Sorren is so cross with us . . . If it upsets him that we're here, well . . .'

'What did he say to you? I tried to phone him but he wouldn't pick up!' Shuna seemed so distressed, guilt clawed at me.

'Just . . . just that we shouldn't have done what we did. We shouldn't have gone into Isla's room and upset you.' Oh, how I longed to explain to her all that had happened. The link between Isla and Ava. But how could I? Her pain was too deep, too raw for me to go stepping in, stirring things up with a mystery I could not solve.

'Honestly!' She rolled her eyes. 'Ava is a child, she is curious! She was . . . exploring, that's all. I'm so sorry, I shouldn't have left you alone with him. I didn't think . . . Let me speak to him. I'll explain.'

'It's too late. He hates us now.' The memory of his quiet voice, so full of anger and upset, threatened to make me cry again. I steeled myself.

'He doesn't hate you, Anna! You must understand. Sorren is very protective of me. *Too* protective.' She shook her head. 'Please, come downstairs with me. We can have a cup of tea, or something stronger, and I'll tell you how things are. I'll tell you about Isla . . . and about Sorren.'

I paused in my frantic activity. Shuna's eyes were still red-rimmed, and there were traces of tears on her face.

I threw the pair of jeans I was folding onto the bed. 'Of course. Let's go.' We still had time before the ferry left, and it wouldn't take long to finish packing.

We sat with small glasses of watered-down whisky –
we both needed it – and Shuna began to speak. It came
out like a flowing stream. I knew she'd been desperate to
talk about her daughter, but I hadn't expected such intensity. It had all been pressed down, constricted, ignored,
and once the lid was removed, everything came out in
torrents of emotion.

'You know, I love talking about her. People are scared
to mention her to me, Sorren especially. They think the
memory hurts. And it *does* hurt. But if I don't talk about
her, if I don't keep her memory alive . . . sometimes it's
like she never came into this world. And she *did*.' Shuna
shrugged. 'She was here, she was mine, and she lived a
lovely, full life before she died. I *want* to remember her.'

'How . . . how did it happen?' I made myself ask.

'She'd gone on the beach without telling us. The tide
caught her. Someone saw it, the lifeboat volunteers went
out. Sorren was so young at the time, so young. He was
on his boat, he tried to save her . . . he ended up in hospital. He still blames himself.'

Oh Sorren. I had no idea. What a burden to bear. 'But
surely it wasn't his fault . . .'

'No, not at all. But he's convinced that it was, that he
should have saved her. You can imagine. A sixteen-year-old
boy, what could he have done? After the accident, he
was in hospital for two weeks. He was in so much
pain, you know. He had been smashed against the rocks.
The rescuers said it was a miracle we didn't lose them
both . . .'

'Oh Shuna!' I said in horror, and held both her hands.

'He kept Isla's wee shoe beside him under the sheets. He thought I wouldn't know it was there. When he came home, he just wasn't himself any more. He was never the same again; none of us were. He became very protective of us, especially me, to the point that I feared he'd never have his own life. I was so happy when he decided to train as a chef in Italy, when he came back with Alessia. She was beautiful . . . she adored him, and he adored her . . .'

I tried to ignore the stab of jealousy. 'Yes. Catriona told me.'

'When Alessia said she was going back, I thought Sorren should go with her. He couldn't live for his dad and me. He had to follow his own dreams, like we'd done at his age. But he stayed. There was only so much I could say or do, you know; my son is his own person. But I couldn't help thinking that his sister's death had halted his life too.'

'I understand.' In my mind, the image of a young boy lying broken in a hospital bed.

'Every morning I wake up and think: *Another day. Another day without Isla*,' Shuna continued. 'But she's always here with me. Always.' She touched her heart softly, then tilted her head, resting her gaze on me. There was warmth in her eyes, and a sense of wistfulness, like she was imagining what could have been. 'She'd be about your age now, just a wee bit younger. Ava reminds me of her very, very much. But had Isla lived, I think she would look a bit like you. She had your lovely dark hair,' she said, and stroked my hair in a motherly way.

Imagine. Just imagine.

To grow up with a mother like Shuna.

'Sometimes I feel like I have to have superhuman strength just to breathe. Who would have thought that being alive could be such an enormous effort?' she said, and it was such a strange statement for someone who seemed so strong, so calm, so cheerful. It broke my heart.

'I'm so sorry,' I said in a low voice. A rogue tear fell down my cheek – I'd cried more tears in the last few hours than in all the weeks after Toby left – but I couldn't help it.

'No, no, don't cry, Anna. We have a good life here. I'm always busy; there is always something to do, something to sort or organise. There are people who depend on me: my family, my friends . . . Everyone expects me to be strong. After all, I've been through the worst thing that can happen to a mother, and survived.' I couldn't believe that the sweet woman I had known for the last few weeks had been carrying such pain inside. Her fingers felt warm in mine, and I held them tighter.

The tears were now falling freely on my cheeks, and I didn't even try to stop them. It was a strange privilege, to be chosen to hold her confidence, the secrets of her heart.

'Isla was our wee miracle, sent to us after many years of longing for another baby and when Sorren was already nearly eleven. Our miracle child, our blessing. After she was gone, I couldn't face getting rid of her things. As you saw, I kept her room exactly as it was. Down to the book she was reading; it's still on her bedside table, did you see it? The notebook with the little hearts, with a list of the friends she was going to invite for a sleepover . . .' she went on, almost dreamily. 'I keep the bed made and ready, the chest of drawers still full of her clothes. Nothing was touched or moved for fifteen years. The day she died, there was a cardigan on her bed, one that her Canadian aunt had embroidered with forget-me-nots and roses and sent over for Christmas . . .'

'Yes. I noticed that.'

'Well, I never touched it. When I air the bed – I don't want it getting damp and mouldy – I move it to the chair, and then back onto the bed. There was a wee handprint on the window . . . I couldn't bring myself to clean it away. I used to hover my own hand against it, as if in a way I could hold her hand. Every day it got fainter and fainter, until it disappeared.'

I could see it. I could see the little imprint of Isla's hand in my mind's eye.

'Every once in a while, when I get a moment of peace, I go into Isla's room and close the door. Hamish and Jane know that there is no disturbing me when I'm there. I dust, and I air the bed; I make sure everything is in its place. I sit at her window and gaze at the sea – sometimes I see dolphins jumping in the distance, and I remember how much she loved them. I look at the photographs on the windowsill and on her desk – Isla as a baby, Isla on her tricycle. Isla at the Highland dance competition, Isla on the beach, with that yellow hat she loved, the one with a flower on the side . . . Isla posing in front of the school play park in her little uniform. Who would have thought that her first day of school would be the last . . .'

I clasped my hand to my mouth. It was too much, too much. I wanted Shuna to free herself of her painful memories, to offload on me, but I was breaking, I could feel it. As a nurse, I often have to listen to painful stories, be still and accepting and slightly detached so as to offer a strong anchor; but my professional self was so much stronger than I could be while listening to Shuna, while sharing her pain.

'The time I spend in her room is my time to grieve. Sometimes I cry, mostly I don't. When I come out of there, I'm ready to face the world again. I've put all my pain in a box and left it there, because I know that if it spills out, I'd simply not be able to keep going.'

'Maybe you should talk about it more. Not keep it all inside . . .' I said tentatively.

'Maybe. Hamish and I . . . Well, we love each other dearly, but Hamish is not one for talking much. And Sorren . . . I worry for him, you know? My Sorren. It's been so hard for him, I don't want to put more weight on his shoulders.' She gave my hand a squeeze. On impulse, I threw my arms around her neck and held her close for a moment, letting her pain flow into me and comforting her the best I could.

But Sorren's words had broken something. And that would not change.

I dried my eyes and looked at my watch. 'We have half an hour. I'd better go get the bags . . .' The change of register, from reminiscing and sharing and floating in a sea of emotions, to the practicalities of leaving, was making my head spin.

'Sorren will regret this. So, so much. I know it.'

I looked down and smiled, a bitter smile. 'It's not like there was anything between us.'

'Maybe. But I saw the way you looked at each other . . .'

'Well. It's all behind us now. Time to leave,' I said.

As I looked up, I realised that Ava was standing in the doorway – and I didn't know how long she'd been there.

'Please don't take me away from here,' she said softly.

And at her words, all of a sudden, I remembered.

I was seven years old, sitting in our filthy living room with my mum on one side and Sam, our social worker, on the other.

'Sorry about the mess,' my mum was saying. 'But you were early . . .'

I cringed with embarrassment. I hated people to see the empty bottles, the dirty plates, the washing piled in a corner of the room. My mum had tried to wake up early to clean, but after ten minutes she'd given up and gone back to bed. At least, for once, she was nearly sober, maybe in a last-minute attempt to keep me.

They were on to us. This was the expression my mum had used when she'd told me about the phone call. *They're on to us, those bastards.* This time it was all Mrs Ritchie's fault. Sometimes it was the social worker's fault, or a policeman's, or her current boyfriend's, or her parents', though they'd been dead years; whatever happened, it was always somebody else's fault.

The current disaster was Mrs Ritchie's doing because it was she who'd phoned Sam. She'd seen me curled up asleep in our tiny front garden, because my mum was dead to the world and I couldn't get back into the house after she'd sent me out for errands. I still remember the cold, and the fear that someone would see me, or even kidnap me like in a film. At first I sat with my shoulders against the front door, trying to stay awake; then, when I couldn't keep my eyes open any more, I slumped on the doorstep and fell asleep there. The next morning my mum opened the door to go and buy cigarettes, and found me there. She just told me to go in and have some cereal. I was numb with cold and exhaustion; out of the corner of my eye I saw Mrs Ritchie staring from her garden like she couldn't believe what she was seeing.

Sam came that afternoon, and the news wasn't good. My mum had gone too far. I was to be taken away and looked after by someone else.

Sam put my little zipped case in the back of her car, and gently took me by the hand.

'Please don't take me away from here,' I whispered. My mum was chaotic and neglectful; but she was my mum, and I didn't want to leave her. Sam just smiled and stroked my back. And then the car started and I was gone.

*

The rain pounded us as we stepped out, gale force winds hitting the island now. The storm was upon us, the air so dark it seemed like night-time. The ferry was there already, swaying and straining against its mooring. Ava and I ran, holding on to each other's hands, until we reached the man who checked the tickets. Ava stood frowning, mutinous, all the weight of the world on her little shoulders.

I slipped my hand into my right pocket. Nothing. There were no tickets.

This was impossible. I had put them in my pocket, I was sure. I checked my left pocket, my handbag, my jeans, the zipped compartment of my case, squinting in the pouring rain. Nothing. How could that be?

'It's okay, come on board,' the man said when he saw me struggling. I breathed a sigh of relief. Ava's hand was wet and soft in mine, her face so mournful I couldn't bear to look at her.

'Come on, darling,' I said, and lifted our luggage to step on to the ferry. The man made a gesture as if to hurry us – maybe even worse weather was coming.

We were leaving. We were really leaving Seal.

My eyes travelled up to the village and the hills behind it – the inn, the high street, Kilpatrick House in the dis-tance: all the roots we had put down, about to be ripped—

I spun round. I thought I'd heard something, but it must have been just the noise of the rain.

'Anna!'

No – it was a voice. Someone calling my name.

Someone stopping me just as I was stepping on board the dancing ferry.

It was Sorren.

He was wearing his usual checked shirt, drenched, his hair flattened and dripping in his eyes. There was a gust of wind so strong we both had to hold on to the steel handrail.

Ava freed herself from my hand and jumped into Sorren's arms. Sorren held her and closed his eyes briefly. 'I don't want to go!' she said, muffled in his chest.

'Coming or not?' the ferryman called to us.

'Give us a minute, Mike,' Sorren replied. 'We just need to sort something out.'

He looked at me over Ava's head, and his gaze seemed almost imploring. I wasn't angry with him, not any more. But I couldn't bear more harsh words, more blame being thrown at me. I was wary. 'Anna, please don't go,' he said, looking down, looking away, looking everywhere but my face.

'Make your minds up! Coming or staying?' the ferryman shouted over the wind.

'She's staying,' Sorren said.

The man wasn't convinced. 'Are you?'

'I . . .'

'Mummy, please! I want to stay!' Ava was still clinging to Sorren.

Suddenly Sorren stepped so close to me I could feel his warm breath in my ear. 'Anna, I was a fool. Such a fool. I'm so sorry. Please stay.' He offered me his hand.

'We're leaving now, miss,' the man yelled at us. 'In or out?'

'She's staying!' Sorren repeated. 'They're staying,' and he looked at me, his big hand cradling Ava's head.

I took his other hand, and he clasped his fingers around mine. Then hand in hand, we watched as the ferry crept away from the island shore.

17

This place I call my home

Sorren

The second she stepped inside my house, the place seemed to come alive. It was her laughter, as she pulled down her hood and wiped the rain from her face with her hands; the scent of her skin and her hair, filling my home and my life with a sweet fragrance. The presence of her, the way she looked around, and everywhere she looked suddenly had a reason to be.

My cold, unlived-in home had been shaken from its lonely sleep and was pulsing in time with Anna's heart.

And to think that I had nearly lost her.

'Sorren? Are you okay?'

'Yes. Yes. Sorry, just . . . It's strange to have you here. I didn't think . . .' I shrugged. 'I didn't think it would happen. Especially after . . . you know . . . But come in front of the fire. I'll pour you a whisky. Or a cup of tea? I'm afraid I don't have much in the house . . .'

'A whisky would be great,' Anna said, and ran a hand through her wet hair. She sat on the floor as close to the fire as she could, hugging her knees. A slight shiver ran through her.

"Is Ava okay?" I asked.

"Yes. I think your mum's hot chocolate *and* chocolate cake did the trick," she smiled.

I poured our whiskies and sat down beside her. She looked thoughtful. Like she had a lot to ponder.

'Anna.' Oh, it was hard to tell her, to explain. To put it all into words. Words seemed so limited, so limiting. I took a breath – maybe I was hoping she'd stop me – but she didn't let me off the hook. She waited. 'I'm sorry for what I said. You know, there are things I didn't tell you . . .'

'I spoke to your mum,' she said, and then she looked into my face. And I read her eyes: compassion.

'Right.' I took a breath. 'She told you about Isla . . .'

'Yes. And she told me about *you*.'

I nodded. For a second, I had to fight the instinct to take Anna back to the inn and then return alone to my silent, safe house where nobody could probe me or ask me things or open old wounds. Old wounds that weren't closed at all.

Instead, I smiled and made light of the moment. 'Let me stop you there. Scotsmen don't talk about feelings.'

She didn't laugh, she didn't smile. She kept looking at me thoughtfully, her head tilted to one side, her damp hair shining with a reddish hue against the fire. She was silent until I couldn't deny the wave of emotion inside me.

'She told you it was me who didn't save Isla.'

'No. She told me it was you who nearly lost his life trying.'

I blinked. There would be tears. There could be no tears. I had learnt with time to hold them back. Whenever people mentioned Isla and looked at me that way, the way Anna had looked at me, I closed all inner doors until I felt nothing, nothing at all. Their pity couldn't touch me. The pain I felt was buried so deep down, it could never come to the surface.

But this was Anna.

And the tears came, secret, invisible, coating my eyes without flowing. I saw her hand extended, coming to hold mine, and I held on to it; I held on to it like a drowning man holds on to a buoy. Her white fingers in mine, her hand so small compared to mine.

'Sorren. Sorren, listen. Your mum explained something to me . . .'

'Yes?'

'She said . . .' She looked into the fire for a moment, like she was gathering her thoughts, or choosing the best words. 'That it hurts her that nobody talks about Isla . . . that she would love to hear her mentioned, that she's happy for Ava to touch her things.'

'I know, and I'm sorry.'

'I'm not saying this for us, for Ava and me. To justify us. I'm saying this for your mum. She needs this, Sorren. She needs that room to be opened up and used, and she needs to share her memories of Isla. I think she'd like to tell you, but she doesn't know how. Because she's scared of hurting you.' I lowered my head. 'You try to protect her. But you can't pretend that it never happened. If you do, you take away the good things with the bad.'

'Yes. Yes. I see. It's just . . . it's hard. So hard to talk about her.'

'I know. I'm so sorry . . .'

I took a sip of my whisky, hoping the alcohol would anaesthetise me. Every little bit of me hurt, but it was a relief to finally feel it, all the pain that had been trapped in my bones, eating me from the inside. Finally it was coming out. Maybe I would be free . . .

Anna's face was exquisite in the light of the fire, her voice like warm water soothing me, healing me. How easy it would be to take her in my arms and kiss her, and forget about everything, everything that ever hurt. To lead her upstairs and keep her with me all night, warming a bed that had been been cold since Alessia had left, melting a heart that had been frozen just as long.

'There's something else,' she said. Her hand was still in mine. I never wanted her to stop touching me.

'I'm listening.'

'It's difficult to explain. Really difficult,' she said, lowering her head and letting her hair fall around her face like a silky curtain. 'You'll think I'm crazy.'

'I won't. Tell me.' I took her other hand, and once we were knotted together, she began to speak.

'Ava's father left us about six months ago . . .'

'Yes, I know. I heard you saying that to my mum. I'm sorry.'

She nodded. 'When he went, Ava was in shock. She

226

just wasn't herself for three days. When she woke up on the third day, she asked for her mum.'

'Oh . . . and where were you? Were you at work?'

'No. I was right there, Sorren. She was looking into my face and *she asked for her mum.*'

'She . . . I don't understand . . .'

'Neither do I, to be honest. That's why we're here.' She took a breath. 'That was just the beginning. She began to ask about her other mother, she drew picture after picture of the sea. She talked about another life she had. I took her to a doctor; he said it was just a way to comfort herself after her father left. The thing was, she kept talking about a specific place . . .'

'Seal,' I said, the pieces of the jigsaw beginning to fall into place in my mind.

'Yes. She told me she used to live on Seal. She had memories of this place, Sorren. When we arrived, she sang along with the Gaelic choir, she knew what the priest would wear at the Fishermen's Mass. She told me she used to go to a play park from which she could see the sea . . .'

'The school play park.'

'The school . . .'

'Yes. You can't see the sea from the park in the high street, but you can from the school. I know because I used to take . . .'

My voice trailed away. We looked at each other.

'Isla,' she whispered.

I got up and leaned on the mantelpiece. My heart was

beating fast. All of a sudden I wanted to run out into the rain, and keep on running, on and on.

'Ava took Isla's dancing shoes from her room. She said they were hers.'

'She just thought they were pretty, Anna. She saw the dancers wearing them,' I said, but I sounded unconvincing even to myself.

'She'd been playing with Isla's fabric scraps,' Anna continued, undeterred. 'She said she used to make clothes for her dolls with her mum.' I felt cold. A memory came back to me – Isla proudly showing me her doll in a green and yellow dress she had sewn herself, tied at the waist with a woollen ribbon. 'But Ava and I never did that. Your mum and Isla did.'

I swayed a little and put out my hand to steady myself. My mind and my heart just couldn't wrap themselves around what I was hearing.

'What are you saying, Anna?'

'I don't know, I really don't. My daughter has your sister's memories. That's all I know. I don't have an explanation . . . I'm looking for one. Or maybe . . .'

'Maybe?'

'Maybe we won't ever find one. Maybe there's no point in looking,' she said in a voice so soft I could barely hear it, like she was talking to herself. 'Maybe we should just try to be happy, all of us.'

But she'd had longer to process everything that Ava had been saying. For me, it was all new, and the shock of seeing them in my sister's room, the argument we'd had, the relief of them staying – and now the strange things she'd said to me . . . everything went to my head more than the whisky I was sipping.

Ava and Isla. Isla and Ava.

The way Ava had clung to me as if she'd known me forever.

The dark-haired girl on the beach the day they'd arrived, the one I'd mistaken for my sister – it was Ava; I knew it was Ava. But for a moment, they'd looked the same, at least to my eyes . . .

And then I was lost.

'I . . . I can't . . . I don't understand. I don't understand.' All of a sudden, my emotions overflowed and I couldn't put them into words. I took a step towards Anna, like a drunken man looking for somewhere to lean. I found her arms, her body – her neck, where I could hide my face.

'Anna. Anna.'

She wrapped her arms around my waist. Her body felt warm and tender against me, and just like I'd dreamt of doing, I took her face in my hands, and then my lips were on her lips, sweet and soft, and my fingers were in her hair, and I wanted her, I wanted her so badly I feared I couldn't stop.

But I did, and she lowered her head, her breathing heavy, then buried her face in my chest and held me against her again.

'I need to get back to Ava.'

'Yes.' I knew it was something else, though, something she couldn't put into words: that she wasn't ready.

'I'm sorry . . .'

'No, no . . . there's nothing to apologise for. Nothing.'

'I know that what I said is quite shocking . . .'

'Well, I'll have all night to digest it, won't I? And tomorrow maybe we can spend the day together, you, me and Ava? Would you like that?'

'I'd love that,' she said. And then I stole another slow, tender kiss, and it was time to go.

There was no chance of sleep for me, no chance. Everything that Anna had said danced in my mind, and neither whisky nor exhaustion would grant me sleep. In my mind, her lips were still on mine, her words floating in the air all around me, her presence, her strange revelation coming to change my life, to change my perception of things, my very core.

Anna, Anna had come.

Anna

Ava was asleep. I was touched to see Shuna sitting on her bed, a soft ray of light from the window illuminating her thoughtful face. 'Hello . . . I hope you don't mind . . .' she whispered.

'Not at all.'

'Did you and Sorren sort it all out?'

I nodded. I was glad that the room was in semi-darkness so she couldn't see the blood rising to my cheeks. I brought my fingers to my lips. Tender skin still smarting from his stubble . . .

'Oh, thank goodness. I'm so glad. Well, I'll let you be,' she said, getting up and tucking Ava in gently with one last loving gesture.

But something was playing on my mind. 'Shuna, have you seen my tickets anywhere?' I murmured.

'What tickets? You mean the ferry ones?'

'Yes.'

'No, I haven't. Did you not have them with you?' We were whispering like two conspirators over Ava's bed.

'I thought I did, but they weren't in my pocket . . . or anywhere. The guy was going to let me on the ferry without them, but . . .'

'Maybe you left them here.'

'Maybe.' I shrugged.

She turned to look at Ava. 'You don't think . . .'

'Ava? No, I don't think so. She wouldn't. Oh well, it doesn't matter any more.'

'No, it doesn't. I'm so glad you're staying.'

'So am I,' I said, and even in the gloom I could sense her smile. And then she hugged me, a warm hug that smelled of clean cotton and lavender and home.

'Goodnight, darling.'

'Goodnight, Shuna.'

As soon as she left the room, I switched my bedside lamp on to get undressed. I was in two minds whether to text Parvati to tell her what had happened, but I decided against it. I sat on the bed and began to take my clothes off.

It was then that I saw it out of the corner of my eye: a flash of white where no white should be. There was something on top of the wardrobe, something that definitely hadn't been there when I left. I stood on tiptoes – I could barely reach – and teased it with my fingers to make it fall. And down it came – an envelope. The envelope with my ferry tickets inside.

How did it get up there? Ava couldn't have reached, not even standing on a chair. And she wouldn't have anyway.

So who would have hidden them? Sure, Shuna didn't want us to leave, but she wouldn't do something like that. And even if she'd had a moment of madness, she would have taken the tickets away, not hidden them on top of the wardrobe like a child concealing the broken pieces of a vase.

Well they couldn't have flown there by themselves.

Add this to the list of mysteries, I supposed.

'We're staying,' I whispered in the darkness, to whoever was listening.

I wasn't surprised when, on closing the curtains, I saw a pod of seals coming to gather beneath our window. *You are staying*, their round black eyes said to me.

18

Paper and seaweed

Catriona

I was getting ready for bed when I heard a noise just outside my door. I thought maybe it was the neighbour's cat,
coming to claim food and shelter while its owners were
away somewhere. I opened the door just a notch – I was
in my pyjamas already – but there was no cat. No cat,
but something on my doorstep: a parcel wrapped in
brown paper, held together with fishing line and decorated with shells. My heart stopped. Who else but Sorren
could have left me something like that? It seemed to have
come straight out of the sea.

I unwrapped it quickly. Inside there was a book called
Making Jewellery, and a box of tiny pearlescent beads.

I was overjoyed, if a bit surprised. How did he know I
wanted to get into jewellery-making? Then I remembered that he'd been there when I'd mentioned it to
Shuna at the school. It felt strange, though – why had he
not just given it to me? Why go about it in such an elab-
orate way?

Was he trying to tell me something?

I sat at the window like I always did when I wanted to

think, nursing yet another cup of tea and absent-mindedly making a bracelet with purple and white beads. If a doctor opened me up, I thought, he'd find that my insides were made of tea. I sipped the warm, sugary liquid and let my thoughts flow, the book and the beads on my lap.

Through the years, even when I was a young girl, Sorren had given me direction – he had *been* my direction. He had been the strong, protective presence in my life who kept me on course; the reason behind nearly everything I'd done since the age of ten. The small decisions as a child and a teenager were shaped by thoughts of him. Going to the ice cream van – would I see him around? Getting my hair cut – would he like it shorter? Accepting an invitation to a party – would he be there? And then, as a young adult, came the big decisions. What course at university would allow me to see him more, would allow me to stay nearby? What hobby could I take up to spend time with him, what could I do to impress him, make him say *well done, Caty*? How could I gain his approval?

My life revolved around him – it was always Sorren and Caty. And it could never be any different.

I had to tell him about my feelings once and for all, I thought as I ran my fingers over the cover of the book he'd given me. As much as it terrified me, I had to.

Maybe this would be the time that he *saw*. The time he understood that all along, while he struggled and toiled, what he'd needed and wanted had always been there.

Maybe.

There was another possibility, though. That I would lose him forever.

But I wouldn't think about that, I wouldn't think about that at all. I'd look for the right time to speak to him, a time just for us.

I would let love guide me.

19

Dolphins

Anna

Sorren was sitting on a stool at the bar, a cup of coffee in front of him. As soon as I saw him, my mouth stretched in a smile. I'd just slipped into jeans and trainers after my shower and left my hair to dry, and I had no make-up on. Simply myself, without embellishment, without disguises. The way I wanted to be.

'Good morning,' I said softly, and 'Sorren!' exclaimed Ava, running to him.

'Hello,' he replied, and he couldn't hide the tenderness in his eyes as he looked at me. 'I sort of made a plan for today. I was thinking of taking you out on my boat.'

'On the *sea*?' Ava said.

'Well that's where boats usually go,' he laughed. 'Unless you want to just sit in it on the beach and have a chat . . .'

'Are you not busy at the restaurant?'

'They'll manage without me for a few hours,' he replied brightly.

'Are you sure?' I said, but it was a formality, because I hoped he would ignore my protestations. I *really*, really wanted to go. It would be wonderful to sail in the aqua world around Seal again.

'Yes, please! Can we?' Ava pleaded, speaking my mind for me.

'Well, it's Monday, and what I usually do on a Monday is take little people out on my boat to look for seals. Every single week,' Sorren said seriously.

'Really?' Ava replied with a delighted smile – she knew he was joking, but she wanted the joke to continue.

'Really. I also get them to catch crabs for me, for the restaurant.'

'Eeeeeew, crabs!' Ava said.

'I bet the crabs say eeeeeew, wee girls! That's before they end up in the pot.'

'Okay then,' I said, excited. 'We'd love to!'

'Super. Let's go play grab-a-crab,' he said, and Ava's laugh resounded once more, making little waves of happiness ripple in my heart.

'I've been on a boat a million times,' she whispered to me as we made our way to the beach.

'No you haven't. You've only been on . . . Oh.'

She said nothing more, and I didn't ask.

The whole world was sea, sky and wind – nothing else beneath, above or around me. I sat with my yellow life jacket on, eyes half closed against the strong gusts of wind, and let the beauty of the seascape sink into me as the boat danced gently over the waves.

'It's quite breezy today,' Sorren said. I smiled inwardly.

Breezy? This was certainly not a breeze! It was most definitely wind. I guessed the islanders were used to the gales coming from the Atlantic. 'I love the wind. The stronger the better,' he said loudly, to be heard over the noise. 'In Italy, the air is almost always still. I lived there for a while . . .'

'Yes, I know.'

He laughed. 'Something else my mum told you?'

His face was the face of someone who spent a lot of time outside – tanned, slightly weather-beaten, a sense of vitality shining from his eyes. The face of someone who would not be caged in. Who would not be tamed.

'Afraid so! I'd love to go to Italy.'

'You should, it's wonderful. I trained there. As a chef. But then I came back to the island. I didn't want to leave . . .' he said, and gestured towards Ava, who was leaning against the ridge of the boat, her chin on her arms. I wondered why he had indicated my daughter. Why had he not gestured towards the island itself, small and green on the horizon?

Maybe because he too had picked up on how Ava was feeling so at home. How she felt the same way as him.

Anyway, I noticed how he'd neglected to mention his Italian girlfriend.

'Oh look!' I called. A pod of seals were resting on a rock, their big, lucid black eyes fixed on the boat as we passed.

'That's called Inis Roan: the Island of the Seals. Though it's not much bigger than a rock.'

'I remember that,' Ava said suddenly.

Silence.

'Have you been here before?' Sorren said, serious all of a sudden.

'I lived here,' said Ava, and my eyes met Sorren's.

'We must have seen it on the way in,' I speculated.

'You couldn't have. Oban is on the other side.'

'We went on a mini cruise. Maybe . . .'

'Don does the mini cruises. He never goes this far from the shore, so no. You couldn't have seen Inis Roan then. Unless he changed itinerary, but I doubt it.'

Right. Our eyes met once again with the weight of a million things unspoken. Oh, the relief of sharing this burden with someone. The mysteries that dotted my days seemed a little less daunting somehow.

After that conversation I simply sat, squinting in the wind, taking it all in. Ava and Sorren were chatting, pointing things out to each other, sometimes laughing. He told her about fishing and about island life, and she listened solemnly. Ava was a little sponge, eager to learn new things, and Sorren seemed to know how to speak to her.

A ray of sun pierced the clouds above the boat, and I closed my eyes to soak it in. At the sound of Ava's squeals, I opened them again.

'Look, Mummy, look!'

I followed her pointed finger. At first all I could see was the expanse of the sea. Then some silvery shapes detached themselves and rose from the waves – dolphins! They followed us for a while, jumping and playing, and Ava and I stood side by side, smiling and laughing, filled with happiness, lost in the moment.

With one last leap that seemed like a goodbye, the dolphins left us and disappeared.

'This place is *wonderful*,' I said, and sighed.

Sorren turned around, his eyes shining blue and clear in the sunshine. 'It is, isn't it? When I'm out at sea, I'm happy. I think I was made to be on a boat more than I was made to be on land.' And he looked it. His eyes reflected the colour of the sea, bright blue in the sunshine, grey when the sky was covered, changing in tune with his words and his feelings. 'Look! Some more friends. The seals love Ava,' he said, and I followed his gaze to a pod – there must have been three or four of them – that was swimming alongside the boat. Ava began waving at them, laughing and calling. At that moment, she was the embodiment of joy.

'Seals, dolphins, they've all come out to see you, Beanie,' Sorren said, and Ava gave him a beaming smile. She came to sit beside him, and laid her little head on his shoulder. I was surprised. It was such an intimate gesture. Sorren slipped an arm around her waist and they sat like that for a long time, Ava nestled into him. As strange as it was to my eyes, I couldn't have separated them – they seemed to fit perfectly with each other.

'Listen, I was thinking. The sky is so clear today. Maybe I can come and get you after I finish at the restaurant, and we can look at the stars . . .' Sorren and I were saying goodbye at the back door, standing a bit closer to each other than two friends would have. There was something in his eyes; something had changed since we'd fought, since I'd told him about Ava's memories.

Like a little door had opened in his heart and in his mind.

Like he was inviting me in, and it was up to me to accept or refuse the invitation.

I held my hair away from my face in the rising wind. 'You mean in the middle of the night?'

'Well, yes.'

'Like naughty teenagers?'

'Exactly,' he shrugged.

'Sold,' I said with a smile.

I watched him walk away, his stride long and fast, in the summer evening. I had no idea where Sorren and I stood; I had no idea what was going to happen next, and maybe it had to be that way. Maybe I couldn't control everything, and life would decide for me.

Maybe I'd been too focused on looking for reasons, for explanations, like everything had to have a name, a meaning, a purpose, when all we really had to do was live our lives to the full and care for each other the best we could.

After all, Ava and I were already living in suspended reality, far away from home, our time on Seal punctuated by Ava's strange memories and recollections. What was one more uncertainty, one more unsigned road?

I couldn't wait for nightfall. I wanted to be with Sorren.

I wanted to stand beside him and look at the cold, cold light of a million stars.

Later on, I took the little yellow notebook out of my backpack, and sat on the bed.

I doodled for a while as I collected my thoughts. I drew a tiny rock with not-so-artistic seals on top. I wrapped the words like a ring around the drawing.

She said she'd been on a boat a million times.

She knew about the Island of the Seals.

All of a sudden, I felt something touch my head lightly, sweetly. I jumped off the bed, smoothing down my hair. There was something hard under my fingers. I lifted a strand of hair and realised it had been braided, the braid now falling apart in my hand. My heart was pounding in my chest, and I caught my wide-eyed reflection in the mirror hanging on the opposite wall.

I laughed to myself. Silly me. I undid the braid and sat back on the bed. Why was I making such a big deal of my hair getting tangled?

Suddenly the scent of the sea was strong in the room. My eyes went to the window, but it was closed. Maybe the salty wind had a way of seeping in; maybe it just seeped everywhere on Seal.

I watched Ava sleeping, undisturbed, her chest rising and falling quietly, peacefully. I laid the notebook and all the mysteries it contained on my bedside table, beside

Sorren's shell, and slipped into bed with my daughter, a sense of perfect peace enveloping me as I held Ava's warm little body close to mine.

And then I heard my phone beeping in my handbag.

I don't know what made me get up and check instead of waiting until the morning. Maybe I thought it might be Sorren.

But it wasn't.

Anna, I hope you and Ava are well, things okay with me, miss you terribly, everything feels wrong. Please reply.

Toby. It was like all the air had been sucked out of my lungs, out of the room. For a moment I felt so helpless, so dismayed that I could have burst into tears. But I didn't.

I didn't reply. I deleted the message and tried to delete it from my mind, too.

We were safe, on Seal. Toby couldn't reach us, not even with his words; he could not destroy the peace I was slowly building for my daughter and me.

20

Cold love

Catriona

There was a blanket of ominous cloud over Seal, depositing torrential rain on us. Sooner or later, the clouds would be swept away by the Atlantic winds, and the beaches would be clear and sunny again, but meanwhile the restaurant was full of tourists wanting shelter from the rain, and we hadn't stopped for a second. As I ran between the floor and the kitchen, my hands full of plates, I managed to catch Sorren alone.

'Hey,' I said with a smile. 'I was thinking, maybe you could come up to my house later on. A drink and a chat, you know. Like old times. We should finish here . . . at some point,' I said, eyeing another group of tourists coming through the door, soaking wet.

'Not so old. I came up last week,' he laughed. In spite of the din in the overflowing restaurant, when he spoke it felt like the place was in complete silence. It was like his voice had a special frequency that was natural for me to hear over anything else. 'Sorry, I can't, tonight.'

'Oh.' I couldn't help wondering what he had planned.

It would be too late to go for a drink with the lads. Maybe he was going to Fraser's house? I didn't want to ask.

'And thank you—' I began, meaning to mention the book he'd left me, but Tatiana's voice interrupted me.

'Catriona! Service!'

I looked in the direction of the kitchen and saw Fraser standing there, watching Sorren and me. Our eyes met for a moment, and then he turned away.

Of course, I ended up bringing the wrong dishes to the wrong people, and giving out the wrong change.

'You okay? You seem a bit distracted,' Tatiana said while scooping some tablet ice cream into white bowls.

'Aye, I'm fine. Honestly, I'm okay.'

'Is it because of Anna and Sorren?' My blood went cold. Tatiana was the only person on the island I had confided in.

'So you've noticed too . . .' I whispered, looking down. Tatiana brought her finger to her lips and disappeared through the door with three bowls of ice cream balanced in her hands. She was back within a minute.

'You are so *blind*,' she hissed.

'What do you mean?'

She gestured towards the window. I followed her gaze and saw Fraser breaking up some cardboard boxes for recycling.

I laughed. 'Fraser? The guy can't stand me. He never even speaks to me!'

'Well he watches you. Every time I'm around you, he's there. Have you not noticed?'

'I think you're completely off the mark,' I dismissed her.

'Maybe. But Anna is going to Sorren's house tonight . . .'

Her words were like a blade in my heart. So that was what he had planned. I walked away, my stomach in a knot, pretending to be so busy I couldn't exchange another word.

The rest of the evening passed in a haze, until finally Sorren and I were alone, closing up, with Fraser in the back courtyard, doing the last few errands.

There was just us in the kitchen, and the silent black world outside. I took a deep breath.

'Sorren . . .'

'Mmmm?' he said, piling up plates in a way that told me how tired he was. Then he looked at me, and his face changed. 'Hey . . . you're pale. And you're shaking!' he said. He put a plate down and held my hands, then caressed my face, tucking a tendril of hair behind my ear. 'What's wrong? Are you not feeling well? Want me to get the car and give you a lift home?'

'No, no. I'm okay. Just . . . tired. I wanted to thank you. It really was a sweet thought.'

'What do you mean?'

'The book. And the beads.'

'I don't know what you're talking about, Caty . . .'

'The present on my doorstep.'

'It wasn't me.'

'Ach, Sorren, come on . . .'

'Really, it wasn't. You must have a secret admirer.' He smiled. 'Are you sure you don't want a lift home?'

'No. No thanks. Anyway, you're busy tonight. You don't want to keep Anna waiting,' I said, and for the second time that day, I walked away from the conversation, sick with sadness.

The walk home from Star was always spectacular, but that night I was simply blind to its beauty, and deaf to the mighty noise of the waves breaking against the shore. Everything I had found out that night was swirling in my mind.

The gift. It wasn't from Sorren.

Sorren and Anna. It really was happening.

I was losing him . . . if you can lose someone who's never been yours in the first place.

Fraser

I heard you and Sorren talking. I can't believe you thought it was Sorren who'd given you those presents. In my mind, I walked up to you and said: *It was me. I left the book and the beads.*

And I left them to make you happy. Because I listen to what you say, though I don't speak much myself.

Because I see *you*. I see you for who you are.

Because Sorren is one of the kindest, most generous people I know, and my best friend, and I'd never say a word against him; but he doesn't see you, he doesn't listen to you. He sees the little girl you used to be, and not the woman you are.

I always felt removed from everyone. Far away from everyone and everything.

Only the sky and the land know who I am.

All I wanted to do was to be in nature, mostly by myself. I don't really know how, but I found myself writing books about what I'd learned, and earning a lot of money, and having people wanting to take my picture. One thing led to another, and I was in front of the cameras. It took me a week to realise that working on TV wasn't for me; I positively hated it. By then it was too late. I'd signed a contract, and I didn't want to let all those people down.

Until I couldn't take it any more.

I didn't even stay long enough to sell the house in Edinburgh, tie up loose ends, sort out things with work. I just left. I drove to Oban and I took the first ferry. I dropped my mobile phone into the sea. All I had with me were two bags, one with clothes, the other with my outdoors equipment, and my 4x4. I remember I drove off the ferry and parked as close as I could to the sea, and then went for a walk on the beach. It was a cold early spring day, but I had taken every layer off, leaving only a T-shirt – I needed to feel the air on me, the wind on my skin. I needed the wind to blow it all away: the wrong turns, the decisions that seemed inevitable, the gazes of people on me, their eyes searching for someone to admire, something lacking from their lives, someone to worship and then tear down.

On impulse, I went for a swim. The water was freezing and it took my breath away, but I liked it that way. When I came out of the sea, I was so cold that my skin was burning.

Reborn.

And that's when I saw you.

I stood there after having shed everything, freezing cold and shivering, with nothing to my name but a car and a tent and a few clothes, and you appeared, you rose from the land like a Celtic goddess. Your red-blonde hair flew in the wind, your step was slow and strong, your body tall and slender. You passed me without seeing me, as I sat on the rocks and watched you walk on the wet sand, keeping a blue scarf closed at your throat, like a stray wave of the sea you had trapped and woven around your neck.

I fell in love with you that day.

21

The Himiko cloud

Anna

Hours trickled by as I sat at the window, looking into the night and waiting for the moment Sorren and I would be alone at last. I was shaky after Toby's text, and I wanted to be with Sorren even more. My phone beeped again.

You're not replying. Have you moved on already? That was fast. Things not working out for me. I miss you and Ava. Talk to me, Anna.

I switched it off.

No more.

No more heartache.

My heart beat in double time when Sorren appeared behind the street lamp in front of our window. Silently, after one last look at Ava asleep in her bed – a pang of guilt, followed by a need too strong to be ignored – I slipped downstairs and stepped out into the night.

A few murmured words, hands that found each other. The sky was enormous and endless, and the darkness nearly pristine but for little lights spread here and there and the round white moon above us. I felt like I should dissolve in the blackness around me, dissolve into the sea, and I held on to Sorren's hand to keep me whole. In London, nature was kept well in check – it sneaked its way in between buildings and along pavements, and even in the parks, the grass and trees were daily cleaned and tamed and watched. But here it was different. The sea and sky ruled the rhythm of life, and you could breathe free in their embrace – but when they weighed on you with all their might and power, you were reminded of how fragile, how small we all are in the face of the forces of nature.

On Seal, sometimes the night was just too big to bear.

As we walked in the darkness, no sounds around but the ebbing and flowing of the sea, I could feel on my skin the dreams of the whole of the island. The moon followed us all the way to Sorren's home, as if waiting to see what would happen there.

Sorren's garden was a patch of land that ended where the beach began. He lived as close to the sea as he could, short of being on a boat. I was aware of the warmth of his body as he leaned over my shoulders, enfolded in the jumper he'd given me against the cold of the night, while I looked into the telescope. The moon seemed so bright, so close – it felt like I could almost touch it.

'Hello, moon,' I said, smiling in delight.

'Can you see why I love astronomy? Isn't that incredible?' he said, his soft voice in my ear as he wrapped an arm around my waist. I was filled with wonder. I couldn't believe I could see the moon so clearly, almost as if I could hold it in my hand.

'But it's not smooth! I always imagined it like a big round jewel. An opal.'

'It's not smooth at all, no. Asteroids hit the moon all the time and leave craters on it. It's because she has no atmosphere to protect her,' Sorren explained.

'She?'

'Sorry?'

'You called the moon "she".'

He laughed. 'Of course. She's definitely a female. Like Venus. I also think of Neptune as female, actually, while Mars and Pluto are most definitely male. Saturn is a cranky old man.' It was my turn to laugh. 'You know,' he spoke again, this time quite solemnly, even dreamily, 'a while ago, scientists discovered something called the Himiko cloud. It's a newborn galaxy . . . not even that . . . It's a galaxy in the process of being born. Inside it there might be a solar system forming, constellations, who knows . . . All in potential. All swirling in this cloud that is eight hundred million years old.'

'That's amazing . . . Like a baby galaxy.'

'Like a galaxy that has just been conceived. All there, waiting to happen.'

I smiled at the passion in his words. 'You should have become an astronomer instead of a chef.'

'I was useless at maths. And I loved food too much to do anything else. What about you? Do you like your job?'

'I love my job. I started out as a hospital assistant, you know, cleaning, fetching stuff for the nurses. I watched the doctors and nurses work and I was in awe of what they could do, of the power in their hands. Look after people, make them better . . . that's what I wanted to do too. So I went back to school, and I became a nurse. That was only last year.'

'Congratulations. You must be so proud of yourself.'

'I don't really have much time to think about it. I'm too busy,' I laughed. 'With Ava and my shifts, you know, I just keep going. But yes, I suppose I am proud.'

'Well I'm proud of you too,' he said in his calm, tender voice.

For a second, time stopped.

Who had ever said they were proud of me?

Nobody, I think.

Not my mum, for sure. Not Toby.

I had to get to twenty-six years of age before someone told me they were proud of me.

'You like looking after people, Anna. But who looks after you?' Sorren said, and he tucked a tendril of hair behind my ear. Our bodies danced an awkward dance, torn between forcing themselves to stay apart, and being drawn to each other.

Wanting to touch.

Finally he looked into my eyes, and his expression, his posture, everything had changed; there was no awkwardness, no shyness left in him. He wrapped his arms around my waist and kissed me, a strong, possessive kiss that was far away from his soft, gentle ways. Our eyes met again, and his were dark and burning. A long shiver travelled down my spine, but it wasn't fear. It was desire.

And then he smiled, and there was something shy in his smile. He was himself again – the Sorren I knew.

'I . . . I need to go. I need to get back to Ava.'

'Yes,' he said. My eyes widened. I was a bit piqued. Would he not try and convince me to stay? He stroked my cheek softly, but did not move.

For what seemed like forever, I stood in the island night, the wind on my face, bathed in the white light of the moon. I was caught in an instant that was as clear as crystal and yet nebulous like a primordial galaxy. Like the Himiko cloud, and all the worlds that could be born from it.

The air was moist, charged with infinitesimal particles of salt water, and in the distance the sea ebbed and flowed, as if it were making love to the land.

You know those moments when your life has come to a crossroads and you can feel it? It was like the sea and the wind were talking to me, under the clear starry sky. Like they were calling my name, beckoning me to a place I didn't know, to a place that was still uncharted.

Somewhere you can't go alone.

Sorren's hand slipped into mine as we exchanged a single look, and wordlessly we made our way inside. We walked in unison, our steps in harmony, in silent togetherness.

I don't know how we got upstairs and into Sorren's bed, but it felt inevitable, the natural conclusion of a magical night. If I had to tell you how it happened, if I had to describe moment by moment how his arms came around me, and mine around him, just as willing – the way we came to each other like a compass needle can't help going north – I don't think I could.

And then he was inside me, making me feel every moment, deeper and deeper, until we were one. I wanted him to stay there. I wanted him with me forever, and with him I wanted Seal, the sky and the salty wind, and the waves breaking one after another within me, making all my sadness and fears dissolve, until I was home again.

Sorren

We woke up entangled, warm from each other's bodies in spite of the chilly night. It was like I had woken from a dream – what had happened was so unbelievable, so amazing. But no. There she was, the sweet scent of sugar and rain seeping off her skin as she slept. She was all curled up, like a baby – her white back, her small hands, the soft curve of her breasts beneath her, the dark shadow of her hair on the pillow. I placed a dozen feather-light kisses on her cheek to wake her up. Her skin was milky white and dotted with freckles, and her hair so black, like a crow's wing.

She opened her eyes – the colour of amber, the colour of tea – and blinked over and over again, like she didn't believe where she was.

'Ava!' was the first thing she said, sitting up in alarm. 'I need to get back!'

'Shhhh, it's okay. It's only half three in the morning.'

'But it's light!' she said, stretching her lovely body in a way that made my heart melt.

'We're in Scotland, remember? Long, long days and short nights.' I went to take her in my arms, but she pushed me away gently.

'Sorren, I need to go back. If Ava wakes up and doesn't find me . . .'

'Of course. Let's go. I'll make you coffee and—'

'No . . . don't get up yet.'

The curtains were open, and I could see the night sky, huge and windswept, and the calm sea murmuring sweetly in the distance. Everything was perfect. I pulled her to me once more, and this time she surrendered. She nestled into me, and as I held her tight, stroking her hair slowly, I realised she was shaking a little.

'Are you okay, my love?'

'I'm fine . . . sorry. Just . . . Oh, I can't put it into words. I never want this moment to end,' she said into my chest. Her bare skin was so warm against mine. How cold my bed had been without her. How long had I slept in a lonely bed.

But not any more.

'Let's just pretend that the way we are now is forever. That nothing else is happening,' she said.

Yes, I thought. Like there was just us left in the world, and all we had to do was be close to each other, and never part again.

22

Turning wheel

Anna

I was exhausted, but every fibre of my being was contented. Pacified.

Being with Sorren had been a time of pure happiness. It reminded me of those first days after Ava was born, when every time I looked at her, liquid joy ran through my veins.

I slipped inside the inn, vaguely embarrassed. Hopefully Shuna wouldn't have noticed that I hadn't come back until dawn. Ava was asleep, curled up under the duvet, her nightlight plugged in. I tried to sleep a little, but it was impossible. I was too full of Sorren, full of what had happened – the enormity of it all. I lay there dreaming, dozing, silently recalling moments too sweet, too secret to talk about. Until finally the island awoke, the steps of the guests loud on the stairs. Jane's voice resounded in the street below as she spoke to her boyfriend on the phone. Soon the first ferry moored at the pier, sounding its horn.

I let myself stand at the window for a moment, contemplating the grey slate that sea and sky had become as a soft mist rolled in. I didn't even think it was possible for a place with such changeable weather to exist. One day it was high summer, the next autumnal mist. The sky opened and closed like an accordion, clear one moment, steely the next, with a million variations in between. I could have looked at it forever, reflected in the sea in its endless manifestations. The tropical green of a southern island, the grey of the north; angry or serene or dancing under the wind.

I sighed, the beauty of the island seeping into me, the memory of Sorren's hands on my skin. Sorren and Seal were melting into one, love and beauty and home enfolding me in a sweet embrace.

I was happy.

Was it possible, to be happy?

Ava began to stretch and yawn, her eyes still closed, and I sat on her bed to give her a cuddle.

'Hello, sleepyhead,' I said, nuzzling her neck, her hair. I stroked her soft face, still dazed with sleep. 'I was thinking. Why don't we go to the Design Gallery for breakfast? Maybe a hot chocolate?'

'Yes! And a doughnut!'

'And a doughnut,' I said with a smile. Hot chocolate and a doughnut – not exactly the breakfast of champions, but hey, every once in a while it was good to just loosen up. Not to be wise or sensible at all.

While Ava was getting dressed, I switched on my phone, hoping Sorren would get in touch. I couldn't wait to hear his voice. As soon as the screen lit up, the phone began to ring. It was a London number; my heart sank as I realised it was Toby's mother. I pressed the red button and tried to forget all about it.

But guilt would not leave me alone. I never particularly enjoyed speaking to Gillian, but she wasn't in the best of health, and her only son didn't seem that concerned, so I kept an eye on her. I felt it was my duty, though she never seemed to get in touch with us, or want to see Ava much. Still, she was an elderly lady and she was alone.

The phone began to ring again.

Wait a minute – what if it was Toby? What if Toby was at his mother's and calling me from the landline? My heart began to pound.

If it *was* Toby, I had to know.

Pressing that green button was like lifting a heavy box – exhausting. My mouth was dry, the tingle of panic in my hands.

'Hello?'

A moment's pause, a moment that lasted forever.

'Hello, Anna?'

I breathed again. It was Gillian.

'Have you heard from Toby?' she asked after we had exchanged a few formalities.

'Not really.' I didn't know why, but I didn't want to tell her about the texts. 'You?'

'Yes. Oh yes. He's . . . fine.'

There was something in her voice, a strange note I couldn't put my finger on.

'Good,' I replied. I didn't want to talk about him; I didn't want to think about him. Why had she chosen today to call me? It was like being woken from a sweet dream with a slap in the face.

'Well, I'm glad you're okay. Take care,' I said quickly.

'Anna . . .' she began, but I pressed the red button before she could add anything. I wasn't in the mood for a conversation about Toby.

'Come on, baby. Hot chocolate awaits us,' I said, but my smile was slightly shakier than it would have been five minutes earlier.

I searched Shuna's face. There was a slight smile dancing on her lips, but she didn't say anything. I wondered if she knew. I blushed anyway – I couldn't help it.

'Shuna, we're going to the Design Gallery for breakfast. Would you like to come with us?' I was actually hoping she'd say no. I was sure that what had happened the night before was written all over my face.

'Thanks, Anna, but I'm waiting for a delivery,' Shuna said, glancing at her watch. 'Wrap up well, though, it's a damp day.'

Her maternal comments always warmed my heart. I followed her advice and wore my jacket and scarf, and buttoned Ava into her red coat. Then we stepped out holding hands, and slowly walked onto the pier to look at the sea. A tiny pod of seals – no more than three or four – sat lazily on the rocks, their black eyes bright in the murk. It was just the time when the first ferry came in from

Oban, and groups of tourists were taking shape as they emerged from the fog and walked towards us.

'Ava, let's go. You can't see where the pier ends and the sea begins,' I said, but she ignored me. She was standing immobile, one arm at her side, the other entwined with mine.

'Daddy,' she whispered, so low I barely heard her.

'What? What do you mean?'

'Daddy has come off the boat.'

'Don't be silly . . .' I began, but she was raising a hand to point at someone. Her face was blank, like she was in shock, like she couldn't believe her eyes. I followed her gaze to a figure who had just stepped off the ferry and was moving towards us. I was ready to look away, to tell Ava it was just a trick of the eye and move on to the café, where we would sit and sip our hot chocolate and everything would be as it was before.

But something in the way the figure walked, something in the way he moved . . . the shape of his body . . . I couldn't look away. My heart began to beat too hard again, and I felt my knees giving way.

I took Ava's arm again, as if to protect her. 'It's the fog, Ava,' I said. 'We can't see properly.' It couldn't be Toby.

It just couldn't be.

'It's Daddy,' she repeated.

I blinked, trying to see better.

The figure stopped. I could see his face now.

He looked at us like he too couldn't believe his eyes.

I knew those big, childish blue eyes. I knew that

stubble. I knew that stance, leaning forward a little, like he was ready for the next adventure. He wasn't wearing a jacket, just a shirt, and he was pale with the cold. How typical. His motto: *Always unprepared.*

There, standing among the tourists, coming to break into my little paradise of sea and sky, was the man who had betrayed us over and over again. And already my daughter had freed herself from my grasp and was running into his arms.

23

What a family is

Anna

'Ava, Mum and Dad need to talk for a bit, okay?' I said. I figured I was probably as white as a sheet – I certainly felt it. We were back at the Seal Inn, and Shuna and Hamish were with us. It was all so surreal, I felt like I was watching it happen to someone else.

Toby was on Seal.

Toby was here.

In the space of a few minutes, my whole world had been turned upside down. Again.

'Go on, sweetheart, just a little while, and then you and I can spend all the time together you want,' Toby said, and his eyes were shining with real affection. He'd left his daughter for seven months, yet it was plain to see that he loved her. In that irresponsible, toxic way I knew all about.

But Ava had subtly changed towards him. Yes, she had thrown herself into his arms, and yes, her hand was in his, but there was a wariness, a slight detachment on her part. Like a puppy who'd been hit once and was now watching her step.

Shuna went to disentangle Ava's hand from Toby's.

'You come with me, darling. Why don't we go and take a cake to Lady Kilpatrick like we planned? I'm sure Hamish can hold the fort here . . .'

Hamish gave her an imperceptible nod. I was so embarrassed to have brought all this to their doorstep; that Toby and I should be having such a conversation in their home.

'Can I not stay with Daddy?' Ava said, and her words were like a knife in my side.

'In a wee while,' Shuna said. 'Just give your parents a bit of time now . . .' She gently led Ava towards the kitchen to get the cake.

'Put your hood up when you go out!' I called after her – the weather was so changeable today, I was worried it would start pouring again any moment. Or maybe it wasn't the rain I was worried about; maybe I just wanted to keep Ava with me, and not be alone in a room with this man who had hurt us so much.

But I had to let her go. I had to speak to Toby alone.

We closed the door to keep the outside world out, and our own disaster in. Toby stood in front of the fireplace, his eyes lowered, like a child who had been caught doing something naughty. Behind him on the mantelpiece was Sorren's cowrie shell.

My new life and the old one standing next to each other.

'I'm sorry, Anna . . . I'm so sorry,' he began.

'You *should* be.'

'I . . . It didn't work out for me in Australia.'

'You messed up?' I said, shrugging my shoulders. It wouldn't be the first time. I knew it was a nasty thing to say, but I was beyond caring. I couldn't be supportive of him any more.

'No. No, I didn't, actually. Everything was going really well. I was working, renting a house with a mate; I was going to find a place of my own. But then I thought, what am I doing? I can build a good life here, but Anna and Ava are on the other side of the world! It made no sense.'

'Right. You had to go all the way to Australia to realise you didn't want to be away from your daughter?'

'It wasn't like that . . .'

'How was it, then? Tell me, Toby. Tell me what went through your mind when you thought it would actually be a good idea to go and leave Ava behind. To tell her she was better off without you. Toby, she's *six years old*! You broke her heart!'

'I *did* think she was better off without me! I left because I hated myself. I couldn't give you and our daughter a proper life. I felt like a complete failure.'

'I never called you a failure, Toby, and Ava thought you were some kind of hero.'

'I know. I don't blame you. It was me. It was me feeling that way. But when I started working over there, when I saw that Australia was actually working out . . . well, I realised I could be a better man. I could be the man I've always wanted to be.'

I lowered my head, trying to steel my heart.

'I couldn't be without you and Ava,' he continued. 'All

of a sudden I could see how stupid I'd been. And I thought that maybe I could be a good partner and a good father, just like I'd always wanted, like you'd always wanted . . .'

'All I wanted was someone who would take a bit of responsibility. Hold down a job, for a start.' I was about to add something about the women, about his cruelty towards me. But I couldn't. It hurt too much, and the fact that I had put up with it hurt even more.

'I know. I know. But down in London, I was suffocated. With you and my mum being so disappointed in me all the time . . .'

'Oh, so now it's our fault?' I felt irritated again, just as I was beginning to soften. After all he'd done, he'd managed to turn the guilt onto me, and onto his mother, of all people. The woman in whose eyes he could do no wrong.

'No, of course not. It was me. I just couldn't do anything for myself, for my family. I felt a total *failure*,' he repeated.

'Stop saying that word! All I wanted was for you to be there for us. I never asked for more,' I said, and then hated myself for it. I didn't owe him an explanation, after all.

'I needed to grow up,' he said. Now that made more sense.

'What do you want from us now? Why on earth did you come looking for us up here?'

'I want to be a good partner to you and a good father to Ava.'

'Don't you think it's a bit late for that?' My hands were shaking. I clasped them together.

'I promise you—' he began, but I'd had a sudden thought.

'How did you know we were here?'

'My mum told me.'

I nodded, remembering the feeling I'd had on the phone that she was about to tell me something. How I regretted telling her where I was going.

'You could at least have *called*!'

'You never replied to my texts. And I was afraid you'd tell me not to come.'

'I would have, yes,' I said, and crossed my arms. This lovely room, the space that had felt so welcoming and serene, was suddenly suffocating me. It was like all our resentments and misunderstandings were filling it and taking the oxygen away.

'But here I am,' he said quietly.

'So I'll go back to my original question. What do you want from us?' He opened his mouth. 'And I mean *realistically*.'

'I want us to be a family again. A proper family. Go back to Australia, start a new life . . .'

'Australia!' I rubbed my forehead.

'I know, I know. But hear me out. I've changed—'

'You have no idea what you did to Ava!' I yelled, resentment dripping from every word.

His face fell. He looked like someone had just punched him, but I didn't care. He deserved it.

'I know, but—'

'No, you don't know,' I continued, forcing myself to

lower my voice. I couldn't have a shouting match in Shuna's home. 'You don't know anything, Toby. After you left, she didn't eat or speak for three days. Three days! Can you imagine how worried I was; can you imagine how upset your little girl was to do something like that?' My chest was rising and falling in a frantic rhythm as I remembered the state Ava had been in.

'I thought I was doing you a favour! I thought your life would be easier without me!'

'Mine is, but not *your daughter's*!'

Toby sat heavily on the bed and buried his face in his hands. For a moment, neither of us spoke.

'Oh God. I didn't think . . .'

'You didn't think that leaving Ava would break her the way it did?' I said quietly. For a moment, I nearly felt sorry for him. It was like he lived in a parallel universe, one where he was the main subject and the rest of us were out of focus. Like he was unable to understand what other people, even people he loved, were going through. I never thought he'd meant to actually hurt us – I always knew it was because he was disconnected from reality – but it didn't make things any better.

'I'm so sorry. I promise you it'll never happen again. I must have been mad . . . I'm so—'

'Stop talking,' I said.

'What?'

'*Stop talking.* I can't listen any more.'

'Well, if you want to dismiss me like this, the father of your daughter . . .'

268

'You're hardly in a position to take the moral high ground. I'm going for a walk, Toby,' I said, and before he could object, I was heading down the stairs and outside.

The beauty of the beach and the immense sky left me cold as I looked longingly towards Star of the Sea.

Towards Sorren.

To my immense irritation, Toby had followed me outside. Now he was walking beside me along the beach, and I cringed every time our arms brushed.

'I've met someone,' I said eventually. Yes. My Sorren. He *existed*, he was precious to me, and I would not deny him, I would not hide his existence.

Toby stopped in his tracks and turned to look at me. 'Well. That was fast.' There it was. Gone was the sweet, conciliatory tone. The Toby I knew was back, his aggression, his dismissiveness. 'Who is he? Someone at the hospital?'

I shook my head. 'He's from Seal.'

'Are you together?' His words were like a whip.

'That's none of your business.' Anger took my breath away.

'Has he been near my daughter?'

Now that was the last straw. Toby had left his daughter without a second thought, and now he had the gall to ask me a question like that.

'He has, yes. He's a good man. I trust him. And Ava trusts him too,' I replied, angry tears gathering in my eyes.

'Does he know I'm here?'

'Probably. If he doesn't know yet, he will soon.'

'Does he know you're going back to London? Well I suppose he'll find out soon enough . . .'

'What? You're just taking it for granted that I'm going, aren't you?'

'Anna,' he said, and took me by the shoulders. 'Ava binds you and me together. She always will. You can't possibly separate us.'

'I didn't separate you. You left her,' I said in a low voice. How many times should I make him face reality? How many times before he would see what he'd done, before he'd stop making me feel like I was failing Ava by keeping them apart?

'I'm here now, Anna. And I won't leave again.'

I had to go. I couldn't look into his face any longer. All of a sudden, my desire to see Sorren was stronger than any confusion I felt. I had to see him, I had to speak to him.

'I need some space, Toby,' I said then, and I turned and walked on, leaving him behind. I heard him calling my name, imploring again, then angry, but I didn't stop.

Sorren

I kept looking at my phone. It kept not beeping.

By now, Anna should have sent me at least a couple of texts to tell me what she was doing. Instead there was silence, and no reply to my own messages. I wasn't sure how, but I felt there was something in the air. When the phone finally rang, her voice sounded a bit strange, and my radar went into overdrive.

'Hey. Are you okay?'

'Not really.' In the background, I could hear the sound of the sea. She was outside somewhere.

'Darling, what's happened?'

'Toby is here.'

'What?' Toby, as in Ava's dad?

'He came to the island.' Her voice sounded cold, controlled, but with a hint of trembling in it. Like someone who felt like bursting into tears but was stopping herself with everything she had.

I was too astounded to say anything. Images of the night before flashed before my eyes – Anna and me close, holding each other, just the two of us in the wide, windy night . . .

'Sorren?'

'Yes. Yes, sorry.' I couldn't tell her how I felt. Although she could probably guess.

Inside, I was burning.

Burning with fear, burning with jealousy.

Fear because now Anna might go; jealousy because she was with the man who shared a huge bond with her – a child. And I couldn't bear it.

A knot of fear twisted my stomach as I imagined the possibility of Anna telling me they were getting back together. Yes, I could just see it in my mind's eye – a phone call, a text, or maybe her standing right in front of me and delivering the news. *I'm sorry, but he's the father of my child. He's Ava's dad, and that can never change . . .*

'Where are you? On the beach? I'll come and get you.'

'I . . . Oh God, I want to see you.'

'Sure, I'm on my way.'

'No, Sorren, not yet. I need to speak to him. I need to try and sort this out . . .'

'Sort it out? What is there to sort out? Just tell him to go.'

'It's not so easy . . .' Her voice was about to break and my heart went out to her. It was true. The guy was Ava's father, and there was nothing I could do to change that.

'Okay. Okay.' It didn't sit well with me. I wanted to see her at once. I needed to feel her close, to feel she was mine.

I stepped back inside the restaurant kitchen with a weak goodbye, and sat down for a moment to absorb the shock.

'Are you okay?' Tatiana asked. 'You are white and concerned.' She always had a creative way of saying things.

'Yes, I'm fine.'

'You're sitting down.'

'Just for a moment.'

'You never sit down when we're preparing service.'

'I . . . I think I'll go for a walk . . .'

'What? Fraser and Catriona aren't here, there's just me! You can't go for a walk!' She crossed her arms.

'Ten minutes, I promise. Just a breath of fresh air.'

My body would not let me stay away. I had to see Anna. I just had to.

''Kay,' Tatiana grumbled grudgingly.

I stepped out into the wind. The air smelled of rain and salt, and the sky was heavy and grey. It had stopped raining, but I knew it would start again any moment. Dark swollen clouds were waiting their turn, and white mist covered the sea and the shore. I closed my eyes for a moment, the cold air on my face and in my hair.

Anna's partner was here. He'd come looking for them.

A sweet, painful memory came to my mind – Anna and me alone in the windswept night, in each other's arms.

Feeling safe at last.

I couldn't let all this go. I couldn't lose her.

My mind kept going back and forth between knowing she needed time alone with him, time to sort all this out, and wanting to run up to the inn and interrupt whatever conversation they were having. I needed to be there, in the equation, in her life. In *their* lives – Ava's too.

I couldn't just step meekly aside.

I would not let her go.

Anna

I'd turned to go back to the inn when I saw a familiar figure in the distance. It was Sorren, walking down the street along the seafront. Clearly he hadn't listened when I'd said I needed time to speak to Toby . . . but I couldn't blame him.

'Sorren . . .'

'Anna, are you okay?'

'I'm fine. I'm fine, yes. I—'

'Anna!' I turned around and saw exactly what I'd feared I would see – Toby, walking towards us. He'd guessed who Sorren was.

And there we stood, the three of us, and the sea.

'Oh. You're the guy, then.' Toby was trying to sound tough, but I could hear the insecurity in his tone. I knew him too well.

'I am *the guy*, yes. And I need to speak to you.'

'Well I don't need to speak to you,' Toby replied. 'In fact, I have nothing to say to you.'

'Sorren . . .' I whispered.

'This is between Toby and me, Anna. Stay out of it,' he said in a tone I had never heard from him before. It silenced me.

'Like I said, I have nothing—'

'Follow me,' Sorren said simply.

To my amazement, Toby did. He turned around for a moment to look at me with an expression that was trying to be reassuring, as if he were saying, 'Don't worry, I've got it covered, I'll sort this,' but actually he just looked scared.

Sorren

'So. What do you need to say to me? What's so important?' Toby said.

I *hated* him.

I hated the artful way he had gelled his hair so it stood up at an angle. I hated the way he was wearing a T-shirt and scarf like someone out of a boy band. I hated the way he spoke, an affected accent that could have been from anywhere, and was from nowhere.

'Not here. Come on,' I said, and made my way further down the beach. He followed.

'What, do you want to drown me or something?' He laughed, a high-pitched laugh that grated on my nerves. 'Well I must admit, this place is lovely. I wouldn't mind booking a cruise or something. Or finding a boat myself . . .' he wittered on.

'You'd be a fool if you went on a boat without know-ing what you were doing,' I said. I had no interest in making small talk with him.

We walked in silence for a few minutes, our feet sink-ing in the sand. Then I stopped and faced him.

'I brought you here to warn you, Toby.'

'You did? Warn me of what?'

'That if you hurt Anna or Ava again . . . I'll find you.'

Night had fallen on that dreadful day, and I was closing the restaurant. I stood in the back courtyard and watched the dark sky for a moment, herds of clouds hiding moon and stars from view. Everyone had gone and I was alone, the silence deep and complete but for the sweet murmur of the sea. It felt like I was the only person in the world.

And then I heard a noise behind me, in the kitchen –

someone was there. I walked slowly inside. My arm extended, I groped for the light switch, thinking that if this was a horror film, the lights wouldn't work. I saw a dark shape move across the room and stand silhouetted against the back door. My heart jumped all the way to my throat and I lost my bearings. I couldn't find the switch.

'Hello?' I called.

'Sorren . . .' I heard a voice say. Immediately, I relaxed. It was Caty.

'Hey, Caty, I thought you'd gone home . . . You gave me a fright!' I tried to catch my breath quickly, and my hand found the switch. In the sudden strong light I saw her beautiful face, her eyes wide like a wee girl's.

'I had. But I came back. Please, turn the light off.'

'Off? Why?'

'Please.'

'Okay.' I shrugged, and darkness swallowed us again. I heard her footsteps move towards me.

'I . . . heard about Ava's dad. That he's here. I'm sorry.' I felt her fingers finding mine.

'Yes, well . . .'

'She'll leave the island. But you and I will stay, like always . . .'

Unexpectedly she stepped closer to me, so close I could feel her sweet breath on my face. Her hands travelled up my arms and rested on my cheeks. Our eyes were nearly level, she was so tall – and then she kissed me. I'd like to say it was a surprise, but the truth is, every cell of my body had screamed at me that it was going to happen. I closed my eyes. Her lips were fresh and soft, tasting of nothing but her, nothing but Caty.

She pushed me away gently, and whispered my name. The look in her eyes was sweet and vulnerable. Then she wrapped her arms around my neck and held me close, like she wanted to feel my body near, like she'd dreamt of this moment for a long time – like she was drinking me in. My hands ended up entwined in her long golden hair.

'Caty . . .' I said, and my voice was darker, hoarser than I'd expected, than I wanted it to be.

No.

I held her for a moment, a moment sweeter than it was allowed to be – she was another sister to me. Then I disentangled myself, and took a small step backwards. I didn't want to upset her, but I couldn't give her what she wanted from me.

'Sorren . . .'

'Caty, I . . .'

'I'm sorry,' she said, and I was relieved. Of course. It had been a misunderstanding. She'd let herself get carried away.

'Don't be silly. It's okay.' I smiled.

And then, before I could stop her, she placed her lips on mine and kissed me again, slowly, deeply – a kiss full of desire, but not only that. A kiss that spoke of love. And for a moment, I could not stop. I let myself fall into her comfort, into her sweetness once again.

It was all wrong, all wrong – I remembered myself and pushed her away again, this time more firmly. I held her by the shoulders. 'Caty . . .'

She didn't say anything at first, but I saw her face shining in the gloom and I knew she was crying. I dried a tear on her cheek with my finger, and she closed her eyes briefly.

'I don't understand. Caty, please . . . I thought we were good friends . . .'

'No, you don't understand. You certainly don't. All these years . . .'

Suddenly the penny dropped.

All these years.

All these years of friendship and chats and late nights, and all the time, while I thought her a sister, Caty was in love with me.

'Catriona, I . . .'

And then every single word I had in my head disappeared, and I couldn't continue.

'*Catriona,*' she said.

'What . . . what do you mean?'

'You called me Catriona. Not Caty. It's the first time since we were . . . I don't know, in primary school?'

'I don't know what to say. I didn't realise . . .'

'I know.'

'I thought we were good friends . . .' I repeated lamely. I knew that nothing I said now would sort things out. Nothing could make things all right again.

Caty laughed bitterly. It was strange to hear something

like that from her, eternally cheerful and generous as she was.

'I thought one day you'd change your mind,' she said.

I took her by the hand. I wanted to keep her with me, talk it all out – the way we did, the way Caty and Sorren had done since forever – but she freed herself and put her hands up. 'Please, Sorren. Let me go. Let me go now. I'll come round.'

'Caty . . .'

'I'm in love with you! Okay? Do you understand it now, do you see it? Now that I've spelled it out? I am in love with you,' she finished softly, sweetly. Just like that. Without hesitation. She was laying herself open for me, vulnerable and defenceless. Caty, my good friend, the beautiful woman whose blue eyes and red-gold hair had turned so many heads.

'I'm sorry,' was all I could say. I couldn't find any other words.

She looked at me, her eyes wide, and at that moment, I hated myself. I hated myself for hurting her, and because it would have been so perfect. Caty, who loved this island just as much as I did. Waking up every morning to a tender touch, falling asleep in her arms. Letting her hair fall on me, silky on my skin. She knew me so well, she knew where I ended and began. She was already part of my family.

It would have been perfect, if I loved her.

But I didn't.

And the truth shouted at me louder than ever, now

that I was forced to look it in the eye. The words I hadn't dared speak for a long time, out of fear, cowardice, some sort of laziness of the heart, which longed to stay calm and sheltered and not to beat too hard any more.

Truth was calling.

'Caty, I'm so sorry.' I shrugged, not caring if the words I was about to say sounded childish, or straight out of a romantic novel. How raw, how infinitely simple feelings were when they were put into words. 'I'm in love with Anna. Whether she stays or goes.'

A pause. A heartbeat, while her face crumpled and something inside me broke for her.

'I don't want to lose you . . .' I said.

'I know. But for once, Sorren, for once it isn't about what *you* want.' And she turned and walked out, out of that bittersweet moment and into the night.

There was silence for a second, like everything had stood still to witness what had just happened. And then the noise of the rain tapping on the roof and windows, a gust of wind rattling the door. I wanted to run after her, to bring her back into the warm, but I knew that if I kept her hope going, if I didn't extinguish it now, I would hurt her even more.

As I stepped out into the rain – the kind of drizzle that soaks you from all sides – my mind returned to Anna, like a magnet goes to steel again and again.

Anna, Anna, said the waves breaking on the shore, shattering hope.

24

Watch over me

Catriona

I made my way to the beach, my tears mixing with the rain. The wind was freezing, but I didn't care. I wanted to feel its harshness; I wanted my body to hurt like my soul was hurting. I sat with my back against some rocks, a small ledge above me to protect me from the rain, gazing at the black expanse of the sea.

All that I knew.

This place, this island, loving Sorren was all that I knew.

Would it ever be possible to go away from here? To leave this island behind, to leave Sorren behind, to be free of this love that brought me nothing but grief?

For the first time in a long time, I let my tears flow freely – only the sea was there to listen to my sobs, so I had no shame, no restraint. All my dreams had been dashed. There was nothing left to hope for. I'd waited so long to tell Sorren about my feelings, and now I knew why: I'd been afraid of his answer. All along, I'd known in the depths of my soul that this was how he felt.

I cried and cried, my face in my hands. And then finally my sobs abated, and a strange calm descended on me. Even the wind and rain subsided a little, and the angry waves diminished. I sat in silence, shivering, my arms around myself.

To live your life in the shadow of one person, and one person only.

To love him more than you love yourself.

To let all your decisions, all your choices, be influenced by what he'd think, where he'd be, what he'd do.

And then to be left without a compass.

It was a cloudy night, and hardly any stars shone above my head. I could see the lights of Eilean in the distance, and on my left, those of Roan. They were so small, lost in a sea of black. The only light in the sky was a bright white moon, frayed clouds spindling in front of it. I was cold in my thin jumper, wet as I was, but I couldn't bring myself to go home, to face reality. To face life, the day after—

'Catriona,' said a voice behind me in the darkness. I jumped up, my breathing ragged. For a second I was so terrified I couldn't speak. A beam of torchlight broke the darkness.

'Sorry. I didn't mean to startle you.'

'Fraser!' I was trembling all over, from fright and cold. 'You . . . you . . . creep up on me on a beach in the middle of the night, and you don't mean to startle me!'

'I didn't *creep*! I walked; you just didn't hear me.'

'You're like a cat!'

'Yes, I've been told that before. I didn't know who it was, I couldn't call your name.' He opened his hands. 'What are you doing out here so late?'

Instinctively I dried my face with my hand. Would he be able to see by the light of his torch that I'd been crying? 'Nothing, just having a walk.'

'You must be freezing. You're soaking . . .'

'Yes, I suppose I am. But what are *you* doing here?'

'I'm sleeping on the beach. Look, my tent's down there.' He pointed to somewhere beyond the dunes. It was too dark for me to see.

What were the chances that among all the beaches around Roan, I'd come to sit just where Fraser had pitched his tent?

'Why don't you stop here with me for a moment, Caty? I'll make you some tea . . .'

I smiled and looked down. He'd never called me Caty before. It was like he and Sorren had swapped places – Sorren stepping further away, and this man who wasn't much more than an acquaintance stepping closer. 'Can you make tea in a tent?'

He laughed. 'You've definitely never gone camping. You need something dry to wear. And I have biscuits,' he said with a small smile.

I hesitated for a moment. I could still feel the flutter of sobs in my chest, and my face was probably a sight. He would certainly ask why I was so upset. A long shiver travelled through me and gave me my answer.

'Okay then. Tea it is.' I couldn't face going home

anyway. I didn't want it to be tomorrow. The day when reality hit.

We made our way up onto the dunes among short, hardy grass, and down the other side, sand slipping in mini landslides under my feet. The sky was slowly clearing and the moon shone brighter and brighter every second.

'Sorry, it's all a bit basic,' Fraser said, taking out a camping stove and ancient chipped melamine mugs. 'Well, I wasn't expecting guests . . .' He smiled again.

'No, it's lovely.' And it was. Like a little house in the middle of nowhere, among all this beauty, all this freedom. How surreal. One minute I was sobbing my heart out – oh God, did he hear me? – the next I was having a tea party on the beach at one in the morning.

'I'll just light the fire. Here, put this on,' he said, handing me an enormous fleece that could have fitted two of me. 'You can go into the tent to change.'

The relief of dry clothes against my skin was wonderful. Seeing Fraser's nest – a sleeping bag and a tartan throw – and feeling the warmth of the fleece as I got changed made me feel suddenly exhausted. For a second I thought I would lay my head down and go to sleep, but I shook myself and went back outside.

Fraser settled me on a waterproof mat in front of a pile of sticks – a fire-in-waiting – and wrapped a blanket around my shoulders in such a gentle way that it made me want to cry again. His fingers brushed my shoulder, and I had the absurd, silly urge to hold his hand and rest my head against his chest – just for a moment, just to feel I wasn't all alone, completely abandoned. He was so strong and I felt so weak, so lost.

But I couldn't do that, of course.

He worked on the mound of driftwood until a tiny flame bloomed like a blue flower. He nourished it, bent over the wee spark, sheltering it from the wind, feeding it, blowing patiently to make it grow, his hands cupping the dry grass like they were holding a nest, until the little bonfire burnt strong and beautiful.

'Oh,' I said softly. I was so full of sadness, but a little blue flame on a dark night, created with such effort and such hard work and against all the odds, was an incredible sight.

Fraser looked at me, his head lowered, and gave me a brief, shy smile.

Shy?

Was he shy?

How come I'd never noticed before?

Finally the flames were dancing, the heat coming off them blissful in the cold night. The wind had blown the clouds away, and above us stretched a canopy of stars.

I didn't feel like talking. I'd let my hair down to keep my neck warm, and it was like a curtain around me. My fingers were wrapped blissfully around the warm cup, and the tea felt good, warming me up from the inside. Fraser was quiet too – nothing new there – sitting calmly with his long legs crossed, his gaze on the fire. The flames created golden shades in his hair and danced on his face, casting beautiful shadows. For the first time I noticed how still he could sit, how still he could *be*. Fraser was someone who never fidgeted – there was a sense of centredness about him.

'What upset you so, Catriona?' he said all of a sudden.

Oh. That question.

'Fraser . . . I don't really want to talk about it . . .'

He nodded. 'I understand.'

'I don't think you do.'

'Caty. I do.' He put down his cup, hugging his knees with his hands, like he was ready to tell a story. 'You know, when I came to this island, I had next to nothing. A tent, some camping stuff, some clothes and a car. No family, no friends, nothing that tied me to anywhere. I'd left it all behind. I started afresh. It was a new life.'

Hearing Fraser speaking at length, albeit in his trademark short sentences, was a new experience; now that I had the chance to actually hear his voice properly, I found it soft and calm, slow and deliberate, like he gave a lot of thought to everything he said. His dark blonde hair was ruffled by the wind, and his eyes were kind, truthful. To me he'd always seemed ageless, but all of a sudden I realised he was probably a wee bit younger than me.

'What happened? I mean, why did you leave everything behind . . . your old life?'

'Because it wasn't good for me. I thought I'd made choices, but I hadn't really. The choices had been made for me. Without me even noticing. I'd got somewhere, somehow . . . I didn't even know how . . . and I hated it.'

I nodded. I could understand that very well.

'You know, I think this is the first time in all the years I've known you that you've spoken more than three words to me.'

'Yes. I suppose I don't speak much. Does it bother you?'

'Well, I thought you weren't particularly interested in talking to me.'

'That's not true,' he said calmly. 'It's really not true at all.' And then, after a wee while: 'Caty . . .'

'Mmm?' My eyes were lost in the flames and their mysterious patterns.

'The book about jewellery-making. And the beads. *I* left them for you.'

I couldn't believe it. I would have never imagined . . .

'You did? But . . . why?'

He opened his mouth to say something, but then he stopped. It was like the words had frozen in his throat. At that moment, a gust of wind buffeted me, the air so cold that my lungs hurt. In spite of Fraser's blanket, I was beginning to shiver again. The disappointment of finding out about the book and the beads came back to me. Clearly I'd got it all wrong. Everything. Hot tears gathered in my eyes once more. Every step I'd taken recently . . . no, forget recently. Every step I'd taken *always* had been a mistake. I felt the tears begin to roll down my face.

I lowered my head miserably.

I'd got it all wrong, everything.

Fraser got up and moved closer, then crouched down in front of me. He raised a hand to stroke my hair, slowly, like he wanted to savour the moment. Then he took my hands and pulled me to my feet. I didn't put up any resistance – I was in a haze of tiredness and disappointment, and there was something about his kindness, his uncomplicated sweetness towards me, that brought blessed relief.

'Caty,' he said softly, and the way he spoke my name was velvet against my skin.

He put his arms around me and pulled me to him, with the wind and the black night all around us. His body was so warm, I wasn't shivering any more. I closed my eyes. I just wanted to rest; I just wanted to be loved.

I led him into the tent, and we lay together in a tangle of sleeping bag and blankets, the wind blowing outside and the sweet light of the fire glowing through the canvas. I wrapped my arms around him and kissed him, sweetly, then more passionately than I'd thought I could. I wanted to lose myself in him; I wanted to forget. He held me to him, so tightly it nearly hurt, kissing me back. A minute of tenderness, of forgetting, like his lips were ether.

Then he pushed me away gently.

'Fraser?'

'I don't want to be just this for you.'

'Just . . . this?'

'The rebound guy. Someone who's there when you hurt. Caty, listen.' The way he said my name. Like he held a precious gem in his hand, or a delicate blossom. *Caty.* 'I'm in love with you,' he whispered. 'I have been for a long time.' I could feel his breath against my ear, the weight of his words seeping into me. 'When something happens between us ... it has to be because you really want it. Because you really want *me.*' He kissed my cheeks and my forehead, then held me tight, holding on to me like he'd dreamt of this for a long time.

I'm in love with you.

Was that what he'd said?

But I had no more energy to think, no more energy to talk. I closed my eyes against him, let him hold me and cradle me like a wee girl, and to my surprise, I fell into a deep, dreamless, blissful sleep.

Anna

That night, Ava and Toby were downstairs listening to the Grants playing, and I was in my room trying to think, trying to digest what was happening. To magic a decision out of the confused and contradictory thoughts that filled my mind. All the while I kept my phone close, hoping that Sorren would call. We hadn't spoken since he'd had that mysterious conversation with Toby, the one that had left Toby white-faced and shaky. I still had no idea what they'd said.

'Anna? Are you okay?' Shuna's voice outside the door. I swallowed and ran a hand through my hair.

'Yes. Yes, I'm okay,' I said, and opened the door. 'Please come in. Sorry . . .'

'Don't apologise . . . What do you have to be sorry about?' she asked in that gentle, caring voice of hers.

'For bringing all this into your home. All this . . . drama!' A fresh bout of tears threatened to choke me again.

'Nobody's life is free of drama. It's just that most of the time it happens behind closed doors. It's not your fault if all this is happening to you now, far away from home.'

'Home?' I said, and the bitterness in my voice startled me. 'My home with Toby?'

The intensity of my words must have startled Shuna too, because her eyes widened, and she placed a comforting hand on my arm.

'Come. We'll have a cup of tea.'

I snorted. Shuna looked at me. 'My granny was the same, you know. I don't remember much about her, but I do remember that she always had a cup in her hand. I think she believed that tea sorted everything.'

'And she was right.' Shuna smiled. 'I'll put the kettle on.'

Shuna and I sat in the family living room beside the peat fire, warming our hands around cups of tea. The wind was blowing strong, howling outside the window. Already I could feel summer slipping away and autumn inching in, a bit more every day. From the pub we could hear a low, sweet tune – the Grants' fiddles had been my soundtrack since I'd arrived. How much I'd miss them when life took me away from here, away from Scotland . . .

Shuna was watching me with her kind blue eyes as my thoughts whirled round and round. She was silent, waiting for my cue. Thank goodness she'd come looking for me; I needed to talk to someone, someone wise who could help me make sense of the mess in my mind, but I simply didn't know where to start. A couple of times I tried to speak, but no words came out. Just more tears that I desperately tried to stop from falling.

'Anna,' Shuna said, seeing that I was struggling. 'Is there anything I can do? Can I help in any way?'

I took a breath that turned into a sigh of pure exhaustion. 'Toby says he's sorry. He wants us to be a family again.'

Shuna nodded. There was a little pause.

'Was he a good father, a good partner to you, before he left?'

'Do you mean was this his first mistake; was abandoning us out of character? No. Even before all this, I was forever mopping up his disasters. Ava adores him, but he doesn't have a clue how to raise a child . . .'

Shuna nodded thoughtfully. 'And what about you? What do *you* want?'

I knew what I wanted. I wanted to put a thousand miles between Toby and me.

I wanted him out of my life.

And I wanted Sorren in it.

I couldn't articulate all that to Shuna. Talking about what *I* desired seemed so selfish when I had a six-year-old child whose happiness depended on me. And I couldn't mention Sorren, either. She had to be aware of what had been happening between her son and me, but we never mentioned it. It was all too delicate, starting out as it had; like a frail bloom that we had to protect and nourish. A bloom that might soon be ripped from its little roots.

'It's difficult to explain,' I said tentatively. 'I can't bring myself to sever this . . . *bond* between Ava and her dad . . .' Oh God. Thinking was so much easier than talking. Fresh tears fell down my cheeks and I dried them with the back of my hand.

'I understand. But you don't have to do that, not at all. Ava and her father can be in touch, they can see each other. Many families work like that nowadays. *You* don't need to be with him for him to be Ava's dad . . . Oh Anna. You can't waste your life with someone you don't love, someone you don't even respect. Who doesn't respect you, it seems to me. Maybe if he was a really good father for your daughter, you could make a sacrifice. For her. But from what you tell me, he isn't. He hurt her very badly.'

I looked down, and Shuna sighed. 'I'm sorry. I'm here passing judgement when I haven't even known you that long. But I care for you. And for Ava . . .'

'I know, I know,' I reassured her, putting my hand on hers. But I also knew that there was a subtext to every-thing she said: Sorren. Of course she would be concerned about him; she was his mother. But I didn't want to cause him even a moment's pain. Just the thought of it tortured me.

The thought of going away with Toby, of leaving Sorren behind.

I couldn't see a way out. I breathed in and looked for the right words, as hard as it was.

'I . . . I always wanted a proper family, Shuna. I never had one. I never knew my father, and my mum wasn't that interested in me. She . . .' I shook my head. I just couldn't tell her, I couldn't tell her what I'd been through. 'I want a real family for Ava. That's why I stayed with Toby all these years, though I haven't loved him in a long time.'

'Oh Anna. I'm so sorry for what you went through . . .'

I shrugged. 'Well, that's just the way things are.'

'I know that nowadays families are broken all too easily. But sometimes it's the only way . . . sometimes people are just miserable together. And their children know it, they are aware of it . . .'

'I'd rather be miserable if it makes Ava happy.'

'It doesn't work that way, sweetheart. If you're miserable, Ava won't be happy either. And you deserve happiness too. You do. And not just you. What about . . .' Her voice trailed away.

I knew who she meant. I knew what she was about to say.

Sorren's name hung unspoken between us.

At that moment, Jane called, and Shuna got up. She gave my hand a squeeze.

'Life has a way of helping us figure things out,' she said, and I was reminded of what she'd told me the night of the ceilidh. Those simple words alone, the reminder to let things flow and allow life to do its thing, helped immensely. 'Maybe not immediately, but with time. I know you and Ava will be fine,' she added. 'You can always count on us, remember that.' A flash of sadness appeared in her eyes, and in a moment of clarity, I realised that it had taken her all her willpower, all her equanimity, not to try and convince me to send Toby away. For Sorren. Maybe for herself, too.

After she left, I sat alone for a while. The fire glowed softly, its beautiful aroma filling my nostrils. The Grants' music, the smell of peat, the sound of the sea – all the things that had punctuated my days since I had arrived on Seal, all the things that without my noticing had unknotted me, soothed me. All the things I'd just been asked to leave behind.

25

Hopes and dreams

Anna

Toby was staying.

For a few days, he said.

Until I decided to follow him, he meant.

There had been no word from Sorren, and I couldn't settle to anything. It was a relief to go and look after Lady Kilpatrick for the day. At least that way I could spend some time away from Toby. On impulse, I decided to take her for a walk by the sea, in spite of Linda's apprehension; it was a mild day, and I was confident that we would be fine.

The sun was shining, the sky blue and dotted with fluffy clouds. A fresh breeze was blowing in from the sea and making the water dance. We strolled arm in arm along the shore – far enough from the water that Mary wouldn't get wet, but close enough that she could walk on the compact sand and not tire her legs too much.

'Thank you for bringing me here,' she said. 'Linda never does. She's scared I'll catch cold, or get too much sun, or fall into the sea!' She laughed as if it was an absurd thought. I didn't want to remind her that I'd found her on the bridge in the middle of the night. I couldn't blame Linda. Sometimes Lady Kilpatrick was perfectly sensible; then all of a sudden she would start talking to someone invisible, or wander off. There was no way she could be left alone near the sea.

'She worries about you,' I said.

'There's no need. You're pale, Anna . . .'

'Yes. I didn't sleep well. Watch your cardigan,' I said, and lifted it back on to her shoulders. It was forever falling down. In some ways she was like a little girl; at other times, her expression seemed so solemn, so knowing. Her prophetess face.

'I hope it was for all the right reasons,' Mary said, perfectly serious. I had to laugh.

'Actually, it was because of all the *wrong* reasons. Worry kept me awake.'

'And what do you worry about?'

'I . . . Oh, I can't trouble you, Mary. It wouldn't be fair.'

'Don't be silly. It's not like I have troubles of my own.' She shrugged. 'All I do is stroll, eat, sleep and take medicine. My life is as boring as they come!'

'I wouldn't mind some boring. My life has been quite . . . entertaining recently. And not really in a good way.'

'I hear that some good things are happening to you, though. That a fine, fine man from the island wants you at his side.'

I smiled sadly. 'How on earth do you know everything that goes on?'

She shrugged. 'People talk to me. But I've been watching you all morning, Anna. I know you are upset. You can't hide it from me. I was only asking to see if you wanted to talk about it. Stella told me everything.'

'Stella told you . . .'

'She said your daughter's father is back on the island. That he wants you to go away with him.'

'She's right . . .' I took a breath. Of course I didn't believe for a moment that it was her dead sister who'd told her that. She must have heard it from the Seal grapevine. 'Ava's dad . . . he left us a while ago. And now he's here.'

'Do you love him?'

'No. Not for a long time. Actually, I want him as far from me as he can go.'

'But . . . ?'

'But he's Ava's father.'

'He won't be much good to her if he's no good for you, Anna.'

'I know. I know.'

Mary stopped in her tracks and turned to me. 'I was with the wrong person all my life,' she said out of the blue. I held my breath. 'My husband, Lord Kilpatrick, was not the man I loved. But he was kind, and he loved me. He would never have abandoned me the way Toby did with you.'

I looked at her, unsure what to say. Silver strands of hair had come loose from her bun and were dancing in the wind around her face; her eyes were wistful, lost in another time.

'All my life I was with one man and in love with another. When love comes, Anna, you must take it as fast you can, because before you know it, it can disappear and be gone.' She smiled a smile that was both sorrowful and sweet, a smile that spoke of loss but also of past happiness. 'And all you are left with is photographs and memories.'

We walked slowly home, both lost in our own thoughts. There was something in her words that was niggling at me – something that wasn't quite right.

I went through our conversation in my mind until I got it.

She'd called Toby by his name.

Fancy that: the Seal grapevine seemed to know all the details.

'Come. I want to show you something,' Mary said as I dished out her evening medication, together with a cup of tea and some hot buttered toast. Soon I would have to go back to the inn and face Toby, and the thought dismayed me.

We sat side by side on her bed. Mary held a wooden box on her lap. She opened the lid and took out a faded photograph.

'This is Eric,' she said. She pointed to a slight young man with fine blonde hair, a small smile dancing on his lips. He was standing beside a taller man formally dressed in a kilt and all the trimmings.

'The man you *adored* . . .' I said in a low voice, nearly to myself.

'Yes. And this,' she said, indicating the taller man, 'is my husband, Lord Kilpatrick . . . Malcolm.' A tender smile was on her lips as she said his name. 'Malcolm and I were engaged when I fell for Eric. Eric begged me to break the engagement and be with him. I said no. I couldn't upset everyone, you see, Malcolm, my family . . .'

'What happened to Eric?'

'He was heartbroken. He said there was nothing left for him. He went to fight in Spain, and he never came back. I lost him.'

'I'm so sorry . . .'

'Malcolm was a good man and we had a happy marriage, but I never loved him, not like I loved Eric. All my life I thought of Eric. Of what could have been. And you know . . . my children never knew about him. They adore their father. They wouldn't understand. They would just blame me.'

It took me a few seconds to wrap my head around what she'd just said. Nobody knew. She'd carried this secret inside her for all these years.

'I want you to take these.' From the box, she took out a pair of silver earrings, similar to the ones she was wearing. They had an intricate Celtic design and a purple stone – I wasn't sure of its name – in the middle. 'Eric gave them to me. I want you to have them.'

'Oh Mary! I can't. Honestly, I can't . . .' I put my palms up.

'Why not?'

'It's not professional.'

'Nonsense!'

'You should at least ask Linda.'

'Why ask Linda? They're *mine*. Linda doesn't even know they exist, and if she did, she wouldn't know where I got them. She'll never know what Eric meant to me. But you do. Please, dear,' she said, and squeezed my hand. 'Take them. Look, wear them now.'

I sat at the dressing table and put the earrings on. I looked at my reflection, and behind me, the wrinkled face of Lady Kilpatrick, her silver hair. The melancholic light in her eyes.

Would I lose Sorren like she'd lost Eric?

Would nobody ever know what I carried in my heart, not even my children?

'It's a leap of faith,' she said softly. 'Take it. If you don't, you'll regret it forever.'

Catriona

I walked home still not quite believing what had happened. When I'd woken up, Fraser was still awake; he'd murmured a few words and held me closer to his chest, then he'd stroked my hair and kissed me gently, chastely, on the forehead before letting me go without a word. I was too confused to talk, and I needed to be alone.

Even my house seemed like a strange place as I slipped in quietly in the early-morning grey, still smelling of wind and open spaces – and of Fraser's skin, his woodsmoke scent. I felt like I was in a dream.

I made myself a cup of strong coffee and sipped it slowly, relishing the caffeine in my veins. I began to undress, throwing my sandy clothes on the floor before stepping under the hot water of the shower.

I wouldn't think of anything. Not of Sorren, not of Fraser's words of love, nothing. Just the warm water on my skin. What was finished was finished; all that was left was me.

And then, all of a sudden, the water felt icy on my body, and I gasped. I tried to jump out of its reach, but I was paralysed. A spasm of anguish tightened my stomach, like all the fear in the world had gathered there. It's difficult to describe if you don't have the Sight – it was an all-consuming feeling of terror, as if I was about to be hit by a car. I stood frozen, panting, my heart racing so fast I thought I would pass out. And then I saw it. There was someone there, a shadow, a silhouette, blurred through the glass of the shower cabinet. A small figure standing in wait.

I clasped my hand to my mouth and closed my eyes. Slowly, deliberately, I took the towel down from the hook and wrapped it around me. Then I opened the door.

There she was, Stella; her big black eyes, her sleeveless dress, her bare feet.

I wasn't afraid of her; I was only afraid of what she'd come to tell me.

As I stood there racked by shivers of terror and cold,

Stella opened her mouth. At once a carousel of images exploded in front of my eyes, each more horrible than the last, until I was on my knees on the bathroom floor.

Finally she spoke.

'*Ava.*'

Right at that moment, I heard the back door open and a man's voice called my name. Footsteps approached, then he was kneeling beside me, taking my hands. I looked into his eyes, and his face came into focus. It was Fraser.

'What's wrong? What's wrong, Caty? I heard you screaming . . .'

'Oh Fraser! She's going to drown!'

'Who? Who is going to drown?'

I stood up. 'Call Sorren. Ava is in danger. You need to go to the Sea Rescue now . . . I'm going to find Anna.'

'How . . . What are you talking about?'

'Fraser, please,' I begged him, struggling to catch my breath, my wet hair icy on my bare back. 'There's no time . . . Please.'

Our eyes met, and his face changed, confusion becoming determination all of a sudden. He believed me. He would listen.

He ran downstairs and out without another word.

26

Keep me safe

Anna

Ava was still in bed, sleepy after the excitement of the last few days. Her face lit up when she saw her father. Toby sat on her bed and held her, both of them lost in each other.

'Daddy!' she said into his neck, her voice muffled against his sweatshirt. It reminded me of when she was a toddler and she'd just learnt to talk. 'Daddy' was her favourite word, and she ran around saying it over and over again, in a tone of pure joy. The innocence of her voice won me over, and I painted a smile on my face, a smile I didn't feel.

'So what are we doing today?' It was Ava's customary question, one that usually filled me with enthusiasm; but this time it was her father who answered.

'Let's you and me go for a wander on the beach,' he said. 'Is that okay with you, Anna? It's a bit drizzly, but nothing much.'

'Sure,' I said listlessly. 'Just don't be long.'

They'd been gone barely an hour, and I was sitting at a table in the pub, gazing silently into my coffee, when

Sorren appeared at my shoulder. I looked at him pleadingly – *forgive me, forgive me* – and he took my hand and led me upstairs. As soon as we stepped into the room, he closed the door gently.

'Anna. Don't go back with him. You don't have to . . . you don't have to . . .' He looked down, frowning. I could see how much saying these words was costing him. If only he knew how much it was costing me to hear them – how every word was a needle in my heart. 'You don't have to choose me,' he said finally. 'Just don't go back with him. He's going to hurt you. I know that. I know that for sure.'

'I know it too. As long as he doesn't hurt Ava . . .'

'He did it before.'

'He promised me he won't leave her again,' I said, and every ounce of my strength went into actually trying to believe those words.

And failing.

'There are many ways to hurt someone other than leaving them.'

'Sorren, please. I . . . I have no choice in all this. No choice. Please stop tormenting me!'

'You do have a choice. This is not some Victorian novel. You can leave your partner and make a life with somebody else.'

'He's Ava's father.'

'You keep repeating this, Anna, like a mantra. You keep saying it like it's the answer to everything. He's her father, yes. He left her and went to the other side of the world. And what about you? What about what happened between us the other night? Did that mean nothing to you?'

Guilt was racking me. With Toby, I'd always been the injured party. I had suffered, but at least it had never been my fault. But now I was the one hurting someone.

Someone very, very dear to me.

I love you, were the words in my heart.

'There's nothing left to say,' was what I actually said.

There was a moment of silence. It seemed to me that Seal was taking a collective breath.

Sorren put his head in his hands; when he looked at me again, he was composed.

'Fine. It seems you have decided. I wish you well,' he said coldly, and turned to leave.

'Sorren, don't be like this. Please . . .'

His expression softened, but he remained aloof. 'I'd like to say goodbye to Ava.'

'Not now . . .'

'Don't worry, I'm not going to upset her.'

'I'm not worried about that,' I said wearily. 'She's out with her dad. On the beach.'

'I just came from the beach. There was nobody there.'

In spite of myself, a little pang of worry tightened my heart. 'They must have gone somewhere in the village, maybe for a juice and a cake. Out of the rain,' I added. I looked out of the window, and that was when I noticed that the light drizzle had turned into proper rain. Not a downpour as such, but heavy enough. Ava would catch cold, I thought, and hoped they were safely inside.

'How long have they been out for?' Sorren said.

'About an hour. Why?'

'I'm going to check again,' he said, and something in his voice made me look up in alarm. I studied his face. He wanted to say goodbye to Ava, that was all; it wasn't that he was worried because he hadn't seen them on the beach. Of course it wasn't. There was no reason to worry.

'I'm coming with you,' I said, and made straight for the door without even bothering to put my jacket on. Something wasn't right, though there was no logical reason to feel like that. Toby cared for Ava; he would never put her in danger. Yet still . . .

We walked out quickly, and Sorren shed his jacket to wrap it around my shoulders. I pulled the hood up to try and shield myself from the rain. The downpour was getting heavier by the minute. Any second now, I would see Ava running towards me, wet but smiling, clutching some little trinket that her father had bought her in the Design Gallery . . .

We stood on the pier and looked around – nobody. Ava's red jacket was unmissable; I would have seen her even in this downpour. I looked up to the sky, rivulets of rain running down my face. A cluster of dark clouds was moving towards us, turning the sky slowly from grey to black, and the wind was turning into a gale.

'Let's go to the village. They'll be there somewhere,' I said, worry gnawing deeper at me. That was when I saw Catriona running up the street towards us, her red-blonde hair blowing around her face; her face white. She was mouthing something, but at first I couldn't hear it over the noise of the wind.

'Caty!' Sorren called, and we ran towards her. She was breathless. Now I could see why her face was so white – she looked terrified.

'Ava is in danger. You need to go to the Sea Rescue,' she said, struggling to catch her breath.

I didn't ask myself how she knew – her expression was such that I believed her at once. My knees nearly gave way. 'Oh my God! Ava!' I gasped, as Sorren began to run. I heard his mobile ringing from his pocket. He answered it quickly, without interrupting his stride, then turned back towards me.

'Someone is in difficulties . . . out at sea,' he said breathlessly. 'We don't know . . . we don't know if it's them. Go back to my mother's.'

'I won't! I'm coming too!'

'No! We have no time for this. Go to my mother's, Anna!' He turned and started running again, too fast for me to catch up.

Catriona reached me and put her arm around my shoulders.

'Come on, Anna. Let's go. She'll be okay, I promise. Sorren and Fraser will see that she's okay . . .'

It couldn't be.

Toby wouldn't have been so utterly stupid as to take a boat out to sea when he didn't know what he was doing, when the weather was so uncertain. And to take his daughter with him . . .

It wasn't possible.

And still . . .

'Maybe it's not her. Maybe it's not her out there,' I said, shaking my head.

The rain was pouring down now, so thick I could barely see. We ran to the inn, wind and rain lashing our faces, and barged inside, wet and distraught.

'Shuna! Is Ava back here?' I called, trying to catch my breath.

'No, why? I thought you said she'd gone out with her father. What's going on?'

'We can't find them. Sorren was called from the life-boat station. We don't know if it's them. Oh Shuna . . .' I clasped my hand to my mouth. A few punters were watching us, but I didn't care.

'It won't be. It won't be. Don't worry,' she said. We looked at each other, and I knew we were both thinking of the same thing: of a day long ago when a little girl went to the beach and the tide caught her out.

I couldn't bear the thought. 'I'm going to look for her,' I said, and ran back out onto the street. As I hurried away, I could hear someone asking Shuna if they could help, if there was anything they could do.

Ava wasn't in any of the shops, so I hurried back down the grassy slope and onto the slippery sand. As I stood gazing helplessly out to sea, I realised that Shuna and Hamish were behind me, holding hands, squinting in the pouring rain. Beside them was Catriona, and some of the locals from the pub.

308

We stood there silently, powerless, terrified.

I slipped my hand in Shuna's, and Catriona wrapped an arm around my waist.

I'd never known fear so great.

And then I saw them among the waves, appearing and disappearing like jumping dolphins, tossed by the anger of the sea, the Sea Rescue boat, and a little white one. The one that was usually tied up on one side of the pier, tiny among the bigger fishing vessels. The one that wasn't there any more, its pole standing bare at the foot of a small grass-topped dune.

And then I knew, I knew for sure that Toby had taken Ava on that boat and onto the livid sea.

27

Icy waters

Sorren

The sea was raging. I blinked the rain out of my eyes as I leant over the side of the *Oystercatcher*, scanning the water for Ava's red jacket. I willed the boat to go faster as the waves tossed us up and down, sea and sky mixing in a whirlwind of grey. Suddenly a flash of red appeared – something floating, something small, something that looked infinitely fragile among all that fury, all that power. I didn't think. I just dived overboard, the icy water taking my breath away, Fraser's cries somewhere behind me, somewhere that seemed far away. My ears were full of water, my eyes were burning. I tried to keep myself afloat as I desperately searched around the boat, half blind, frozen. Were they underwater already? Were they fighting to stay afloat? I couldn't see. The sea was empty.

And then I spotted something – someone waving his arms. He was submerged by a huge wave, and when he reappeared, I could see that it was Toby. I grabbed him from behind, my arm around his chest. I was furious, furious that I should find him and be obliged to take him to safety when Ava was still in the water. For a moment

I contemplated letting him go – every second was precious – but I couldn't bring myself to do it.

Suddenly Fraser appeared beside me and took Toby from me. I turned away and resumed my search for Ava. Maybe she was floating somewhere, maybe she was unconscious. I would find her, I would save her . . .

'Ava! Ava!' I called, swallowing salty water with each cry.

There was no red to be seen anywhere in that empty space of blue and grey. There was nobody, nobody left. *It's finished*, said a voice inside me.

Isla was dead. No, Ava was dead.

They were both gone. I had failed again, just like back then.

I looked up to the sky, rain flogging my face, and wished for the water to swallow me. For it all to end. I relaxed my limbs, I let myself go; no more energy, no more fight left in me. I would sink beneath the waves and reach Isla and Ava, wherever they were . . .

I gasped, spitting water, lifting my chin, rubbing my eyes. There she was, standing on a rock – long black hair, one shoe on and one off. The rain was so thick and the waves kept splashing, so that everything was blurred and I couldn't see her face, but if she was standing, she was fine, she was saved!

Relief filled me, but as I began to swim towards her, I caught a glimpse of red floating in the water once more. Ava's jacket . . . her arm . . . her head, semi-submerged, dark hair floating like seaweed, and the girl on the rock was gone – maybe a wave had dragged her down, maybe she had fallen . . . I swam furiously until I reached her, the little body turning and bobbing in the angry water, the tiny white face nearly translucent against the black waves. I held her tight and swam on, and despair filled me, because she wasn't breathing. She was pale and motionless, the waves hitting her one after the other as she lay in my arms. Over the noise of the rain I could hear my own broken sobs. It had happened again, like a curse. She was gone, gone forever.

I couldn't save her.

With what remained of my strength, I lifted Ava up towards safety. Anna had come down on to the rocks – I wanted to tell her it wasn't safe, to shout to her to climb back, but I couldn't. She leaned forward and took her daughter from my arms. I could hear her sobs, her cries, and every one was a blade to my heart.

I'm sorry, I'm sorry, I'm sorry.

I'm so sorry, I couldn't save her.

I leaned over Ava's unconscious body and took a breath – still watery, still ragged. I spat out some water and tried again. I breathed life into Ava's cold blue lips and pressed on her chest, horrified to hear a crack as I did so – her ribs must have taken a battering – then again, and again. Anna was crying and screaming: *Please, Ava, please!*

Ava lay silent and still.

I couldn't stop. I breathed into her once more, and pressed on her chest, and I was ready to go again when she spat out water, coughing and coughing.

I felt my consciousness ebb away – I could rest now, I could rest – but before everything went black, I saw someone beside me: a slight girl with long black hair . . . And then I saw and thought no more.

The hospital was quiet. Everyone and everything was hushed, even the sound of footsteps on the lino floors. We sat in silence, Anna, my parents, Caty, Fraser and I, waiting for news of Ava. From the window, we could see the helipad – the helicopter that had flown Ava, Anna and me was still there. They'd persuaded me to get changed into dry clothes, but I would not go and get my bruises seen to until we had news of Ava.

Time passed slowly, dense, charged, unbearable. Every once in a while my head spun and I coughed so hard, so painfully, I thought I had probably broken something too, but I didn't care. Anna sat rigid, her hands clasped on her lap. Suddenly, abruptly, she covered her face with her hands, her shoulders trembling. My mum reached out for her, stroking her back.

'I shouldn't have let her go . . .' Anna said desolately. I bit my lip. I wanted to take her in my arms, I wanted to tell her it would be okay – but I couldn't, I couldn't tell her that, because I didn't know if it would be. Ava had been in the icy water a long time.

'You couldn't have known . . .' my mum said.

I found Anna's fingers and entwined them with mine. 'It was my fault, not yours. I should have found her earlier . . .'

My mum shook her head, and my father protested. 'You found her. You gave her a chance,' he said. 'Now stop, both of you. Neither of you caused this.' Both Anna and I looked at him – my father spoke very little, but when he did, everyone listened.

Now we could only wait. Anna's hand felt icy in mine – I never wanted to let it go.

It seemed like forever, but finally a smiling nurse came to talk to us. Anna didn't speak when she heard that Ava was going to be fine; her face just melted into tears of joy and relief. She came into my arms and held me close for a long time, shaking, while my mum patted my back and hers. My mum was crying too, and Caty. Fraser and my dad hugged us all, one by one.

'You can see her now,' the nurse said.

Anna kept her hand in mine and took me with her to Ava's room. I hovered in the doorway while she held Ava and kissed her and cried, all her fear and her love pouring out of her like a waterfall.

As soon as we had a moment, I took her aside.

She stroked my cheek. 'Are you okay? All that cold water . . . are you sure you don't want the doctors to look you over?'

She didn't know that underneath my clothes I was black and blue. She didn't need to know. 'I'm fine, I'm sure. Listen, Anna . . . Something happened . . . something I can't quite explain.'

'What do you mean?'

'I saw a girl on the rocks. I thought it was Ava. But then I realised that Ava was in the water. She had the same long black hair . . .'

'You saw a girl on the rocks?'

'I think so. I was scared, I was cold, I was struggling to breathe. I don't know. But I think I saw her, yes.'

'Who was it? Who did you see?'

I couldn't answer.

It was time for us to go. Anna would sleep at the hospital with Ava, and I had arranged to stay on the mainland with friends. My parents were going home – they were both exhausted.

On the way out, before we reached the dark car park, my mother stopped me. Without a word, she threw her arms around me, and we cried together, in relief for the girl I had saved and in grief for the girl I couldn't. The past and present merged together; the sorrow of yesterday and the joy of today mixed forever in our hearts.

Catriona

When the nurse told us that Ava had woken up, I cried. Ava would live. Ava was saved. I was full of relief for the pain they were spared; full of relief that Anna's lovely, sweet wee girl was out of danger.

Anna and Sorren were in each other's arms, and it hurt, it hurt so much. I slipped outside and breathed in the cold night air, drying my tears. Fraser came looking for me, the warmth of his body beside mine palpable as I stood alone. He didn't say a word; he just took both my hands. Our eyes met, and I felt like dying inside as I saw such love in his gaze. The kind of love that is born out of time and thoughts and a long togetherness, not just a wee spark like the one he'd used to light our bonfire. I could feel it – his love for me was deep and true, and I was shocked by its very existence, and shocked that I'd never realised.

A love that listens when you speak, like your words are precious.

A love that takes the cold off your bones.

A love that gives you blue flames and tea in melamine mugs, and a nest made of a sleeping bag and two strong, tender arms to sleep in.

A love I could never return.

I wanted to be free, but I couldn't be.

'You were right. I can't do this to you,' I said, and tears gathered in my eyes again. 'You can't be some sort of rebound for me. You deserve better.'

'Caty, listen,' he whispered. 'This is a cage with an open door.' He took hold of my elbows in that gentle, strong way of his.

I took a breath. His words seeped into me and I blinked, as if I was trying to process them and not quite managing. Could my life really change? Could what had always been not be any more?

And then all the tiredness of the world fell onto my

shoulders, because of what had happened to Ava, because of Sorren, because of everything. I just wanted to close my eyes and sleep and sleep. Oh, to let myself lean on Fraser's chest and forget about everything . . . Strange how I felt that way when he was around. Like I was tired, really tired, and had been for many years without noticing.

My shoulders hunched. I felt overcome. 'I'm sorry, Fraser. I am so sorry.'

He didn't reply. He just looked at me, a long, long look that went all the way into my soul.

And I saw myself in his eyes. I saw myself lonely and lost and forever chasing what was not mine, what would never be mine. More tears fell down my cheeks, tears of sadness for him and for me, both looking for love where no love could be found.

He leaned towards me and dropped a slow, gentle kiss on my forehead.

Then he left, and I was alone.

28

The end and the beginning

Anna

I didn't want to spend a single minute away from Ava, but there was something I had to do. Something that couldn't wait.

'Toby?'

He was as pale as the sheets he lay on, and he looked very alone, defeated. And still I had to squeeze my hands into fists and hold them there before I could come close to him. This was the man who had nearly got my daughter killed. There would be no second chance for him, never. Hypothermia and two broken ribs was nowhere near enough to settle the score. I could have strangled him with my bare hands for having put Ava in danger; but she was safe now, and I would not make the same mistake twice.

'Ava?' he asked, grimacing as he tried to sit up.

'She's fine. She's sleeping. Nothing broken, just a slightly cracked rib. As fine as she can be after spending so long in the freezing water.'

'Oh God. I'm sorry . . . I'm so sorry, Anna!' He struggled to get his words out, as if every muscle, every nerve in his body was sluggish, almost paralysed. That's what hypothermia does to you, I suppose.

'I know you are. But we won't talk about this now. Not here.'

My daughter nearly died! You nearly killed her! I could feel my breath becoming quicker. Why oh why had I ever listened to him? Why had I fallen for it again? I struggled to remain calm.

'I came to ask if you need anything,' I said.

He seemed confused. 'What?'

I could feel my whole body trembling. 'If you need any-thing. I won't phone Gillian, she doesn't need to worry.'

'I . . . Thanks.'

'So? Do you need anything?'

'I need you! And Ava!' Tears began to fall on his cheeks. I felt nothing.

'I asked Sorren to bring a change of clothes and some toi-letries for you. You're leaving as soon as you're on your feet.'

And then the old Toby was back. 'When will Ava be able to travel?'

I took a breath. 'Are you joking?'

'You can't . . . you can't keep her away from me . . .'

I didn't hear any more, because I was out of the room and gone. Nothing he said, nothing he did would keep me tied to him this time.

When Toby came to the Seal Inn to gather his things, I had them all ready in his bag. I didn't want to waste a minute – I wanted him out of there, and out of our lives.

I would have preferred never to speak to him again, but it was important for me to see him off. I wanted to look him in the eye and tell him to stay away from us, I wanted to see the ferry carry him away. There was no way back from what had happened.

I walked to the pier with him, and the air and the sky spoke of summer gone, of autumn coming. Toby was a pitiful figure, the bandages that kept his ribs together making his clothes bulge. Even the way he stood, the droop of his shoulders, the tilt of his head, told me he knew that he had lost us. And lost us forever.

'Anna . . .'

'Yes, Toby.' I was surprised at myself. Surprised I still hadn't screamed at him, not at the hospital, not here. But my rage was so deep, so white-hot, not even screaming could have expressed it.

'I can only say I'm sorry . . .' he began. But I had no time for his apologies. They meant nothing to me.

'I want you to stay out of our lives.'

His face fell. 'But Ava . . . she'll want to see me . . .'

'You'll see her, of course you'll see her.' I shook my head in frustration. Had it been up to me, they would never have met again, but I couldn't do that to Ava. 'God, Toby. You nearly killed her.' I was whispering – clusters of people waiting for the ferry littered the pier, and I didn't want them to hear me. 'Do you actually *understand* that? Do you?'

'I do. I do. I was an idiot. I'm sorry.'

I sighed. I was just repeating the same things over and

over again. I had a million questions, too – did you ever love me? Do you actually know what love is? Why did you put me down all these years; was it so that you could feel better than me, stronger than me?

But then again, there was no point.

'Good luck, Toby,' I said, and turned around.

'Anna?' He put a hand on my arm. I shook him off and kept walking.

That was it. No more words, no more explanations, nothing he could cling to and manipulate and use against me to keep me close. I walked away, and as I did, I felt Lady Kilpatrick's earrings dangling at my ears.

I'd walked away once before.

That day four years ago, I'd gone to see my mum, laden with groceries she'd probably be too sick to eat, a Boots bag with medicines and toiletries, some cleaning stuff to make the place as decent as it could be. I hadn't planned to say goodbye forever; I wasn't even thinking of it. It was just a visit, really, to make sure that at least she lived some-where adequate, that she wasn't too ill to get out of the house, things like that. I did it every few months, to check on her; she moved around a lot, and sometimes it was tricky even finding her. I had to track down her friends, most of them as wasted as she was, and ask where she'd moved to. Sometimes she had a flat, sometimes she had a room, or a sofa. Or a portion of floor.

I knelt on the spotless lino of my mum's kitchen. Wher-ever she was, she'd scrub the kitchen until it was perfectly clean and shiny, not a spoon, a cup, a bag of pasta out of place, the floor gleaming, the dishes put away. Weird, isn't it? Mounds of dirty clothes everywhere, empty bottles lined up on every surface and rolling underfoot, carpets covered in stains – and still her kitchen was always pristine to the point of obsession. As a child, I watched her scrubbing the stove, the ends of her hair white with Jif, her hands red and raw. She hadn't changed her clothes in days – she'd even slept in them – and rubbish sacks had accumulated in the spare room; but I had to take my shoes off to step into the kitchen, and then, on all fours, wipe away my footprints from the floor.

'What are you here for? I didn't ask you to come,' she said as I pushed a load of dirty clothes into the washing machine. The kettle was on to make us both coffee – extra strong for her, for what it was worth. She'd need a lot more than coffee to shake off her perpetual hangover.

'You never ask me to come. I come anyway.'

'Just get out, Anna!' She slammed her hand on the table, making me jump. I pursed my lips.

Okay. She was having an angry day. I'd ignore her. I was used to it.

'Sure, after I finish this and clean a little. I brought you some microwave meals; all you have to do is—'

'You think my life would be this way now if I hadn't had you?'

I froze. She'd never said that before.

'So now it's my fault that you live like this, Mum?' I said. I hated myself as I heard the pleading edge to that word – Mum. I hadn't called her that in years; Karen seemed more fitting. But not today. *Mum, please – be a mother to me still.* 'What exactly have I done?'

'You were born,' she said.

And at that moment, I knew.

I knew it was all over, and there would be no coming back from there.

Slowly I placed the washing powder on top of the machine. I left the door open, the stinking clothes piled inside. I left the groceries in their bags and the medicines on the coffee table. I left the mug with the instant coffee and sugar inside, as the kettle boiled and switched itself off. I left my mum sitting unawares, a cigarette in her hand, because she'd said so many cruel things through the years, she didn't think this time was any different.

But it was.

I walked out of her house, taking my jacket and my handbag as I left, closing the door carefully behind me, without noise. I don't know if she called me back; if she did, I didn't hear her. I couldn't hear her voice any more, like I'd shut her out forever.

I never saw her again.

I stood on a sand dune, the wind in my face, and watched the ferry slowly leave the dock, taking Toby with it. But it wasn't thoughts of rejection or abandonment that filled my mind – it was thoughts of freedom and hope and love that bloomed there like a rainbow in a stormy sky. Ava and I were home.

29

The blood is strong

Anna

Linda was chairing a meeting of the local tourism board that night, so she asked me to look after her mother. I was tidying Mary's things – the books, the magazines, her medicines – as she sat by her beloved window, watching the sky getting darker and darker. The view from Kilpatrick House was breathtaking as always.

She looked frail in her dressing gown, and more tired than usual. Her hands felt cold, so I'd made her tea to warm her, and brought some shortbread to keep her strength up.

'You know, Anna. It feels like you've been here forever,' she said. She leaned her head back on the armchair with a small sigh.

I smiled. I was exhausted myself after the emotion of seeing Toby off, but too relieved to care. 'That's true. I can't believe I found this place . . . I feel so lucky.'

'It wasn't luck. It was Leah.'

I stopped in my tracks, one of the novels I was lining up for her in mid-air. 'Sorry, Mary, what did you say?'

'Stella told me. It was your grandmother, Leah. She brought you here.'

I placed the novel down and stood. 'My . . . granny Leah?'

'Oh yes. Leah McAulay. I remember her . . .'

I think I actually felt my mouth fall open as I blinked over and over again. I pulled a chair across and sat in front of Mary. Okay, weird things kept happening to me on the island – fine. But what did my grandmother have to do with it all?

Wait. Stella had told her, so clearly it was one of Mary's illusions.

But how did she know my grandmother's name?

'You . . . remember her?'

'Of course I do! I remember things from long ago better than what I did yesterday. Leah was a friend of Stella's. Her family took her away to England, and we never saw her again. I think I have a picture somewhere . . . Darling, would you mind getting my photo album, the black one with the pictures of Stella and me . . . Yes, that one. Let me see . . .' She thumbed through the pages until she got to a picture of a young girl and her mother, both in cotton dresses, standing together in front of the door of a white cottage. 'There you are. The wee one is Leah.'

'That's my granny?' I said. Mary nodded. I had only sketchy memories of my grandmother, but I recognised her black hair, the same as my mother's, mine and Ava's. 'And she was from Seal?' I asked in disbelief.

'Born and bred. She used to live in a cottage not too far from Roan, near the sea. It's in ruins now, sadly.'

I stared at the picture for a few seconds, trying to take it all in.

And all of a sudden it came back to me – Ava standing on Don's boat, pointing at a place on the island, somewhere barren and bare . . . but for a ruined cottage.

'So both Ava and I . . .'

'Have Seal blood. And you must remember, my dear. The blood is strong.'

That night, I heard her once again, my granny Leah.

I heard her humming, a sweet tune with words in a language I didn't understand, a language that flew like a singing stream.

30

Notes to a hungry sea

Anna

Finally Sorren's house wasn't an empty shell any more. We were all there, in his kitchen, gathered to enjoy the summer evening. The scent of fresh hot bread and of a hearty roast filled the air. Sorren was standing beside the stove, Shuna and I were sitting at the table, cups of tea in front of us, and Hamish was in the armchair, a warm, silent presence. From the French doors we could see Ava, skipping with a rope Sorren had bought her, like a bright flower among the broom and the rhododendron and the other strong, hardy shrubs Sorren had in his Hebridean garden.

It was our time, our moment of peace and togetherness.

'Well, we'll be counting the days till you come back,' Shuna said, and gave my hand a squeeze.

'So will we,' I replied.

Seal was going to be our new home. The immensity of the change should have flustered me; instead, all I felt was peace, and trust that everything was going to fall into place. But there were still a few things to sort out, a few loose ends to tie up. Ava and I were to go to London to settle our affairs, and then Sorren would drive down to help us with the move. I was also going to say good-bye to Parvati, though not for long – she'd promised she would come and visit us with the twins during October half-term. I was already planning what we could do: take the boys to play on the beach, a trip out on Sorren's boat to see the seals and the dolphins, hot chocolate and cake at the Design Gallery, and of course all the music sessions we could find. I couldn't wait to show them my new life.

'It won't be long,' Sorren said, taking the roast from the oven.

'I'll be spending all my time on paperwork, I suppose,' I said, getting up to help Sorren serve. 'And packing. So much to sort out . . .'

'It'll all fall into place, you'll see. It'll be easier than you think,' Shuna said, slicing Sorren's freshly baked bread. The aroma was mouth-watering. I smiled to myself – being with a chef had its advantages.

I called Ava in from the garden and sent her to wash her hands; she came in still skipping. She looked healthy and happy, and showed no sign of having suffered any after-effects from the accident. Only a few days before, as I was giving her breakfast, she'd spoken about what had happened.

'Mummy . . .' she'd said, stirring her cereal.
'Yes?'
'The waves were very high, and I couldn't breathe.'
I felt cold. I didn't want to remember. 'But you're fine,

now, sweetheart. It's all over and you're safe with us. There's no need to be afraid.'

She shook her head. 'I'm not afraid. This time it was okay.'

This time? What did she mean?

'Yes, it was okay,' I said.

'I didn't die.'

'No, you didn't.' I was choking up, and hoped she would get off the subject, but I didn't want to cut her off. If she needed to talk, to tell me what it had been like, I wanted her to have the chance to do just that.

'So this time it was fine,' she said, and took a spoonful of her cereal.

She said nothing more, and I didn't ask.

Apart from that episode, she seemed not to have retained any trauma. If anything, as strange as it might sound, she seemed in even better form than before – cheery, sunny, her old self, like before Toby had left. Like a huge weight had been lifted off her chest.

After dinner, we sat around the peat fire for whisky and more chat. I sat on the carpet in front of the fire, Shuna and Hamish on the sofa, and Sorren took the armchair, because he had a little girl hanging from his neck, tired and sun-baked. Slowly the sky turned from white to lilac, and then purple. Night was falling. I surveyed the scene with grateful eyes: my family.

My family.

'This wee girl needs her bed,' Sorren said, stroking Ava's hair.

'I'm not sleepy,' she replied, in such a sleepy voice that everyone laughed.

'Come on, darling, let's go home . . . I mean, back to the inn,' I said, and smiled.

'I'm happy for you to call it your home, sweetheart,' Shuna said.

Ava and I stood in the garden, in the soft dusk. The sea was at our backs, lapping the shore in a peaceful, tender rhythm. As we said our goodbyes, Sorren took us in his embrace and gave us both a kiss.

'See you tomorrow,' he whispered, smiling at me, his eyes full of love. But the smile died on his lips as he looked at Ava, his eyes wide.

'What's wrong?' I said, but he kept on staring, mute. 'What's wrong?' I repeated, my heart thumping.

And then Shuna gave a little yelp, like a wounded animal. I turned towards her, and I saw that all the blood had drained from her face. Even her lips were pale. For a moment, I worried she was going to faint.

'Shuna, are you okay?' I said, wrapping one arm around her protectively, holding Ava with the other. She opened her mouth as if to speak, and then closed it again. 'Shuna? What's going on?' My gaze went from her, to Hamish, to Sorren. And then I realised that all eyes were on Ava, in my arms.

I turned my face towards hers, resting on my shoulder. Ava wasn't Ava.

The girl in my arms was not my daughter.

She had a different face, her skin fairer and without

freckles, her nose smaller and rounder, her lips pink like a rosebud. Her hair was still dark, but longer, silky strands on my arm, on my shoulder.

I knew who she was.

I was trembling all over, too astounded to move. I just stood there, breathing heavily. The girl extended her hand towards Shuna like she wanted to touch her, so I put her down. I was shaking so hard, I thought my knees would give way.

Shuna crouched, her arms held out in front of her.

'Mummy . . .' the girl said. She walked to her calmly, dreamily, and dried a tear from Shuna's cheek with a little finger. 'Don't cry.'

Shuna gave a small, strangled sob, and the girl came into her arms. I watched them hold each other, Shuna rocking gently.

'Isla,' Sorren whispered, and I looked at him, standing on the doorstep, his hands at his sides. His face was pale in the dusky light.

If that was Isla, where was my Ava?

Where was Ava?

I turned my head back towards Shuna and the little girl, slowly, slowly, afraid of what I would see.

But I saw a waterfall of black hair, and Ava's freckled nose and tanned little face. Shuna's eyes were closed, but somehow she knew that Isla had gone. She gave a long, long sigh, then lifted her hand and stroked Ava's cheek.

'Thank you. Thank you, my love, for bringing her home,' she said, smiling amidst her tears.

31

A cage with an open door

Catriona

Dear Inary,
  With all that happened . . .
  I think it's time . . .
  I had a look at the council website, and it seems there are quite
a few vacancies . . .

I tried and tried, but for some reason the email I was
trying to write just didn't want to come out. I'd made a
decision. I couldn't remain on Seal, not after all that had
happened, not to watch Sorren and Anna together. Glen
Avich, in the north-east of Scotland, seemed the best
option for me. I had family there, especially my dear
cousin Inary. She too had the Sight, and we'd been close
since we were children.

Yet still I didn't seem to be able to start making
arrangements. Even writing a simple email was a huge
effort. I couldn't weave my thoughts together enough to
make a plan.

It's because you don't really want to go, I could imagine
Fraser saying.

Fraser?

Why did he keep coming back into my thoughts?

I hadn't seen him since Ava's accident, when we were both at the hospital, but the memory of the night we'd spent in each other's arms, and his words – *this is a cage with an open door* – kept coming back to me.

I rubbed my temples with my fingers. The letter would not get written tonight, that was for sure.

I gave up and switched the laptop off. I was so tired I couldn't keep my eyes open. I was about to go to bed and just crash when I heard a noise outside. When I opened the door, a gust of cold, salty wind took my breath away.

On the step there was a parcel, safely wrapped in a poly pocket and kept together with twine. Threaded in the twine was a sprig of seaweed – a sort of sea flower. Inside the parcel was a tiny book – *101 Survival Techniques* – and a note:

If you need to make a fire and I'm not around. F x

In the black, windy night, holding the salt-smelling parcel, my face broke into a smile and my thoughts fell into place.

I walked along the shore in my pyjamas, a cardigan wrapped around me. The sea was black and furious, but inside I was glowing.

I wondered how many seal eyes watched over me as I went.

The lights in Fraser's cottage were still on.

I walked slowly, deliberately, a secret smile on my face.

I was unafraid. And when he opened the door, tall and strong and astonished by my sudden presence, I stepped in and wrapped my arms around his neck, lifting myself on tiptoes. I looked for his lips with mine, but he was faster than me, kissing me deeply and passionately, one hand on the nape of my neck, the other around my waist, holding me close like he never wanted to let me go.

32

Isla's song

I knew I had to go. I had realised slowly that I could not be here forever, that the reason for my coming back was not for me to stay, but for my family to fill the hole in their hearts, and for Ava and Anna to find a home.

I thought that leaving them again would break my heart, and it did, but I had brought Ava and Anna to them to fill the emptiness. I couldn't stay, but Ava could.

Sea, sea, I'm coming to you at last.

One last touch to my mother's face, and I was gone.

I float above the waves and I let myself fall, and the waves rise up to take me. I am not going back to the soft, foggy, lonely place I was in before, because the golden light is there for me, glimmering underwater, and it is full of the tender voices of those who've gone before me. It is full of love, emanating from it like a warm current that takes me and swirls me, swirls me around.

I am not a child any more. I am a spirit who has lived and who will live again. I am a spirit who had something to do, and she has done it.

Epilogue

Anna

Since everything that happened, I often think about fate. Was Ava supposed to go back to Seal? Was there a design, a force – fate, or destiny, or who knows – that somehow used us as its tools to take a little girl back where she belonged? Was it really my grandmother's spirit, guiding us to the home she knew?

I watch Ava play and do her homework and get ready for bed; I watch her running on the beach, the green sea behind her, and I wonder – is Isla still inside her? Still hidden somewhere, even now she's home at last?

And how did Isla's memories seep into my daughter in the first place?

Idle questions. Because we'll never have the answers.

All I know is that I was a woman alone, barricaded by her own loneliness and fears and caution, never having known the love and comfort of a family; and now my daughter and I are surrounded by love, breathing it in all around us.

A little girl lost, sweet Isla with her dolls' dresses and

her dancing shoes, had taken us home. She had filled her mother's heart again and relieved her loneliness.

She had given her brother the chance to put things right. To rescue her, to bring her ashore.

The little girl who drowned off the coast of Seal fifteen years ago had brought us all together.

Nobody could save her; but she had saved us all.

Acknowledgements

With love and gratitude to Sherise Hobbs, Ariella Feiner, Vicky Palmer, all at Headline and at United Agents, Ivana Fornera (Mum!), Edoardo Sacerdoti, Francesca Meinardi, Irene Zaino, Phil Miller, Gabriela Veres and Simona Sanfilippo.

And, as always, to Ross, Sorley and Luca. For everything.

To the following readers: Carol Taylor, Kerri E, Zoe Horne, Trudy Davies, Cristina, Diane, Mary Foresti, Sue Eddy, Shell, Cathy, Joanne Baird, Blanche Gallagher, Michelle, Hazel Lees, Jan Cumming, Anne Henderson, Lusa Wall, Pauline Hatherley, Duncan, Lindsay Cogan, Anne Mairi Anderson, Mairi Wallace, Zoe Braycotton, Sweeet83 and Rachel Kennedy.

Thank you for all your support. It means the world to me.

Journey further into the world of Daniela Sacerdoti

with these mesmerising digital shorts . . .

Your Hand in *Mine*

Sylvia has devoted her life to providing a safe haven in the village of Glen Avich for her daughter Pamela, a happy little girl with a big heart. Since her daughter's medical results came in and Pamela's father Douglas walked out, Sylvia has vowed that no one would hurt Pamela again, least of all Douglas's bully of a father, who forbade his wife Morag to have anything to do with her granddaughter.

When Sylvia loses her mother, and her brother moves away, she finds herself alone and longing for a family for Pamela. So when a letter arrives from the recently widowed Morag, inviting them to visit her at home on the tiny island of Seal, Sylvia agrees to go. Will it be another failed attempt to build bridges with Douglas's family? Or is Seal waiting for them with unexpected gifts?

REVIEW

Calling *You* Home

Can a frozen heart be brought back to life?

Viola's heart was torn apart once and she has never quite recovered. The love of her life was out of reach, so she walked away and never looked back. Now, visiting the beautiful, snowy village of Glen Avich for Christmas, Viola is shocked to find him here, staying only metres away. Can she risk heartbreak again?

Inary Monteith's life is at a turning point – a surprise baby has come to upset her plans and open the door to a whole new world. But as her bump grows, fear trumps over love and Inary feels completely inadequate to her new role. As she and her cousins, Eilidh and Viola, gather for Christmas lunch, no one could expect what lies ahead, least of all the arrival of a mysterious visitor who delivers a gift for them all . . .

REVIEW

'As life-affirming as it is heartbreaking'
Lancashire Evening Post

'I can smell the loch, taste the scones, and feel the chill from the vivid settings. Adored it!'
Reader Girls Blog

Poignant and beautifully crafted. Impossible to put it down'
Novelicious

'A beautiful story of love, loss and never forgetting who you really are'
Debbie Flint

'Poignant and romantic, laced at times with sadness, but full of hope'
Owl Music

'So moving in parts that I could not breathe. Marvellously uplifting'
Kim the Bookworm